HARD TRUTH

A DCI JAMES HARDY THRILLER

JAY GILL

BOOKS BY JAY GILL

Knife & Death

Walk in the Park
(A Short Thriller)

Angels

Hard Truth

Inferno

A bonus chapter is available for each book.
For more information visit, www.jaygill.net

CHAPTER ONE

Kelly Lyle swam a final length of the pool and climbed out. It was late evening, and the heat from the Italian sun felt exhilarating on her naked body.

The villa, with its mountainous backdrop, overlooked Lake Garda. Lyle stood for a moment to take in the warmth of the evening and gaze down at the shimmering lake. The scent of lemon carried on the fresh mountain air. This was currently her favourite retreat. It had many benefits besides its beauty, not least of which was its seclusion.

Leaving her robe and shoes on a recliner, she crossed the warm tiles and entered the rear of the house through large sliding doors.

She scooped crushed ice into a chilled glass and added gin and tonic. Sipping her drink, she sat for a while watching Carlo as he slept. Lyle let her eyes wander over his firm, tanned body. She smiled at the thought of their many evenings together.

His conversation was interesting and the food he'd

cooked her had always been exceptional. He was also a very thoughtful and attentive lover.

It was a shame their time together had to end so abruptly, but it was important she return to England and get her plans underway.

Drink in hand, Lyle walked over to the sleeping Carlo. Drugged, gagged and bound to a dining chair, his body slumped forward. Lyle lifted his head and kissed his eyes.

"Carlo. Carlo, my prince, it's time to wake up."

She took some ice from her glass and ran it over his broad, tanned shoulders. "*Sveglia, sveglia, sorgi e splendi!*" she said. "Wakey, wakey, Carlo."

Carlo opened one eye and then the other.

"There you are," she said. "Welcome back to the land of the living." She chuckled at her little joke.

Puzzled, he looked around wildly. His foggy mind was trying to figure out what was happening. He tried to move. He tried to speak. He started to rock back and forth, almost toppling over in the process. His eyes widened further and his face grew fierce with anger.

Lyle poured herself another gin and tonic to give Carlo a moment to simmer down and accept his predicament. "I am sure you have lots of questions, and I wish I had more time to go into all the details of why this is happening to you, but the truth is, I don't. I have a flight booked to England first thing in the morning, and between now and then there is a lot that must be done. So, forgive me if I gloss over the niceties. What I will say is that, despite how this is going to end for you, I've had a lovely time. I think it's important you understand that what's coming next isn't about you. It's about me. Although, in reality, I'm sure that offers little comfort."

Carlo watched as Lyle pushed a hostess trolley in front of him. On the bottom shelf sat a few marble coasters, some napkins, a roll of cling film, an ice bucket and a pair of silver tongs. It was the top shelf that caused him to strain at his ties. From behind the gag he let out a long, pitiful moan. His pleading eyes were met with a coldness he hadn't seen in her before. Fingers that had once caressed him now danced over a range of glistening surgical tools.

With a look that suggested the choice was of vital importance, Lyle said, "Perfect. This will do."

She held up a surgical scalpel. Carlo pressed himself back in the chair. Lyle started to smile as she showed it to him.

"This? This is just my little joke. You're so jittery. I'm not going to use this on you, Carlo."

With a flourish, she lifted a napkin off a lime and said, "This is for the lime. A gin and tonic just isn't the same without lime, wouldn't you agree?"

Carlo attempted a smile. Perhaps, this was all just a sick prank. Maybe he would be okay after all.

"Carlo, look at me." Lyle snapped her fingers. "None of these are for you. I don't have time for blood and body parts scattered here and there. Do you understand?"

Carlo nodded.

"All that would mean a lot of cleaning up. I've told you, I'm on a tight schedule. For that reason, I intend something far less messy for me, and you'll be pleased to know it means next to no discomfort for you." Lyle reached into the ice bucket and took out an ice pick.

Carlo started to scream.

Lyle stepped close and, after a brief hesitation – she was undecided as to which eye to stab – she changed her mind entirely and plunged the ice pick through Carlo's temple and deep into his brain. She quickly wrapped his head in kitchen cling film, ensuring his nose and mouth were covered.

"There; we're done."

Lyle kissed Carlo's broad shoulders and ran her fingers over his tanned, muscular, still-warm body one last time. *It would have been nice to keep him a little longer*, she thought.

After a long, comforting shower, she finished packing and checked the flight times. Later, she would drive to the lake and take a short boat trip. Carlo would then join the others at the bottom of the lake.

CHAPTER TWO

"You're twisting my words. I didn't mean that. That's not what I said." David Howes was feeling pushed into a corner. From the moment Emma Cotton had stormed through the door, he knew he'd picked the wrong day for this job. He had seen "bad mood" written all over her face.

It was too late to back out, so he pressed on and blurted out his story, which was, broadly speaking, the truth. Naturally, he couldn't tell her everything. If he told her what was really going on it, would immediately escalate this whole shit storm from a category 2 to a category 5. He knew she'd find out the truth eventually. He just hoped he'd be long gone by the time the cat was out of the bag.

Dave thought he understood how this would play out. He'd gone over and over it in his mind. Rebecca had even helped him rehearse what he was going to say, but somehow Emma still had him going around in circles. Emma had him doubting what he'd said and what he'd meant by what he said.

He was ready to leave, but she wasn't about to let him

just walk out the door. Not yet. His problem was, the longer he stayed, the deeper the hole he dug for himself. He was terrible at lying. Feeling nervous caused him to ramble.

He could picture the storm forming in her head. The storm she'd soon unleash on him if he stuck around. Menacing grey clouds full of buzzing electricity waiting to release deadly verbal lightning bolts. He tried staring at her breasts to calm his nerves. She was still hot. That was never the problem. The problem was she was hardly ever home anymore, and when she was, she was either sleeping or a real super bitch. He stopped staring. She'd seen him looking and not listening. He cleared his throat and pretended he had a tickly cough. She looked like she was ready to punch his lights out. She wouldn't. She couldn't. Could she?

"Let me get this straight. Look at me. After being together for over five years, engaged for almost two, you wait for me to announce the date of our wedding before deciding this isn't what you want. You wait until I've told all my friends and all my family and every bloody person at work before making your grand announcement. And where do you choose to tell me about this change of heart? You make me trek to a shitty little pub in the arse end of nowhere."

"I'm sorry," said Dave in a hushed voice. He hoped Emma might lower her voice. He could see people looking.

"How does this make me look? I've sent out the fucking invitations. Do you understand that? You even bought the sodding stamps. To top it all off, this isn't just cold feet. Oh, no – poor little Dave is feeling 'trapped.' He wants to spend time apart. I believe you said, 'It would be good for us both.'

"And on top of that, you want to move out. You

suddenly have the urge to go 'travelling.' Yet, the furthest I've ever seen you travel is to the fucking freezer to get a fucking pizza. Finally, and imagine for one second I'm not a complete idiot – not that I'd need to be; any fool could see through your bullshit – you want me to believe that you're not seeing someone else. Is that right? Let me know if I missed anything."

"I don't want to argue," said Dave weakly.

"Argue? You're so pathetic. We haven't even started." Emma glared at him.

"Let's take some time. Space will be good for both of us. Give me an hour, and I'll get some of my stuff from the house. I'll call you in a day or so."

"You don't want to talk about it now? Why is that? Are you just going to leave? No proper explanation?" She stared at him. "Of course you don't want to talk about it. You've already planned this out. That's why you arranged to meet here in public. You think I won't make a scene. And if I do, you don't know anyone. You must have mistaken me for the world's biggest idiot."

"I've tried to talk to you. More than once. You won't listen," said Dave.

"When? When did you last try to have a proper conversation? You're so full of shit, David." Emma reached for her purse and said, "I need another drink."

He got to his feet. "I'll get it for you."

"No, you won't. You sit right there. We haven't finished."

Dave watched as Emma walked to the bar. He flicked through messages on his phone before sending Rebecca a text.

CHAPTER THREE

Emma stood at the bar and gestured to the barman. She put their empty glasses down in front of her. "One pint of phlegm and spit for him and one large house white wine for me."

The barman smiled.

Beside her, she could feel the appraising eyes of the man on the bar stool beside her. His dirty white t-shirt had a rip down the side, and his shoes and trousers and fingernails suggested he'd been painting; he was possibly a painter and decorator by trade. His glazed eyes told her he needed to go home and sleep off one drink too many. He looked around Emma to his friend, who was perched on a bar stool the other side of her. The friend looked older and was also dressed in working clothes. In addition, the friend had fine speckles of paint on his face and arms, suggesting he had recently been using a paint roller.

The first man spoke to his friend, loud enough for Emma to hear. "Lovers' spat? What do you reckon, Scotty?"

"Looks that way, Johnster." Scotty twisted on his barstool and leaned back. He looked over at Dave, who was spinning his mobile phone on the table. "Look at that poor sod. He looks like he's hoping the ground will open and swallow him up. He's got his hands full with this one." He looked Emma up and down.

She said nothing. She looked over at the barman, who was on his way back with her drinks but had stopped to chat.

"If he's not making you happy, love, perhaps I could give it a try," said Johnster, a wide grin on his face. Pint in hand, he slid off his stool and leaned against the bar. He pressed his leg against hers. Scotty sipped his pint and looked on with amusement.

"No. I'm not interested," said Emma. She handed the barman the money, thanked him and picked up her drinks.

"I guess you're not her type," said Scotty. "She sounds a bit posh for you."

Johnster put down his pint and stepped in front of her. "So what is your type? The wee man at the table obviously isn't. Perhaps it's time you tried a real man. A big man, if you know what I mean. They don't call me Johnster for nothin'." He stuck out his arms and wriggled his hips. "It's because of this monster between my legs."

"And there was me thinking you were nothing more than good looks and charm," said Emma with more than a little fire.

Scotty laughed and nearly spilt his pint. Johnster continued, oblivious. "Come on, gorgeous. Wouldn't you like a bit of rough? I hear you posh types like that." Johnster looked past her to Scotty for backup. "I bet she'd like it. Deep down they want a bit of rough. Especially these good girls. And she definitely looks like a good girl."

Emma looked Johnster in the eye, "No. Go home. Or finish your drink. Just leave me alone. I've had a shitty day, and you're making it worse. I just want to get my drinks and go back to my friend. I've asked you nicely, and I won't ask nicely again."

She held up her drinks and tried to push past Johnster. He moved in front of her and placed his hands on her hips, then started to slow dance.

"Johnster's just being friendly. He wants to know if he's your type, darlin', that's all. We both do, for that matter," said Scotty.

"What's my type? It might be easier if I tell you what my type isn't. Your wedding rings tell me that, surprisingly, you're both married. Lucky ladies. Sorry, boys. Married men are a no-no for me. I'm also not keen on men who drink themselves stupid after work or have bad breath, bad manners, body odour and the obsession of a squirrel."

Scotty and Johnster looked confused, so she added, "Squirrels? They're obsessed with just one thing – burying their nuts."

She pushed past and left the two men laughing as though she'd just paid them some kind of compliment. Dave had moved outside to the pub's garden. His mobile phone was pressed to his ear. He was deep in conversation. She had little doubt who he was talking to; she had ideas about who the woman was. Emma's fury reached a whole new level. It was time to get the truth out of Dave. As much as she didn't want to hear it, she knew she had to.

She slammed the drinks down on the table. As she did this, she felt a hand on her backside. She turned to see Johnster with a ridiculous grin on his face.

"Wow, you're persistent, aren't you? And clearly more stupid than I thought," said Emma. "Does the local circus know one of their clowns has escaped? You did hear me say no, didn't you?"

Johnster smiled, "I did, but I thought— "

Emma stepped close and swiftly raised her knee to connect with Johnster's balls. As he doubled over in agony, she raised her elbow so it connected with his nose. Blood gushed down his face. Stepping behind him, she lifted her foot and launched him forward. The top of his head caught the edge of the table, where he crashed to the floor. The two drinks she had just placed on the table toppled and spilt over his neck and shoulders.

Scotty appeared beside Emma and looked down at his friend. "Hey, what the hell's the matter with you?"

He reached out to grab her, but she took his hand and with one smooth movement twisted his arm up and behind his back. The surprised Scotty yelped and groaned.

Emma whispered in Scotty's ear, "Are you going to behave?"

Scotty nodded. "Yes, yes! You're hurting me."

She released the pressure on Scotty's arm and said, "Is that my phone ringing? Can either of you morons hear a mobile phone?" She let go of Scotty's arm and, keeping an eye on the two men, reached into her back pocket and pulled out her mobile phone. She swiped a finger across the phone to take the call and said, "Detective Inspector Emma Cotton speaking."

Scotty and Johnster looked at each other in dismay. "Shit," muttered Scotty as he massaged his shoulder.

Emma heard the voice of her boss, Detective Superintendent Calvin Etheridge. She listened and then said, "Yes, sir, I understand. I'll be there. First thing in the morning."

She turned off her phone, coolly slid it back into her pocket then turned back to Johnster and Scotty.

"You know I can't just let your Neanderthal-like behaviour pass, don't you? While we wait for the landlord to call for a police officer to take statements, which one of you two is going to apologise first? You also owe me two new drinks."

CHAPTER FOUR

Kelly Lyle pulled her jacket close. It would take a day or two to readjust to the British climate. The greyness made her shudder. She stood at the window and watched the tide returning along Sandbanks Beach. In contrast to Italy, the sea here was slate grey. It would eventually turn a crystal blue, but for two days there had been unseasonably lousy weather with rain and high winds. Out at sea there had been storms, and debris was scattered along the beach. A spot of rain hit the window. The forecast for the next few days looked grim, and further storms were expected along the south coast.

The Sandbanks peninsula had the largest concentration of expensive properties outside London and, although she was trying to hide it, the property agent's voice revealed her excitement.

"You must have a guardian angel. You couldn't have timed it better; this property only became available this morning."

Lyle thumbed the business card to remind herself of

the agent's name. She had picked up the false sense of authority in the woman's voice and found it endearing.

When she didn't respond, the agent added, "It's dramatic, isn't it? Such an amazing position. Personally, I love watching the storms. My favourite time is at night. Lightning strikes over the ocean at night look so dramatic. And the thunder crashing all around, so loudly it rocks your whole body. Nights like those can make me feel so insignificant. Vulnerable."

Lyle smiled and turned to the young woman. "You're a romantic, Sienna."

Sienna blushed. "No one has said that about me before." Lyle tucked a strand of Sienna's short hair behind her ear. She stroked her cheek tenderly and gazed into her eyes. "You're also incredibly beautiful. What I wouldn't give to have your youth."

Sienna was unsure how to respond. She hadn't been hit on by a woman before. Is that what was happening here? She wasn't sure where to look. Her heart was beating hard in her chest. Her mouth felt dry. Was it wrong that she was enjoying the attention?

Picking up the file containing the property details, Sienna said, "Do you like it? The house, I mean?"

"I do. It's perfect. I'll pay the asking price, in cash."

"Really? That's wonderful news." Sienna passed her a business card. "If we go back to the office I can…"

"Actually, I'd like to stipulate one condition," added Lyle. "You must have dinner with me tonight. I have a reservation at Rick Stein's restaurant. You can tell me more about the area I'll be living in, and I'd like the opportunity to find out more about you, Miss Sienna Lasota."

Without giving herself time to make excuses, Sienna said, "Yes, I'd like that."

Lyle held Sienna's small chin and gave her a tender

kiss. "I'll see you at eight. Unfortunately, I've got to go. I'm running late for another appointment. I'll be moving in here immediately, no matter the cost. Bring whatever paperwork needs signing with you tonight." Lyle wrote a telephone number on the business card. "This is the number of my accountant. He'll handle the financial arrangements. I need you to make sure it happens this week. Can you do that for me?"

"Yes, of course."

"I know you will. I can see there is more to you than meets the eye. Underneath that beautiful exterior is a strong and determined young woman. I see that you just need to believe it." Lyle opened her purse and took out an envelope, which she handed to Sienna. "It's close to a thousand pounds. Buy yourself something stunning for tonight. Expensive clothes and shoes will give you confidence. I'll see you tonight."

CHAPTER FIVE

Lyle pulled the car onto the hard shoulder and turned on the hazard lights. She climbed out and looked over the bridge to the Fleetsbridge roundabout below.

It was a perfect spot. The evening rush hour traffic was building, and as the cars sat nose to tail, waiting for the traffic lights to change, the audience below would get front row seats.

Behind her, cars flew past, paying little attention to the parked vehicle. Why should they? She'd spent good money to have the car look like a paramedic's rapid-response vehicle.

She straightened the Batgirl mask she had put on, took a selfie and opened the back of the car. The young couple on the back seat began moaning and crying hysterically. Their hands were tied behind their backs, and over their heads they wore hoods.

"I'll be back to let you go in few minutes," promised Lyle.

She pulled out two lengths of rope and a small stepladder. Next, she pulled out a vinyl banner and fastened it to the railing before pushing it over the side to reveal its message.

Almost immediately, the first car honked its horn. Lyle smiled to herself.

Closing the rear door and opening the side door, she helped the young couple out. She could feel them trembling.

"Justin, sit there. Rachel, you sit down next to him." Obediently, they crouched below the railing.

"Please let us go. We won't tell anyone. Just let us go," pleaded Rachel. "We haven't seen your face; you can just let us go. We're wearing hoods. We can't see anything."

Lyle ignored her and opened up the stepladder. She tied two lengths of rope to the railing.

"Let us go, you freak," yelled Justin.

Lyle pressed two fingers into the back of his head.

"Don't shoot me. I'm sorry. I didn't mean that, but you've got to let us go."

"That earns you the opportunity of going first. Take my hand, Justin. If you don't, I'll shoot you in the head right here and now."

She didn't have a gun, but Justin didn't know that. Slowly he got to his feet.

"Do as I say, and I'll let you both go. Put this on. It's for your safety."

Lyle dropped a noose around his neck.

"Now, climb three small steps. You do that for me, and you'll get your freedom. I promise."

"I can't see?" said Justin.

"I'll help you."

With a great deal of coaxing, he did as he was told. Lyle held his arm and helped him up each step until he reached the top. Lyle looked over at the traffic below then up at the hooded Justin.

"Can you hear the car horns, Justin? They're for you."

He turned his head towards her voice. "Please…"

Lyle stepped behind him and pushed him over.

He vanished over the edge. The rope around his neck trailed behind him before snapping taut, instantly crushing his neck. Justin swung under the bridge like a pendulum.

From below came the sound of cars colliding. Car horns blared.

Lyle moved the ladder to the right side of the banner.

"On your feet, missy. Your turn."

As Lyle dropped the noose around Rachel's neck, Rachel pushed back and tried to run.

Lyle grabbed her arm and said, "Oh, no you don't. I need you to go this way."

Rachel smashed against the railing as Lyle shoved her. Forgetting the ladder, Lyle squatted down and grabbed Rachel's ankles. With considerable effort, she tipped Rachel over the railing.

She looked over the side at the couple swinging back and forth below. The traffic was now gridlocked, and people were out of their cars and gazing up. Lyle waved and watched with amusement as onlookers waved back. She blew a kiss and gave a thumbs-up to someone filming. She pointed to the banner and gave a farewell wave.

Returning to the car, Lyle started the siren and disappeared into the fast-flowing traffic.

CHAPTER SIX

Emma stopped her car outside the house of James Hardy. She grabbed the security envelope from the passenger seat and walked as quickly as she could up the driveway.

Her boss, Etheridge, would go nuts if he found out she was once again bothering the retired detective.

As light-footedly as possible, she climbed the steps and reached for the letterbox. The door opened.

"He's not here. And from what I understand, you're not supposed to be here." Hardy's girlfriend, Monica, looked down at her.

Monica was the woman he'd changed his life for. He'd given up being a detective for her. Hardy had changed his whole life for Monica, and now Monica stood not two feet away as Emma was trying to coax him back. She felt like a drug dealer leaving a free sample for a reformed addict.

"I'm sorry. I just wanted to drop this off." She held out the envelope.

Monica took it and said, "He's trying to put this behind him. I believe he spoke to your boss about you dropping these off."

"I'm just looking for pointers. Anything he can offer me. If he could just take a look and let me know what I'm missing."

"You know damn well it doesn't work that way. It's all or nothing. That's why he doesn't open any of the packages you deliver. You need to stop coming here. He's conflicted and needs time to decide for himself what he wants. You do know he only just survived the last investigation he was on? His daughters nearly lost their daddy."

Emma nodded and said, "I'm sorry. I just..." She turned to walk away.

Monica's tone changed. "Are you okay? If you don't mind my saying, you look like shit. I've watched you deliver these envelopes before. Today you don't seem yourself. Less energy, less zing."

"It's just been a tough few days. As well as work, I have some personal stuff. My fiancé seems to have had a change of heart. It seems every way I turn I seem to be lacking." She wasn't sure why she was telling this to a woman she didn't know. Confiding in strangers must be an indication of how crap her life had become. She needed to be careful she didn't start seeking counselling from anyone who would listen.

"I'm sorry. Why don't you come in? I'm a good listener. I could also use a break; I'm an English teacher and have been marking student papers all night. James is out. Alice and Faith are visiting their grandparents. It's just me and the dog." Monica could see Cotton was tempted. "I just opened a cold bottle of Sauvignon Blanc. I have some chilli con carne I can warm up for you. Come in for a bit. It's been a while since I had some adult female company."

. . .

As they chatted and sipped wine Emma could see why a man like Hardy had fallen for Monica. Not only was she beautiful, but she was one of those women who could pull off intelligent, maternal and sexy with complete ease. There was a confidence about her that suggested she had life under control. Monica had a way about her that immediately put you at ease. A casual manner and an aura that made you feel you could trust her with your deepest secrets. She felt like a friend she'd known her whole life.

Monica asked about the investigation, and although Emma couldn't tell her much, due to it being an ongoing case, she explained the dead ends they had encountered. It didn't take her long to get around to explaining how she thought Hardy could help. Monica listened attentively and gave nothing away about how she felt.

"You do realise I have no sway over whether he ever goes back to active detective work, don't you?"

"I wasn't suggesting you try to persuade him. I wouldn't do that."

"I know. I can see your heart is in the right place. It was his choice to leave. He did it for his daughters, Alice and Faith. After their mother died, he became increasingly concerned that if anything happened to him, they'd be alone."

"I heard you were the other reason."

Monica smiled a wide, beautiful smile. "The romantic in me likes to think so. The romantic in him likes to think so too. Hardy is the sweetest and most honest man I have ever met. He's smart, dedicated, passionate and loyal to those he lets in. If you do work with him, don't ever lie to him. You won't get a second chance."

CHAPTER SEVEN

Opening the front door, she felt her heart tighten in her chest. Her evening with Monica had been enjoyable, but it also emphasised how crap her life was right now. *You can't have it all*, she thought, *but just some of it would be nice.* In her head, her mother's voice was reminding her how being a detective was "no life for a woman," and "You'll get to forty, and you'll be too old for kids." And "You know how long I've dreamed of grandchildren."

During the drive home, she replayed the conversation with Dave over and over. She wondered whether he genuinely did just want a little breathing space. For a moment she wondered whether he had simply got cold feet. Then she scolded herself for being so stupid. There was no doubt he was seeing someone else. She'd suspected it for a while, but being so busy she'd put it to one side, hoping his indiscretion could be ignored and would pass.

Emma tried to calm herself. "I won't cry. Do not cry." She checked each room and could see he hadn't been back to collect his stuff. That set her mind racing as to where he was, who he was with, why he didn't need his clothes or any of his stuff. She pushed the thoughts away.

Watson appeared at the window and started meowing and pacing up and down. "Hello, boy. Have you come to say hello to Mummy? Come here. I need some love."

She opened the back door and Watson padded in.

"Still refusing to use the cat-flap, I see. Still feel it's beneath you?"

Emma stroked and squeezed him and gave him a kiss on the top of his head before he wriggled free. Her eyes began filling with tears. She fought them back. She opened the fridge and took out some cold chicken. Her voice breaking, she said, "Are you hungry? Dave won't be coming back today. We won't need all this chicken. It's just you and me from now on. Is that okay? You can have some." She broke a chicken breast into pieces and put them down for Watson.

A sob forced its way out. Then another. She had fought hard, but she couldn't hold her emotions back any longer. Tears overwhelmed her. Having let her guard down for a moment, the distress and upset, which had rumbled away inside, finally erupted like a volcano. She ran to her bed and flung herself on it the way she had done as a little girl. Unable to control her feelings, she had no choice but to let go and let them out. The rawness of her pain and her inability to control her tears surprised her. Were these feelings of loss? Or feelings of failure? Or was it the hurt of his betrayal? Her mind was dark and confused, and everything felt blurred.

Curled up on the bed, she imagined his warmth behind her and his arm around her. She could smell him on the duvet. Feel his kiss on her neck. She pushed his pillows off the bed onto the floor, turned over her own tear-soaked pillow and fell into a deep, heavy sleep.

Watson watched her for a time from the end of the bed before he too curled up and went to sleep.

CHAPTER EIGHT

Detective Superintendent Calvin Etheridge ended the call and dropped the phone in his jacket pocket. Ideally, he would speak to DI Cotton today, but he'd had enough for one day, and she appeared to have a life outside work. Lucky her. *At least someone did*, he thought.

Instead of working late again, Etheridge had decided to go home. Lifting the bottle of brandy from the passenger seat of the Audi and checking the car was locked, he began the short walk along the river.

These days, home was a caravan beside a half-built house on a piece of land he'd paid too much for. The Wreck, as he called it, made him feel sick to look at. It had been meant to be their dream home. He and Kate had planned on building it together; it was to be their fresh start. Instead, it was now a leering, taunting monstrosity. It represented the state of his life. Kate was gone, and the partly built house was nothing more than a constant and expensive reminder of their failed marriage.

He'd heard some couples would have another baby in the hope of rekindling their relationship. He and Kate had

had the crazy idea of idea working together on designing and managing the build of a new home in which they could both grow comfortably old together.

Ironically, Kate did live in a dream home now; it just happened to be with Patrick, the site manager he'd hired. As he'd overheard one of the workmen say with a laugh, "Instead of laying bricks, Patrick's laying the wife. He's doing it while the poor bugger is paying him, too."

Etheridge stepped inside the caravan. He threw his jacket on the back of a chair. It slid off into a pile on the floor. He reached into the sink for a glass and half-heartedly ran it under the tap. Without bothering to dry it, he filled the glass with brandy. He drank half the glass and topped it up. He sighed heavily and pushed the front door open with his foot. He leaned on the doorframe and looked out.

He felt lonely; drink did that to him – amplified what he was already feeling. He thought about phoning Kate. Maybe she was ready to come home. He didn't feel ready to pick up the phone. What if she sounded happy? He didn't want to hear *that* in her voice. What if Patrick picked up the phone? Could he text her? Maybe later, after another drink or two.

A voice caught his attention. He leaned out and looked back up the path he'd just come down. The footpath was a public right of way, but he'd never seen anyone else use it. He stepped down from the caravan to get a better look.

"Ruby!" called the woman. She had the brightest red hair he'd ever seen. She wore blue glittery welly-boots, blue jeans and a jacket the same red as her hair. "Ruby! Where are you?" The woman looked his way and immediately waved and called to him. "Woohoo! Hello!" She started to trot towards him. He wanted to back himself into his caravan and close the door, but it was too late.

26

"She's about this big, brown, with one white foot and white down the front of her face." The woman, who was a little out of breath from trotting over to him, was one of those very animated people who were fun when you were in the right frame of mind. She was now crouching down and using her hand to demonstrate the size of the dog. "Please say you've seen her. Please tell me you've seen my little Ruby." She tilted her head and gave him her pleading face.

Etheridge hid the glass of brandy behind his back. "I'm sorry, I haven't been home long. I've only seen you. Sorry – I didn't mean you're a dog." He smiled with amusement, but she seemed oblivious to his poor choice of words.

He watched as this wacky woman started looking behind and under the caravan and the surrounding area. It was like she was moving in fast-forward while talking incessantly. "I've never walked this way before. It's a beautiful walk. So secluded. No other dog walkers. I thought it would make a change for Ruby. I can't believe I came out without my phone. Poor little Ruby. I'm sure she must be lost. She must be frightened. I hope she's not hurt. She's only just back from the vet. Cost me a fortune. The only time I don't have my phone; can you believe it? I love little Ruby to bits. Do you have pets? I've always had a dog. My whole life. I can't imagine life without one." She started calling again. "Ruby! Ruby! Ruby!"

Etheridge thought about it for a moment then said, "Would you like to use my mobile phone? You won't get a signal here, but we could walk back up the path together."

"I don't want to be any bother, but…" Her face was beaming, and for a fleeting moment Etheridge thought she looked familiar. "I'm at my wits' end with worry," she insisted. "I can phone my husband and children. They can help me search. Ruby couldn't cope alone out here at night. She might be eaten by foxes or badgers."

Etheridge felt sure foxes and badgers wouldn't attack and eat her dog but said nothing. "Give me a second. I'll just get my phone." He stepped inside the caravan, bent over to pick up his jacket then called out over his shoulder. "Do you live very far away? Perhaps Ruby went home."

When he turned and straightened up, she was there in front of him. Uncomfortably close. "Oh, you're there. I thought you were still outside. Sorry, the place is a mess." He smiled awkwardly. She smiled back. He watched as she pulled off the red wig. He searched his memory for where he'd seen her before. *Holy shit.* As he lurched forward, she fired the taser. Every muscle in his body seized. He let out a pitiful groan before collapsing to his knees. He fell sideways, his head bouncing off the chair on the way down. She shocked him again and again. Everything went black.

CHAPTER NINE

Etheridge touched the cut on his head. He was on the floor. He tried to sit up. His body ached and he felt bruised. He got to his hands and knees and threw up beside the armchair. His head was spinning as though he were drunk. The room was moving uncontrollably. He was trying to remember what had happened. He pulled himself up onto the armchair. On the worktop next to the sink he could see the red wig. The woman. Kelly Lyle. *The Mentor*. Where was she? And what was that smell? Gas? The air was thick with gas.

He put out a hand to steady himself. Leaning heavily on the armchair, he pushed himself up to his feet. Stepping forward, he knocked against something metal on the floor. A saw. A surgical saw. Where had that come from? Had she left it? Had she intended to use it on him?

He needed to get out before she came back. He'd seen the sick and bloody things she'd done to her victims. Etheridge lunged forward and nearly fell flat on his face. He was chained around his ankle. *What the fuck?* He kicked his leg, and the chain rattled. It was short, like a leash.

There wasn't enough chain to reach the kitchen area to turn off the gas. Could he even reach the door?

His head was pounding. The cooker hob hissed. His vision was blurred. The room swayed. He needed to move. He must open the door. He needed fresh air. Oxygen. He got down on his belly. Staying low, he crawled to the door. He reached up for the door handle. He pulled the handle. His fingers slipped. He reached again. The handle didn't move. The door was locked. She'd locked him in. *Shit. What now?*

Etheridge looked around for ideas. He turned to the window behind him. It was locked. The key was gone. He grabbed a dining chair and smashed it against the window. Not even a scratch. The thick, modern insulated window wouldn't break; he knew that. She knew that. He was caught like a rat in a trap. Etheridge's eyes scanned the room. They eventually fell upon the key hanging from the handle of a kitchen cabinet. The key was so far beyond his reach it might as well have been on the far side of the moon.

There must be a way out. *Think!*

An alarm sounded then stopped. *What now?* On his knees, he looked towards the sound. Next to the sink he could see a timer. He strained his eyes to see it clearly. The digital numbers were counting down. Counting down to what? Wires ran from the timer to a gas torch. He was in one of Kelly Lyle's perverse games. His imagination told him that when the timer reached zero, a switch would ignite the gas torch and... *boom!*

This couldn't be happening.

Panic set in. What could he do? *Stay calm and think. The saw.* He grabbed it and started sawing frantically at the heavy chain. The alarm beeped again. He stayed focused on the chain. Sawing like a madman. *Keep going! Keep going!*

He stopped and examined the chain. Barely a scratch. The saw was no good for cutting metal. He threw it down. It was a surgical saw. Lyle knew it wouldn't cut through metal. It was merely meant to taunt him.

He sat back. *Think.* It was no good. He would die. How long did he have? Minutes? Seconds? He tried desperately to see the timer, but his eyes were failing. He was starting to lose consciousness. He didn't want to die this way. He didn't want to die.

He found himself staring at the saw. It was medical. The sort used for cutting bone. He laughed hysterically. He understood now. Lyle had left the saw for him. The saw was his only means of escape. He started to sob as he reached for it.

Saw in hand, he looked down at his foot. Should he cut above or below the shackle? Could he do it before passing out and before the timer finished? Was he really considering this?

Yes. He needed a tourniquet. Etheridge took off his shirt and wrapped it around his leg as far down as he could. It was nowhere near good enough, but it was the best he could do.

He pressed the blade just above his ankle. He winced and sobbed and yelled and screamed. He couldn't do it.

He had to do it. A rat would gnaw off a trapped leg to survive. He had to decide how badly he wanted to live.

The timer sounded. He heard a click. Then the *crack, crack, crack* before the flame was lit.

Etheridge panicked and started sawing at his leg. Screaming and sawing. Sobbing and sawing. Blood poured. He kept sawing.

The blast was heard for several miles.

From her car Lyle watched the smoke rise high above the trees.

CHAPTER TEN

Emma stared at photos of Scrabble letters as if staring at them hard enough would magically reveal their meaning. A Scrabble piece had been left at the scene of each murder. T, C, H, I. She moved them around. HICT, CHTI, then CHIT. Perhaps, the word was CHRIST and the letters R and S were missing. *Maybe there are two more bodies, and they haven't been found yet.* And if the word was CHRIST, what did it signify? Was the killer some religious nut? She was clutching at straws, and she knew it. She squeezed her shoulder muscles and twisted her neck until it clicked. She sighed long and hard.

The time was 9.34 a.m. Etheridge was late. She sipped her coffee and pulled out the photos of the five victims. It was nearly a year since the first body had been revealed by the retreating tide under Boscombe Pier. A few weeks later a second body was discovered beneath Bournemouth Pier. Back then she had been a detective sergeant, and she'd had no idea it was the beginning of a serial murder investigation.

About six months back, she'd taken the decision to call

retired DCI James Hardy on the off chance he'd take a look at the case. It seemed the right thing to do considering the way the victims had been mutilated and the bodies left. She'd read about the type of cases he investigated and of him leaving New Scotland Yard to live in Dorset.

Looking back, she'd been naive to call him. She'd acted out of emotion. Secretly perhaps, she'd hoped she'd get to work on the case with him. She was lucky Etheridge was a decent boss and hadn't been offended. Etheridge, too, was more interested in bringing the perpetrator to justice than worrying about anyone's ego or an outsider coming in and stepping on his toes. She liked him for that. At the time, he had seemed distracted by stuff in his personal life and had said very little about her going over his head. She got nothing more than a word of warning to never do it again.

The day Martin Burke was discovered mutilated and tied to a pillar under Bournemouth Pier was the day she'd first met Hardy. Before that, she'd spoken to him briefly on the phone, but meeting him at the crime scene had left quite an impression.

He was confident without being an arrogant prick like some senior detectives she'd met. He'd spent a lot of time listening to others and offering his perspective. Hardy looked relatively young, and she wanted to understand more about why he'd retired so early. She also recalled, with embarrassment, thinking he was handsome in the way older men who stay in shape and look after their appearance sometimes are.

She'd watched out of the corner of her eye as he spoke at length to Etheridge about both murders. Later, she'd heard he and Etheridge had visited the scene of the first murder at Boscombe Pier. Later, Dylan Durrant, too, had been mutilated and tied to a pillar under the pier. He'd been there a while before being discovered, and it was hard to stomach. Every fish and crab for miles had taken a nibble at his corpse.

Etheridge had obviously hoped he'd be able to convince Hardy to work with him – everyone had – but it hadn't panned out that way. She'd never learned why. All she knew was that one morning Etheridge had come into the office in a foul mood. He'd assembled the team and informed everyone that, despite the rumour, Hardy was unavailable for the foreseeable future. When she'd pressed him, he told her Hardy had insisted "it was better he wasn't involved." Whatever the hell that meant.

What they did get from Hardy was a name, a suspect they needed to consider. That was the first time she'd heard of Kelly Lyle.

Lyle was known to Hardy, the London Metropolitan Police and Interpol. Although she worked alone, Lyle was nicknamed "The Mentor" for the way she coerced others to kill on her behalf. She was known to assist other killers by offering them advice and support in an exclusive online website community she controlled. It had never occurred to Emma the killer might be a woman.

She leaned back in her chair and looked out into the main office. As she chewed her pen, Detective Phil Gross walked past. She smiled and held up a hand. Gross opened the door and stuck his head into the office.

"Morning. You okay?" said Gross. He had a mouth full of breakfast roll. She could smell the greasy bacon. Her stomach rumbled.

"Have you seen Etheridge?" she asked him.

Gross wiped tomato sauce off his mouth with his wrist then licked at it. "Now what have you done?" He took another bite, careful not to lose any of the dripping egg.

"Sod off. He wanted to see me first thing. Probably another promotion."

"Yeah, right, and I'm dating Jennifer Lawrence."

"Who?"

"If I see Etheridge, I'll let you know. And, Cotton, you really need to get out more."

"You might be right."

"How are the wedding plans coming along? I haven't had my invite yet."

"Thanks for reminding me." The knot in her stomach tightened at the mention of it. She still hadn't called her mum to tell her it was off.

"That bad?"

"Worse."

"Sorry to hear that. Look, I've got to go. Something is going on. I'm getting waved at. Catch up later, yeah?"

Emma watched Gross push the last of his sandwich into his mouth and disappear along the hallway to his office. She got to her feet to see if she could see what was happening.

She stepped out of her office and looked around. There was a lot of commotion. Something felt wrong. She watched as people ran this way and that.

Gross came running back towards her. He was struggling to get his arm in the sleeve of his jacket.

"What's going on?" she asked.

"We just heard. It's Etheridge. He's been killed. Some sort of gas explosion at his home."

"Oh, my God." Her mind skipped back to the last time she'd spoken to him.

Gross leaned close and spoke quietly. "That's not all. First indications are it wasn't an accident. They're saying some sort of incendiary device was used. He was murdered."

CHAPTER ELEVEN

Tears and hushed conversations were everywhere. As soon as the fire brigade and forensics teams established Etheridge's death was no accident, a wave of shock had passed through the station.

Rumours spread like wildfire. Whispers and theories permeated every office and every corner.

I heard the killer kept him alive while cutting off all his limbs.

I heard it was Lyle. If she can kill Etheridge, then she could pick off any one of us.

She tortured him for hours.

They say she wears disguises. You don't know it's her until it's too late.

She's only here because of that ex–Scotland Yard detective. How come she killed Etheridge and not him? Surely that's a bit weird?

Emma heard it all but said nothing. She hated herself for not intervening. She looked around the office and felt ashamed. If it had been one of them who'd died, Etheridge would put a stop to the rumour mill. He'd also know what to do next. The feeling of being in limbo pissed her off. When she could stand it no longer, she grabbed her coat and walked out.

She needed to see Hardy. Bring him up to date and let him know how out of control this case had become.

She crossed the station car park. The only thing darker than her mood was the dark clouds overhead. Fumbling for her car keys, she noticed an envelope tucked under the windscreen wiper. It was addressed to her. It felt lumpy.

Without thinking, she ripped it open. She got into the car and poured the contents onto the front passenger seat. There was another Scrabble piece. This time the letter E. There were photos too. They were of Etheridge. He was asleep or unconscious on the floor of his caravan. A close-up of the chain around his ankle. A close-up of his face. She flicked through the images. Why was Lyle communicating with her? Did she want something from her? Had she killed Etheridge to slow down the investigation? Or had she done it just to show she could, to tell them she could reach anyone?

She pulled a forensics bag from the glovebox and dropped the Scrabble piece and photos and envelope inside. It was definitely time to talk to Hardy again.

CHAPTER TWELVE

I felt like the luckiest man alive as I walked along the Sandbanks promenade with Monica beside me. We talked and watched Alice and Faith down on the beach as they played beside the ocean. They followed the withdrawing waves then turned and ran as the returning waves chased them back up the shore. Sandy barked and bounced around with excitement, occasionally veering off to chase another passing dog.

Monica leaned into me and tilted her head. "Are you happy?"

I lifted her hand and kissed it. "Completely. Moving here was the right thing. I love it. Alice and Faith have settled in and are happy. I don't remember the last time I was this relaxed, and the icing on the cake is I'm completely in love with a loving, sexy, smart, patient and caring woman who seems able to tolerate me."

"She sounds like she must be a saint; I'd like to meet her."

"Next time I see her I'll mention it."

Monica gave me a playful prod before wrapping her

arms around my shoulders and kissing me. Down on the beach, we could both see Alice and Faith looking mortified at what they'd consider our gross display of affection. It made us laugh, so we played it up. Holding her in my arms, I tilted Monica backwards and kissed her passionately. Looking up at me with smiling eyes, she lifted a leg for extra effect. Although we couldn't hear it, we could see Alice and Faith's embarrassment as they gasped and screamed in horror. They ran along the beach to put as much distance as they could between themselves and us. Laughing and kissing, we held the pose for as long as we could before laughter got the better of us and we had to stop.

Joking over, we continued the walk, and Monica asked, "Do you miss it? Being a homicide detective?"

"Not one bit," I answered without hesitation.

Monica said nothing. Instead, she looked at me in the way she does when she needs convincing. "I've found it more difficult than I was expecting, that's all," I added. "I don't mean stepping away from active duty. I mean emotionally. The darkness of the cases must have got to me more than I realised."

She looked down at the ground. "How do you feel now?"

"It's as if I'm punching through the darkness and seeing the light and feeling the warmth of it for the first time in a long time."

Monica lifted her head and looked at me. "You never told me that."

"I wasn't sure how to put it into words until now."

"Do you think the lecturing and consulting work will be enough?"

"Enough? Yes, it's good money. And the advance on my book was a nice surprise."

"That's not what I meant, and you know it."

"I know."

This conversation had been brewing for a while, and Monica wasn't going to let me off the hook that easily.

"You're a detective," she said. "We both know you're one of the best in the country. I know it's sometimes dangerous. I know you've almost died on more than one occasion. I also know you've given it all up for us, Alice and Faith especially. I understand all that. And going back to pursuing psychopaths is the last thing I want you to do. I want you here, with me, safe. You know I do. But I'm also worried about what it'll do to you. Maybe not today, maybe not tomorrow, but over the years to come. I'm worried some regret will eat away at you. I just don't see how you can simply stop being what you were clearly meant to be."

"I didn't know you felt that way," I said.

"I'm not sure how I feel. I don't want you dying at the hands of some crackpot killer, but I also know what you've given up for me is a part of who you are. I suppose I want to make sure you're content."

"Every day people have a change of lifestyle. That's all this is. The way I see it is that I'm still catching the bad guys. The only difference is that I'm doing it by educating other detectives. I'm teaching them what I've learned so that I don't have to be out there."

"What about these local murders? That young detective, Cotton, implied you know the killer. Is that why she leaves the files?"

"She's young and ambitious. I've spoken to her boss again. She won't be doing that anymore."

A mobile phone started to ring, and instinctively I reached into my pocket. Monica waved her phone at me.

The call was for her. Old habits die hard, and receiving emergency calls was something I still expected.

I left Monica chatting to a girlfriend. I ran down on to the beach to search for shells with Alice and Faith.

"Daddy! We're looking for treasure," said Faith. "These shells, the pearly ones, are what we need."

"We're going to make a mosaic with them for Nana Hardy."

"She'll love that. Let's see how many we can find."

Monica's words buzzed around my brain, and I swiped them away. Looking back, I could see how far down the rabbit hole I'd fallen and the mistakes I'd made. I was a different person now. I had to be.

CHAPTER THIRTEEN

The driveway was empty. Emma parked the car across the street and watched the house for any sign of someone being home. It was a hot and humid day, and all the windows were closed. If Hardy or Monica were home, then at least one window would be open.

She checked her watch. Three-fifty p.m. She'd sat there forty minutes. "Christ's sake. Go get a sandwich and come back in an hour," she told herself out loud.

The bakery had a small seating area, and she sat alone and sipped her coffee. She wetted her finger and picked up the last few crumbs of chocolate cake. She sucked her finger. She was tempted to get another slice.

Two teenage girls came in and ordered caramel choux buns. Their uniforms told her they were from the local grammar school. It got her thinking about the choices she'd made since leaving school. She'd always wanted to be a police officer, in particular a detective. Her parents had tried to persuade her to go into medicine, but it held no appeal. All those years ago this wasn't how she had pictured her life: working every hour, jilted just weeks before her wedding day, avoiding her mother and only a cat for company.

What was she doing here? Did she really think she could persuade a man like James Hardy to do anything? To him, she must look like a woman obsessed. *Leave the poor man alone*, she told herself. Did she really think she could ask him to get involved in the Lyle investigation? The man had decided to leave active policing for good reason. Who did she think she was even to try to change that? Was she doing it for the sake of the victims or for her own benefit? There was no denying she wanted to work with him. If he wouldn't help now, he never would. This was her final attempt. How should she approach it? If she came at him head-on, he'd back off again for sure.

It was just after 5.30 p.m. when she parked outside the Hardy house for a second time that day. This time the family car was in the driveway, and the doors and boot were open. She watched for a moment. They'd been to the beach. Monica was the first to spot her. She watched as Monica spoke to Hardy. Emma realised she didn't feel guilt at being there; she felt determination.

Monica looked over again, and Emma offered a smile and lifted a tentative hand to wave. Lifting a cool-box out of the boot, Monica called the girls to her and ushered them inside. Alice looked back over her shoulder at her dad and then at the stranger in the car, and the younger one was clearly asking Monica lots of questions. Monica kept them moving.

Hardy didn't look over as Emma approached. Instead, he shook and beat the car mats to get the sand off. He then started pulling together the last few items left in the car.

She stood beside the car and watched Hardy's hands as

he reached for two small brightly coloured buckets full of shells. She wondered if she should speak first, perhaps offer to help. She didn't know the right words or even where to start. Instead, she stared at the sand, which would be impossible to remove from the inside of the car completely.

CHAPTER FOURTEEN

"I've been expecting you," I said without looking up. "I'm sorry to hear about Etheridge. I liked him." Cotton's bright eyes fixed on mine, and I wondered what she was thinking. Did she blame me for Etheridge's death? If she did, I wouldn't entirely blame her. I know I blamed myself more than a little.

Etheridge and I had spoken a lot over the last few months, and I'd got to know him well. He was going through a rough patch. As well as the multiple-murder investigation, which was chewing away at him, he'd opened up about his marriage break-up and his financial circumstances, which weren't great due to a house he'd only partially built and no longer had any passion for completing. Somehow, we always managed to find some light during our conversations together. We laughed, told stories and filled his bin with a considerable number of empty beer bottles.

He'd also talked about the rising star in his department, who stood beside me now. He told me Cotton was going to be a great detective. She was sharp, dedicated, with instincts that couldn't be taught and that all the best detectives had.

Cotton was unaware of our friendship. Etheridge had asked I keep our conversations private, and I saw no reason to betray that trust now. If anyone asked, we were merely two seasoned homicide detectives letting off steam and throwing around theories. I was going to miss him, and I shuddered when I thought about his final moments. No one should go out like that.

"You heard? He was well liked," said Cotton. "This has to stop."

I shook the sand off a tartan picnic blanket, folded it and passed it to her. I piled a few things on top, then put a beach chair under each arm and closed the boot. I tucked a pink baseball cap under my chin, picked up a canvas bag I'd loaded with buckets and spades and shut the car door with my backside. "You had better come in."

"You're with your family. I don't want to intrude," said Cotton. She knew how ridiculous that sounded. I didn't reply. She followed me into the house.

Out of the corner of my eye, I watched her taking in the chaos of the Hardy family home. The house was full of noise and energy, the way I liked it. With two children, their friends, a crazy dog, grandparents and neighbours in and out, there was always some excitement. Never knowing what might happen next was part of the fun and reminded me of my own childhood home.

Upstairs I could hear Alice and Faith arguing about who was going to shower first. All the while, I could hear the shower running – by the time the decision was made, there would be no hot water left.

Monica was also upstairs trying to calm the situation while searching for a new bottle of shampoo. I heard her telling Faith that Sandy was a dog and wasn't allowed in the shower with her. In fact, Sandy shouldn't have been upstairs at all.

"Take a seat," I said. "Let me sort a few things out and then we can talk." I loaded the washing machine with beach towels. In the kitchen sink, I rinsed sand off the girls' beach shoes. "Have you eaten?"

"Yes, thank you. I'm fine."

I finished going through the beach bag and went outside the back door. I needed a few minutes to think. It was crunch time. I opened and closed the utility room door to pretend I was doing something out there. I came back into the kitchen and went upstairs to speak to Monica.

As I came back down the stairs, Cotton was typing a message on her phone. I could see she was pretending she hadn't been trying to hear our conversation, which had been conducted in hushed whispers.

"Do you have any more case files with you? I want to see everything," I told her.

I looked back up the stairs to where Monica stood. She winked, tossed her hair and carried on as though nothing had changed.

Everything had changed.

Cotton had to fight back a huge grin. "Not with me. I can organise that."

"Good. Follow me. I have an office out back. You can bring me up to speed. Are you sure you've eaten? How about a drink? Tea? Coffee? I have some cold beers in the office fridge."

"Cold beer sounds good."

CHAPTER FIFTEEN

"First, I want you to understand my talking to you doesn't mean I'm involved in this investigation. If I decide to get involved, and I'm not saying I will, I'll re-examine case files and present my findings. I'll offer my thoughts, based on my experience, for your consideration."

Cotton nodded.

"If it's critical to the investigation, I'll sit in on interviews," I said.

Cotton let me talk.

"I promised my daughters and Monica and myself I was done with it all. I have no desire to return to active duty."

Cotton said, "I understand. Completely."

I scratched the back of my head and could feel sand in my hair. I thought about Etheridge. "That said, if I have a lead that's worth following up, I'll check it out. I want to be able to do that. You'll need to get that authorised."

Cotton made an almost inaudible 'Uh-huh' that suggested she didn't believe this conversation was purely theoretical. Maybe she was right. I knew all too well where all this was headed. Why else would I have let her into my office? Why else did I spend so many hours reviewing case files and pretending I didn't? The truth was, I was hooked from the moment I saw the first body under the pier.

Cotton said, "If we do it, we can do it on your terms. I'd just appreciate you looking over the files, that's all. Let me know what you think. You can tell me what I missed."

I watched as her hungry eyes took in the details of the room. She had the look of a child who'd just entered a magical toy shop. She didn't know where to look first and wanted to examine everything. She pointed to a photo pinned to a map of Greater London I had fastened to a wall. "Are you working on a case? Is that your late wife?"

I closed a file on my desk and put it away in a filing cabinet. "Why don't you take a seat? I'll listen to what you have to say, and then you can leave. I'll tell you exactly what I told Etheridge: I've given more than my share to policing. I've lost too much already. I can't lose any more." I felt bad about what had happened to Etheridge, but it changed nothing. It only underlined my resolve to stay away from active police work.

"You've lost too much? What about Etheridge? He's lost more than any one of us. I stuck my neck out and called you after the bodies of Martin Burke and Dylan Durrant were found under the piers. You came and took a look, no doubt tossed Etheridge some of your wisdom, then walked away. Together, you and Etheridge might have caught the killer. Etheridge might still be alive. And the families of the victims might have answers." Cotton wasn't shy about speaking her mind. I might have felt angry, but I admired her tenacity. "The way I see it, you are involved. You've always been involved. Whether you like it or not."

"What does that mean, exactly?" I asked. Her eyes were everywhere except on me.

"I have a theory Kelly Lyle is killing to get your attention. I don't know why. I don't understand what there is between you two." The thought that this could be Lyle's motivation made me go cold. I let her continue. "If not to get your attention, then why would she start killing here in Dorset? There is nothing that links her to this part of the country. Nothing except you. I don't pretend to understand what she hopes to gain by doing what she's doing. Unlike you, I'm on the outside looking in. What I do know is that the longer you leave getting involved, the more innocent people are going to lose their lives. How can you live with that and do nothing?" She didn't wait for my response. "Has Lyle contacted you?"

I overlooked her outburst. I had a feeling it had been building for quite some time. It was better it was out in the open. I answered the last question. "She sends me a postcard from time to time. The last one was from Italy. Nothing on the card suggests she has anything to do with the murders. No bragging or brinkmanship. I passed the cards on to Etheridge."

"What do you make of the Scrabble pieces?"

"They are new. As far as I'm aware, she's never left anything similar at a crime scene before. They could be a red herring. They could be a game that we don't understand yet. They could be misdirection. They could be anything her mind wants them to be."

"Is she crazy?"

"How would you categorise crazy?"

"Oh, I don't know. How about stripping a middle-aged man naked then tying him to a pillar beneath a pier before cutting his stomach wide open to reveal his guts. Then leaving him to either drown from the rising tide or bleed to death." Cotton watched my reaction. She was testing me. Etheridge was right: she was tougher than I'd first given her credit for. I could almost picture him looking down and saying with a laugh, "Good luck, buddy. She's your problem now."

"You don't need to tell me what she's capable of. And, no. She isn't crazy in the way you mean. She's complex. She is not a standard serial killer in that there is no pattern to whom she kills or how she kills them. She does not fall into the most common definition of psychopath; she shows signs of empathy for a select few. She's possibly the smartest multiple killer I've come across. She is very much in control of both herself and her environment. Which is how she's evading arrest."

"You've studied her?"

"That's my job." I corrected myself. "That *was* my job."

Cotton reached into her thin jacket and pulled out an evidence bag. She showed it to me. "The inscription on the back had us stumped for a while. It was on Etheridge's wrist. I'm guessing the watch belongs to you and is part of Lyle's game?"

The glass was damaged, and the watch was dirty-looking. I recognised it immediately as a gift and knew without looking what the inscription read: *Forever, Love Helena.*

"Helena is my late wife." I felt like my heart was being crushed as I held the watch in my hand again. Memories of Helena flooded back. Her smile as she watched me unwrap the watch on my birthday. "I thought I'd lost it when we moved from London. I can't tell you how much it means to get this back."

"Why did you tell Etheridge to consider Kelly Lyle as a suspect? How do we know I haven't wasted all these months investigating the wrong person?"

I was pleased Etheridge had taken my advice and kept

my theory from his team. I perched on the edge of my desk while Cotton sat in my tattered old comfy 'thinking' chair. It had been a battle getting permission to bring the chair with me from London, but after some tough negotiations with Alice and Faith, they had allowed it into our new home.

"I encountered Kelly Lyle, The Mentor, during a separate investigation into a serial killer called Simon Baker. I had no idea who or what she was at the time. It wasn't until much later that I discovered her involvement in that and many other cases. As I said, she's complex."

"You sound like you admire her."

I ignored the remark and continued. "Lyle's a collector. She takes a souvenir from each of her kills. Usually a piece of jewellery, but she's also been known to take hair or a finger or toe or eye. Keeping a souvenir or trophy is very common. It's been well documented."

"So, you think Lyle did it because you saw something was missing from each of our victims?"

"Not this time. Etheridge let me see the personal effects from each victim. Martin Burke had a St. Christopher necklace, which his family said was not his. I suggested it came from the victim of a completely separate case. Dylan Durrant had a wedding ring, which, again, was not his. Both items could be linked indirectly to Lyle. I suggested he speak to an old colleague of mine at Scotland Yard to confirm my suspicions. Etheridge must have done so and been convinced enough to pursue that line of enquiry."

"I was the only one he put on looking at Lyle. Nobody else," said Cotton. "Etheridge said he didn't want all his eggs in one basket. I told him Lyle was a dead end." She looked at me accusingly. "You're the reason Etheridge had me spend months chasing my tail, getting nowhere. He must have known I'd find nothing."

"Etheridge chose you for a reason," I insisted. "I don't think it was because he was sidelining you. From what I know of him, my guess is he was putting one of his best detectives on the toughest part of the case." I could see Cotton wasn't convinced. "With so many lines of enquiry to pursue, Etheridge had a lot of tough choices to make."

"Why didn't you offer to help? I just don't get it. You could have consulted in a small way. If you had helped, Etheridge might still be alive." Cotton sighed heavily. She rubbed her nose and choked back tears. "I'm sorry. I didn't mean that."

"I'm sorry about Ethcridge. I was in a very dark place for a long time. After my wife died, I was on full throttle for too long. Those who care about me helped me realise I needed to stop. Before it was too late. I came here for the sake of those I love and for my own health. For the record, my state of mind at that time is not something I hide, and at the same time it's not something I talk about."

"I'm sorry. It's none of my business." Cotton checked the time. "I'd better go."

I showed her to the door. I was starting to see why Etheridge had held her in such high regard. She was fearless.

"Emma," I called after her. "I've tried to be straight with you. As honest as I can. I'm going to sleep on it. No promises. I want to speak to my family too. This isn't just about me. I have them to consider. In the meantime, you look into whether you can get clearance for me to put in a few hours. I'll review the case files and make some calls. Maybe I can put in a morning a week. Like I say, I'm going to sleep on it."

Cotton's face lit up, and she stood a little taller. "I'll call the chief now. Thank you."

"It's getting late. Maybe call him in the morning?"

"Not a chance. If you decide to help, I don't want to waste a minute. I'll call you as soon as I know. What's your mobile number?"

That got me smiling. She really was a go-getter. "I'll call you, if... Give me a few days."

"Yeah, yeah, I got it."

I left Cotton sitting in her car at the end of my driveway speaking to her boss. I was feeling apprehensive and, I had to admit, secretly thrilled. I now needed a serious conversation with Monica.

CHAPTER SIXTEEN

Lyle woke with a start. She leaned across to the bedside table and checked the time on her watch. She'd overslept for the first time in a very long time.

She looked back across the bed at Sienna, who lay beside her, then leaned over and kissed her on the shoulder, neck and breasts. Sienna turned to face Lyle and smiled. She lifted herself up onto her elbows and kissed Lyle firmly on the lips. Lyle gently pulled back.

"Yesterday and last night were wonderful. You're a sweet young thing, but now is not a good time for me. You should leave today."

Sienna sat up straight. "What? What do you mean? Are you kidding?"

"It means there can't be anything more than last night."

"That's not what you said. It wasn't what we felt last night, and you know it. Do you think this is the sort of thing I do all the time? You told me I was important, that we had something special, that you understood me. You were right. What has changed?"

"I'm sorry, but you must leave."

"I get it. You told me what I wanted to hear to get me into bed. You were lonely, and you wanted sex. The thing is, I don't believe that. Not for one second. If you can look me in the eye and tell me that's true, I will leave. You'll never need to see me again."

"That's not it. Believe me when I say the reason I'm asking you to leave is *because* you are important to me." Lyle looked at Sienna's slim neck and thought about how easily she could choke the life out her. She wouldn't do that. Not today. There was something about Sienna that made her feel different. Alive and warm. Seeing Sienna's indignation as she put her point across, her anger, her passion and the fire in her eyes, made her feel something again. Something long buried. She wanted to explore it. It scared her.

Sienna was kneeling on the bed now. Lyle allowed her to dominate the space between them.

"That's rubbish, and you know it. That just doesn't make any sense. If this is because of the small age difference between us, then I don't have a problem with it. If this is because you've been hurt before, then I'm not that person who hurt you. I'm me. You cannot deny there's something between us we can build on."

Lyle rose to the same height as Sienna. Her fingers tidied Sienna's hair and soothed her. She looked deep into Sienna's eyes. She kissed her with tenderness and memorised the sensations that reached every part of her body. She closed her eyes and traced her fingers over Sienna's body one last time then got out of the bed and went to the door. She turned and looked at the woman that had captivated her.

"Take your time. I'll be out all day. Just make sure you're gone by the time I get back."

CHAPTER SEVENTEEN

"She left you another envelope a few days ago. I put it on your desk. Did you see it?" said Monica as I entered the kitchen.

I nodded and gave her a face that said "Thank you."

She pointed to a large pile of post, bills mainly, that I'd done my best to ignore.

I filled Sandy's bowl with fresh water and put a few biscuits down for her. I sat on the floor beside her as she lapped at the water a couple of times then came over for a stroke.

Monica waved a tea bag, and I nodded. "Yes, please."

"She's not going to leave you in peace, is she?"

"Who?" I said, trying to sound innocent. "Detective Inspector Cotton?"

"Not her. The other one." Monica looked at me seriously. "Should we be concerned?"

I got up and stood behind her. I wrapped my arms around her and kissed her hair. "I made a promise."

"I know you did. And I know you meant it. But what if Lyle comes after you or Alice or Faith or your parents?"

"She won't do that." I knew I was on shaky ground making a statement like that.

Monica brushed me off and looked angry. "Can you look me in the eye, your daughters in the eye, and tell us that this... this Lyle who has killed God knows how many people will not come near you or your family?"

"Why are you getting angry with me?"

Monica crossed her arms. "Because I don't know what I want. I don't want you in danger. I never want to go through feeling I might lose you ever again. But all the time she is out there, I don't feel safe. And..."

"And what?"

"I hate to say it, but you need it. I can see it now. You're not the same when you're not all... I don't know. All high-octane, Mr Sheriff of Dodge City."

"Mr Sheriff of Dodge City?" We both laughed. "Where do you get this stuff from?"

"You know what I mean, though, don't you? I don't want you in danger, and I need you to promise you'll listen to me and not go all mean and moody. I won't stand for it."

I pulled Monica close to me and kissed her. "I thought you liked me mean and moody."

"I'm being serious, James. I think it will do you good to take a look at the investigation. Speak to Emma Cotton. Help her out. It will also make me feel safer to know that you're involved in trying to stop this crazy bitch before she turns on us. Just don't get completely sucked in by it all. Learn to moderate."

She was right. A part of me had hoped by staying out of the investigation I'd be left alone. I'd be keeping my family safe from Lyle. In truth, the more it went on, the more personal the investigation had become. It was time to stop hiding and push back instead.

"I'll offer advice and maybe make some calls. I'll get involved," I said.

"Maybe you'll stop moping around," said Monica with a grin.

"Moping around? What do you mean? I've never *moped* in my life."

"Come on, James. That big brain of yours needs a proper challenge. Preferably before you drive us all crazy." She pinched my waist. "Getting out of the house a bit more will help in other ways too."

"Hey! That's not fair. I'm the same weight I was when I was twenty-one."

I started tickling her.

"Yeah, right." Monica tried to escape.

"Why do I think you and Emma are ganging up on me?"

Sandy started barking and jumping up as I tickled and chased Monica. She slid to the floor and Sandy licked her face. The barking and laughing brought Alice and Faith into the kitchen. They cheered and helped me tickle Monica, who was now crawling on her hands and knees across the kitchen floor trying to get away.

"Get her," called Faith eagerly.

"I've got her leg," shouted Alice. "Daddy, you stop her."

"I've got a better idea. How about I get you two? Rooagh!"

The girls squealed and ran upstairs into Alice's bedroom. The door slammed. Monica and I smiled at their giggles.

"I'm coming to get you," I called. "Wherever you are. You can't hide from me. I'm coming to get you."

CHAPTER EIGHTEEN

Lyle had spent the day preparing the farmhouse. She'd gone over every scenario in her mind and felt confident that, whatever happened, she'd come out on top. Sustained success doesn't happen by chance.

Having driven around for a while, she was satisfied she hadn't been followed and headed home. Close to home, she once again circled around several times before finally pulling into the driveway and parking the car.

She opened the front door and immediately sensed movement in the house. She gently shut the door behind her and looked around for something she could use as a weapon. If the police were in the house, she wouldn't go quietly.

Lyle pushed off her shoes. She moved silently.

From the other room, she heard singing. She relaxed, a curious smile spreading across her face. Stocking-toed, Lyle crept to the kitchen.

She had told Sienna to leave, but apparently this young woman had a mind of her own. It was time to see what she was made of. Lyle crept up behind her as she added sauce to a tray of pasta.

Absorbed in the music playing and her own singing, Sienna had no idea Lyle was behind her. She slipped an arm around Sienna's neck and pulled tight. Sienna gasped, dropped the tray and tried to release herself from Lyle's grip. The arm was too strong.

Lyle released the hold a little. Interpreting her embrace as playfulness, Sienna turned to face her.

"Please don't be angry," she said. "Let me say something."

Lyle let Sienna continue. She'd better make this good.

"I know what you said, and I don't believe you. We had fun, and I find you incredibly sexy and interesting. I thought perhaps you are scared of getting hurt. I wanted to let you know that I am too, and perhaps that means we made a connection. Maybe that's why we're both feeling apprehensive." She got up on tiptoes and kissed Lyle, then unfastened several buttons on Lyle's blouse and softly kissed each breast.

Lyle watched Sienna and said nothing. She enjoyed the soothing pleasure of her touch while listening to her point of view. She felt conflicted. There was something about Sienna that, for the time being at least, was intriguing.

Sienna looked up into Lyle's eyes and waited for her response. Instead, Lyle ran upstairs, leaving her alone and confused.

CHAPTER NINETEEN

Lyle slammed the bedroom door behind her. She paced the room, her mind racing. How could she complete her game with her mind drifting to thoughts of Sienna? Lyle knew what she *should* do. But Sienna fascinated her. She liked her spirit. To avoid killing her she needed to prove to herself that keeping Sienna around wasn't a mistake.

She lifted her head. Listened.

Silence.

Then the sound of a cupboard door slamming. Sienna.

Lyle smiled.

Did she need this complication in her life right now? Lyle could run through the pros and cons, but ultimately there was no escaping the fact that for the first time in a very long time someone had touched her heart. The trouble was, she knew very little about Sienna. Would she be willing to accept Lyle for who she was and understand her the way Leanne Dupres had? Lyle had not said that name out loud in a long time. Everything she had planned, the game she was playing, she was doing was for her. And yet, until now, she had been unable to speak her name. She was changing. She could feel it.

If Sienna became a threat to her or her plans, could she move fast to dispose of her? It would be safer to have no involvement at all.

Lyle went back downstairs to the kitchen.

Sienna was slicing salad, loudly. She picked up the chopped leaves and dumped them in the salad bowl. Lyle walked up behind her and took the knife from her hand.

"I'm a very private person, and I cannot afford to allow just anyone into my life."

Sienna lowered her head. Lyle put the tip of the knife under Sienna's chin and lifted her face. Lyle looked her straight in the eyes.

She said, "I never want another living soul to know about me. There are things about me that I don't expect you to understand, things I must deal with."

"If that's how you feel," said Sienna, "if that's how you truly feel, then I'll leave. I was wrong about us."

"You haven't let me finish. I'd like you to stay for a while, but there need to be certain conditions. There must be rules.

"First, you will never disobey me again. If I tell you to do something, you do it. Second, you must never discuss me, what we do together, or what I do. I never want another living soul to know about me or us. First thing tomorrow you will go and collect your passport and bring it here to me. It might be necessary for us to leave the country at very short notice.

"I need you to think long and hard before you agree to these rules, because if you break any of them there will be consequences, the sort of consequences you won't enjoy and could be very final for you." She stroked Sienna's throat with the blade of the knife to emphasise her words.

"My life is mundane," said Sienna. "If I don't make changes, there'll be more of the same. You thrill me. With you, I see a future of excitement and risk. I can't go back to the mundane, not now. I won't. I want to be with you. I want to be with you for as long as possible."

"In that case," said Lyle, smiling triumphantly, "we'll have to see how exciting we can make the future for us. I can promise you it won't be mundane."

She took the knife and cut the straps on Sienna's dress and let it fall to the floor. She pulled her to her and kissed her shoulders, then put the knife down on the worktop and ran her fingers tenderly down Sienna's soft back.

"I must work tonight. But I have a few hours before I need to leave." She gently lowered Sienna to the kitchen floor, where she kissed every inch of her body.

CHAPTER TWENTY

"There's a good spot just up ahead. Why don't we pull in there?"

"Just here?" His hand trembled.

"That's it, sweetheart. You seem a little nervous. Don't be. I'll look after you. We're going to have a lovely time. It'll be something you'll remember for the rest of your life, I promise. What's your name, darling?" She ran her hand up the inside of his thigh.

"Lee. Lee Nunn." His voice trembled, and his heart was drumming out of his chest. The anticipation sent adrenaline coursing through his body, making him feel lightheaded. He felt like he might overheat. His skin was moist with sweat. He opened the window a little.

"Are you still at home, darlin'?"

"Yeah." He laughed it off. "Getting my own place soon as I can get the deposit together. Been doing double shifts at my shitty job. Working weekends too."

"You don't need to tell me. I know how difficult it can be. I bet your mum looks after you really well, doesn't she? A sweet boy like you."

Nunn wanted to change the subject.

"I… I haven't done this before. This is my first time. With anyone. It's my birthday today, you see. I'm…" He hesitated, embarrassed to say it out loud, but he liked her, so he continued. "Thirty."

He'd spent quite some time studying her profile online before choosing her. He knew what she was. His mum called them tarts and whores. Then again, she insisted any woman in a short skirt or low-cut top was flaunting it. She'd say, "Stay well clear of women like that. You get mixed up with a tart like that, she'll get herself knocked up. You won't even know if it's yours. She'll demand child support, then she'll be off with the next fella she meets with more money or a fancy car. I've seen it happen time and again. You'll find a nice girl. Be patient." He'd waited. And now, on his thirtieth birthday, he was in a car with Jo-Jo Rox.

He was a pragmatist. He knew Jo-Jo Rox was being nice because of his money and hoping he might become a regular. Which he might if it all went well. She was a bit older than him, mid-forties at a guess, but that was okay. She was very attractive, and he didn't want anyone his own age or younger. That would feel wrong. No, she was just right. Just how he'd imagined. Her lips were glossy with lipstick. Her nails were painted, and her hands looked soft. He glanced at her breasts. He swallowed hard, and his breathing became jerky as he exhaled. He hoped it wouldn't be over too quickly. That would be embarrassing.

"First things first," Jo-Jo said. She put out her hand.

"I'm sorry. Yes, of course."

He got out the money, and she tucked it into her purse.

"Thank you. Now, no funny business. We discussed earlier what I will and won't do within your budget." Jo-Jo winked at him. "Look, it's your first time, and it's your birthday, so perhaps I could throw in a little extra. Something I save for my regulars. How does that sound?"

Lee nodded. He didn't know what that might be, but he wasn't going to refuse.

"Don't look so nervous. We're going to have fun – I promise."

His chest was pounding so hard and his head was spinning so fast he wasn't sure he'd heard what she said. He smiled and nodded again.

"How about you unzip yourself and pull down your trousers and undies for me. Get yourself comfortable. I'll find us some protection. Don't be shy, handsome. It's why we're here."

While Jo-Jo rooted around in her purse, Lee did as he was told. He pushed his seat back and reclined it.

"Is Jo-Jo Rox your real name?" asked Lee.

She laughed sweetly. "That's my working name. We all have working names. It's sexier than my real name. Do you like it?"

Lee nodded.

"Having a street name or online name – I do a lot of online work for fans as well now – keeps us safe from the nutters too. You wouldn't believe the nutters you meet doing this job."

Lee thought that perhaps he would.

Jo-Jo unwrapped the condom then leaned over and rolled it on. "Lovely. We're good to go. I'll let you in on a little secret. My real name is Kelly, but I prefer it if you call me Roxy or Jo-Jo. Are you ready?"

Lee groaned as Jo-Jo used her mouth on him. He thought he might be in love. He was definitely in love. He loved her.

Jo-Jo reached back for the scissors she had in her purse.

Opening the blades, she lifted her head and said, "Everything okay, Lee?"

"Uh-huh. Don't stop. Whatever you're doing, keep doing it. You're amazing." Lee pushed back in his seat, his eyes tight shut. This was the best birthday ever.

"That's what I like to hear. Lyle."

"What's that?" said Lee.

"My real name. Kelly Lyle."

"I like that name. It's nice," said Lee. His eyes were shut tight. At this moment in time, he didn't care what the hell her name was. She could call herself whatever she wanted. All he could think was he didn't want her to stop.

Jo-Jo brought the scissors up close, the blades wide open. She took a firm grip of Lee again. He moaned with pleasure. She held him steady and with only three strokes cut his penis clean off.

Unsure what had happened Lee opened his eyes and looked at Jo-Jo. He was hurting. Something wasn't right. In the darkness of the car, he couldn't see the blood; he only felt its warmth as it flowed between his legs. Lee flicked on the car's internal light. There was blood on him and on her hands.

"What happened? Are you okay? Is it me?" Lee checked himself. His brain was confused. He caught a glimpse of the scissors. "What did you do?" he demanded.

Kelly Jo-Jo Rox Lyle opened her hand and showed him what she'd cut off. She showed him the scissors. "Snip-snip, snip-snip."

Lyle drove the scissors deep into Lee Nunn's neck. She did it again and again and again. Savage repeated thrusts. Finally, she pressed the scissors deep into his left eye, where she left them.

"Sorry, Lee, you picked the wrong woman tonight. I'm not sure how your family are going to react when they hear the circumstances surrounding your death. It's going to be embarrassing, to say the least."

Lee was grasping at his throat. He tried to speak but only managed a deep, guttural choking sound. He kicked out at her in anger. His hand reached for the door handle. The door swung open, and he fell out onto the pavement. He tried to crawl away, but his foot was trapped behind the hinge of the door. He didn't have the strength to move it.

She walked around the car and leaned over him. The moonlight lit up his face, the scissors protruding from his eye socket. "That looks painful. Does it sting? I'm going to leave you shortly. You've got to admit it was fun while it lasted. Anyway, I'll post your dick to your mother. I'll make sure she gets it the day after your funeral. Just when she thinks things can't get any worse, she'll get your manhood in the post." She held up a clear zip-seal bag holding his penis. "I'll include a note from yours truly telling her all about tonight."

Lee spluttered. His lungs gasped for air and his one eye stared.

"I'd love to be a fly on the wall when she realises the rest of you has been buried, and now she's got to decide what to do with this little dinky of yours."

Lee's efforts to get to safety stopped. Fighting for breath through all the blood was his only concern. The blood looked black in the moonlight.

Lee put out his hand to Lyle. He tried to say "Help." Lyle crouched down beside him and watched him drift away.

She stayed with him until it was finally over. She checked his pulse. Nothing.

"Goodbye, Lee. We had fun, didn't we? Happy birthday."

She looked up at the moon and the stars. She looked

around and regretted picking this spot for the death of Lee Nunn. It would have been interesting to come back and observe the crime scene when DI Cotton and friends were doing their thing, but this spot would not allow her to observe from afar without being noticed.

CHAPTER TWENTY-ONE

Emma's mobile phone buzzed and its face shone bright. She reached out in the darkness and knocked the phone to the floor. She scooted around and reached down. Still leaning over the side of the bed, she looked at the message. It was from Dave. It said, "Can we talk? Soon." No kiss, she noted.

She guessed he was ready to collect his stuff. He could wait. She didn't reply to the message. They were over, and she was okay about it. Probably for the best. Probably. She rolled into the centre of the bed and pulled the duvet over her head. She tried to sleep. After forty minutes of tossing and turning, she dressed and went for a run.

After showering, she put on her dressing gown and stood by the oven waiting for the croissants to warm. Watson padded over. He rubbed himself against her leg.

"Hello, boy. Do you want some breakfast? Here you go." Emma put some foul-smelling canned fish down for him. "Yum."

Watson seemed to like it.

"It's just you and me now. We'll be okay, won't we?

How are you doing with the ladies? Any romance you want to tell me about? I bet you love 'em and leave 'em, don't you?"

Her phone beeped and so did the oven. She pulled the croissants out and checked the phone message at the same time.

"We're going to have to pick this conversation up again later, Watson. I've got to go." She continued in a Sherlock Holmes voice. "Seems there's been a murder. Prepare the carriage. We leave at once."

Watson ignored her and licked his paw.

"Christ, I'm already trying to joke with the cat. I need to get out more."

Thirty minutes later, Emma stood beside the police cordon and could see the victim's car. It was parked a few hundred yards away, and the driver's door was open.

She looked up and down the closed road. High up on her left, hotels loomed, their windows looking blankly onto the scene below. To her right was a fenced-off clifftop, the fence punctuated by entrances to steep, winding steps leading to the promenade and beach below. A footpath ran behind the fence, parallel to the cliff's edge. A wooden bench sat high above the ocean, where an early-morning mist hung over the water. The mist would burn away as the sun rose higher in the sky.

"How long until we can get the area completely sealed off? I can see the body from here."

The fresh-faced officer looked nervous. "They'll be here any second, ma'am. I've kept everyone as far back as I can. It's not ideal, I know."

"Okay, okay. Well done."

Emma recognised the quiet clifftop as somewhere youngsters came for some privacy. At night the road wasn't busy. If they'd been drinking and having a good time in

Bournemouth town, it was just a short drive. She started walking towards the scene.

"It's really bad," the officer called after her.

She put a hand up to indicate she'd heard him.

An hour later she pulled out her mobile phone and hit speed dial. Hardy answered, his voice croaky and tired-sounding. She'd woken him up.

"We have another one," she told him. "I've just arrived. It's fresh. It's really nasty." Emma glanced inside the car at the objects arranged on the dashboard. "There's an envelope with your name on it. Literally, your name is written on the front. You want to take a look?"

She waited for Hardy to say something. He didn't.

"You've been temporarily reinstated. The paperwork just needs your signature. I can give it to you when you get here."

There was silence for a moment, then whispering. She guessed he was talking to Monica.

"Where are you?"

He didn't sound happy. So what? This was as much his case as hers.

CHAPTER TWENTY-TWO

"Excuse me. I need to get through." I pushed past onlookers, their excited whispers at odds with the grisly scene only a few hundred metres away.

The road was cordoned off, and the area was buzzing when I arrived. I turned my back on the media. A cameraman I recognised spotted me and nudged a colleague who was on the phone.

Crap.

I introduced myself to a young constable. He knew who I was and that I was expected. I made the long walk to the victim's car.

Cotton was crouching down next to the victim when I arrived.

"Sorry to call you," she said.

"No, you're not." I crouched down beside her.

Cotton said warmly, "You're right. I'm not." Then more seriously, "This is Lee Nunn. Killed less than seven hours ago. As you can see, it's a mess. There's blood everywhere. Inside the car is just as bad. Looks like he dragged himself out of the car for some reason."

"You think Lyle did this?"

Cotton tied her hair back into a ponytail. "Yes. At the moment I'm thinking she ticks all the boxes."

I glanced inside the car and could see the driver's seat was soaked in blood and there was arterial spray over the dashboard and windscreen. The pavement where he lay was worse still.

Looking at the bloody, lifeless body of Nunn I was shocked by the savagery. Why had she mutilated him in that way? I'd not known her to do that before.

I shook my head and said, "This is what you see when the perp is angry or has a bloodlust."

"She will have got blood all over her in this confined space," said Cotton. "It's like she didn't care."

"This is more brutal than the others."

"I agree. It was also riskier. There could easily have been a passerby, either in a car or on foot – like a late-night dog-walker. There was any number of ways this could have gone wrong."

"Lyle is brutal, yes. She's also usually clinical in her execution."

It seemed an odd thing to think, but I could see no finesse. There also appeared to be a lack of forethought.

"This road," I said to Cotton. "Just the one way in and one way out?"

She nodded.

"Any security camera on those hotels?"

"We're looking into it."

I walked around the car. All the doors except his were closed. His foot was trapped in the hinge of the door.

"The attack happened inside the car. It looks like Nunn tried to crawl away. That would indicate either he met someone here and they got into the car, or he brought them here. Has anyone spoken to his family? He might have told them who he was meeting. Check his phone. Check his computer. Speak to his family. Speak to work colleagues. There is a possibility he told someone who he was meeting. I want to know all his movements."

CHAPTER TWENTY-THREE

I was feeling like I'd never been away. I was back. Cotton was smiling.

"What?" I asked.

"Nothing."

I guessed she was pleased with herself for bringing me out of retirement. I didn't care. I was where I belonged. I was going to stop the monster that had done this.

"You mentioned a note. What about a Scrabble piece? Anything else that indicates Lyle did this?"

Cotton took out her phone and said, "Forensics have it all. They didn't want it getting contaminated. Here – I took photos. Lyle left another piece. The letter R this time."

I read the note a couple of times and then looked at the seemingly ordinary Scrabble piece. "Okay. I don't need to see any more."

Cotton held up her hand and waved her fingers, and the team came over to start the process of moving the body.

My mind was racing with questions. I didn't like the

way this killing had escalated. There was no subtlety to it. It didn't feel like Lyle had done it, although I had no doubt she had. I was lost in my thoughts and didn't hear Cotton calling me.

"Hey, hey, Hardy. You saw that she cut his dick off, right? They thought it might have been under his body. They just lifted him, and it's not there. Would she have taken it as a trophy? I know you mentioned she took trophies before."

"Souvenirs. They were more like souvenirs. It was thought she took them as reminders rather than trophies. They were always things like necklaces, bracelets, rings, earrings, books sometimes. That sort of thing. Not body parts or body fluids. She never took anything like that before, as far as I am aware."

Cotton said, "Why would she change?"

"Perhaps it was just a matter of time."

Cotton started throwing question after question at me. "So why the frenzied attack? Why in such a public place? Why the body part? Aren't serial killers creatures of habit? Perhaps Lyle's gone so far off the rails that she's finally lost it. What do you think?"

"It wasn't frenzied. It might look that way because of the volume of blood, but she was in control the whole time. Never forget she is in control."

Cotton looked at me and then back at all the blood.

I pointed to the crime scene, my throat and my eye as I said, "We're here because Lyle wanted us here. The stabs to the throat hit main arteries. The scissors left in the eye socket was part of the message. The note said, 'Hardy and Cotton, SEE what you made me do? I have a VISION of our future together, and you're both invited to the party. When we're finished there won't be a dry EYE in the house. KL xxx.' Lyle doesn't lose control. Look around."

Cotton's eyes moved over the circus around us. The police and tech teams. The onlookers and media.

I put my hand on her shoulder. I was trying not to sound like I was schooling her and spoke my next words more quietly. "This was a way to get you here, get me here and create all this."

Frustration was apparent in my voice. I knew I wasn't in control of my own decisions; I was back looking at another dead body because Lyle had put me here. She had upped the ante.

If the death of Etheridge hadn't already made it clear, then for her own safety and the benefit of the investigation I needed Cotton to understand she was in the big league now.

"Right now, Lyle is deciding what I do, where I go and who I see. She's taking me away from my family. You might not see it yet. With all due respect, you need to wake up. You're still being naive. If we don't get out in front of this, I don't want to think where we might end up."

I was suddenly feeling conflicted. What was I getting into? The feelings from past cases and the memories of how they had taken over my life flooded my mind. Did I really want this?

Cotton was confused, and so was I. I could see I'd overstepped the mark. She was a very capable detective, and I knew I'd said too much. She wasn't having any of it.

She said, "Let's get one thing straight. No one is asking you to do anything you don't want to do. I don't need you holding my hand. That's not why I asked you here. I know you usually work alone – well, tough; you want to work the case, we're working it together. You want to walk away? Fine, walk away. I've had just about enough of your crap. And I certainly don't need you treating me like a kid. I've seen enough and done enough to know how this world works."

I sank my hands in my pockets. I'd just had my butt handed to me.

Cotton kicked a small stone and stared at the ground. "I don't know everything that happened to you in the past. I'm sorry you got hurt. I was told you were one of the best detectives at Scotland Yard. *The best* serial-murder investigator. I want to catch Lyle. I know you do too. The fact you're here shows me you want her stopped. So let's get her. Together."

She pushed her hands deep into her pockets.

We walked over to the cliff's edge and looked out to sea.

I spoke softly. "If I do this, I want to know you're in it too. For the long haul, I mean. You need to understand that this game of hers is leading somewhere, and I don't know where. That scares me. It should scare you."

She could see I had concerns she didn't fully understand.

She said, "Yes, I'm in. I've always been ready to do whatever it takes."

I'd cleared the air and laid my cards on the table. I said, "I'll see you in the morning." Cotton was growing on me. Her straight talk, tough love and grit were infectious.

A part of me felt like it had been rekindled. And seeing Lee Nunn's blood-soaked and mutilated body and knowing that Lyle might come after my family were the impetus I needed to put early retirement behind me – at least for a while. I was ready to take on The Mentor, Kelly Lyle. I hoped Detective Emma Cotton was ready.

Neither of us was truly prepared for what was coming.

I should have been.

CHAPTER TWENTY-FOUR

Monica and Alice finished lighting candles on the cake while I stood back with my phone set to video. Mum and Dad were keeping Faith occupied. I discreetly gave them the thumbs-up when we were ready to parade in with the birthday cake.

The excitement on Faith's face was magical. We sang "Happy Birthday," and she prepared herself to blow out the candles and make her wish. "I want Alice to help me blow out the candles," she insisted.

"Are you sure?" said Monica. "That's really kind. Don't forget to make a wish."

Alice and Faith blew out the candles while we cheered and clapped, then Faith made her wish.

Alice handed out plates then gave Monica her secret sign. Monica and Faith cut the cake.

Monica passed everyone a piece and then announced, "There is somebody I need to introduce, someone with incredible powers, who has been practising her illusions for almost a week and a half."

Faith's eyes widened, and a smile spread across her

face. She could barely contain her excitement as she waited for her big sister, who had vanished from the room, to prepare herself.

"I wonder what this is all about?" asked Dad.

"It's a magic trick, Grandad. Alice has been practising and practising. She wouldn't let me see what she was doing. She said it was a surprise."

"What a wonderful idea," said Mum. "How exciting."

"I'll just go and check to see if she's okay," said Monica as she disappeared upstairs. The wait added to the anticipation.

A few moments later Monica reappeared halfway down the stairs. "The Astonishing Alice is now ready, so if the ladies and gentlemen of the audience would please take their seats. Our magician would also appreciate complete silence while she performs *the disappearing coin trick*."

We giggled and whispered to each other before falling silent.

Alice appeared in a long cape, a black t-shirt, black leggings and her black school shoes. She narrowed her eyes, which were made up with dark eye shadow to make her look more mysterious. Stepping purposefully down the stairs, she entered the room with a sweeping arm gesture quickly followed by a low bow. By this point, Faith was on the edge of her seat, and I put my arm around her and hugged her.

Alice pulled a wand from her sleeve then held up a coin and showed it to everyone. She tapped the coin on the table to prove that it was real and then, without speaking, gestured for Monica to once again check that it was real. Monica agreed it was. Alice took Monica's hand and placed the coin flat on her palm. She placed her own hand on top and Monica placed her other hand on top of Alice's.

Now Alice spoke for the first time. "Would the birthday girl, Miss Faith Hardy, please say the magic words?"

Faith looked at Grandad, who nodded encouragingly. Faith said, "Abracadabra."

Alice waved her free hand over the top of the three flat hands then tapped them three times with her wand.

Monica took her top hand away. Alice removed her hand. Monica showed everyone that her hand, which had only moments ago held the coin, was now empty. The coin had vanished.

The whole room erupted with excited gasps and applause.

Monica pointed to Alice and said, "The Astonishing Alice!"

Alice walked over to Faith and, with a flourish, pulled the coin from behind Faith's ear. She executed a confident bow, waved her cape again and left the room to rapturous applause.

"Again, again!" cried Faith. "That was amazing! I want to see it again."

Alice reappeared a few moments later without her cape and agreed to do the magic trick again very soon but not straight away, as there was a little bit of preparation to be done before the trick could be performed again.

We all spent the next while happily playing board games, which was Faith's favourite thing to do on her birthday. Finally, I gathered the dirty plates and took them to the kitchen, where I interrupted Mum and Monica having a quiet conversation.

"Whatever you two are plotting, it won't work," I joked.

The two women looked at each other. Mum grabbed

my cheek and gave it a loving pinch. She winked at Monica and left the room, leaving the two of us alone.

I put my arms around Monica and gave her a kiss. "Mum's excited about something. What was that all about?" I asked her. "I swear she was skipping as she left the room. The last time I saw her like that she was tipsy on New Year's Eve."

"There's something I've been meaning—" started Monica.

Music from the other room was getting louder and louder as Alice and Faith found some karaoke on the TV.

Monica took my hand. "I've been waiting for the right time."

The TV suddenly got much louder. I stepped into the other room and gestured to the girls to lower the volume. "I think that's a little too loud, girls. Can you *please* turn it down?"

I stepped back into the kitchen. "I'm sorry. You were saying?" My phone began to ring on the worktop. I ignored it. "You were about to say something," I said.

"It's okay. It can wait. We'll do this another time. You'd better get your phone. It could be important."

I kissed Monica and grabbed my phone. "It's probably Cotton. She said she'd call if Forensics got a hit."

We both thought Forensics finding anything was a long shot, but Cotton had said she'd call either way. I stepped outside for some quiet and had a long talk with her.

CHAPTER TWENTY-FIVE

I spent a couple of hours in my study before bed. I flicked through notes I'd made on the case reports while I'd been on the phone with Cotton. We could have gone on all night, but I was aware we both had a busy day coming up.

Trying to shake off the stresses of the investigation and allow my mind to change gear for a while, I took Sandy for a late-night walk.

The air was cold and refreshing. There was a beautiful, clear night sky. I looked up at the stars and searched for the one I always thought of as Helena's. I blew her a kiss. The tranquillity and feeling of solitude felt almost spiritual.

Back home, I gently closed the front door and slipped off my shoes. I checked the rooms downstairs and then crept upstairs, trying not to disturb anyone. Sneaking into the bedroom, I could see Monica was fast asleep. I shrugged off my fleece jacket and placed it on the back of a chair.

I went to Faith's bedroom to say goodnight and, finding the room empty, I made my way to Alice's bedroom. Faith was snuggled up next to her. She usually climbed into bed with her big sister when she had something on her mind that was worrying her. I needed to talk to her in the morning to find out what was going on.

I knelt down beside the bed and gave my two girls a kiss good night. "Good night, Faith, my little birthday girl. Good night, Astonishing Alice."

I sat and watched them sleep. They looked so peaceful and angelic.

"Is that you, Daddy?" asked Alice sleepily.

"Yes, it is, sweetheart. I didn't mean to wake you."

"That's okay. I wanted to see you." She looked at her sister. "Faith wanted to get into my bed. She said she was scared you wouldn't come back. She said she had a bad dream and that a bad person wouldn't let you go."

I felt choked inside. "I'm sorry I'm doing this. I know I told you I wouldn't do any more investigations. I really wanted that sort of work to be over."

"It's okay. We both know that you've got to do it. Nana told us that what you were doing is important and that only you can do it. Monica said you wouldn't do it unless you really had to. She told us you don't want to do it, but you have no choice. She also said it will be over soon and we shouldn't worry. I'm worried you might get hurt again. I don't want you or Emma to go to hospital."

"Things are different now. I won't get hurt. I'll make sure Emma doesn't get hurt." I tucked Alice's hair behind her ear.

"Can Emma come here again soon? She looked nice."

"We'll see."

"That means no," said Alice.

"It means we'll see."

I straightened Alice's blankets and put Faith's teddy bear sitting up next to her.

I said, "I need to work with Emma to make sure this

person we're investigating stops doing the bad things they're doing. You're such a clever, brave little girl. You are both brave. We're so proud of you. You've both been through so much. I love you."

I leaned over and gave Alice another kiss and a hug.

"Do you have enough room? Would you like me to take Faith back to her bed?"

Alice wriggled and smiled. "No, she's okay. It's a bit of a squeeze, but I like having her here with me."

I said, "You'd better get some more sleep. It's really late."

I left the girls to sleep and closed Alice's bedroom door, leaving just the slightest gap, the way she likes it. I went back to my bedroom and found Monica climbing back into bed.

"Were you spying on me?" I leaned over and gave her a kiss.

"Not so much spying as checking out who the dishy stranger was in my house." She pulled me down onto the bed, rolled me over and climbed on top of me. She gave me a long, deep kiss.

"I'm not sure who that was, but this dishy stranger is still fully dressed and in need of a shower."

Monica started unbuttoning my shirt. "You'd better go and take a shower, then. If you're quick, perhaps we can do a little catching up." For fun, she flicked her hair and slipped a strap of her nightdress off her shoulder. "But you'd better be quick."

I rolled off the bed and ran for the door. "I can shower and be back here in under a minute. Don't go anywhere."

I could hear her laughing as I grabbed a towel from the airing cupboard and ran for the shower.

CHAPTER TWENTY-SIX

Emma threw her car keys down onto the coffee table. They landed with a loud clatter, a sharp reminder she was returning home to an empty house.

There was an unsettling stillness about the house. Everywhere she looked were memories of Dave. Although he was gone, his presence lingered.

She flicked through her music collection and put on some ABBA. "Mama Mia" never failed to put a smile on her face. With a wiggle and clapping hands, she went to the cupboard, took out a bottle of red wine, poured herself a large glass and took a small sip. She considered phoning her mother or a girlfriend but decided against it. She cranked up the music then took her glass of wine upstairs and ran a hot bath.

Later that evening, she sat surrounded by case files. On the coffee table in front of her was a near-empty bottle of red wine and the remnants of an M&S microwave-ready meal.

The doorbell rang.

She looked at the time on the wall clock, but the hands

wouldn't stay still. She frowned at the bottle of red wine. *Damn it.* Red wine always went straight to her head when she was tired. She made a mental note to stop drinking alone.

She squinted at the clock again. It read 11.45 p.m. She shoved herself to her feet and went into the front hall. Leaning against the door, she peered through the spyhole. It was Dave.

Her heart skipped with excitement. Had he changed his mind? Did he want her back?

In an instant she remembered all he'd said and the pain he'd caused. *What the hell did he want at this time?*

She partially opened the door, which was still on the chain. Through the gap she said, "Hello? Yep?" *Damn it, she sounded drunk.*

Dave looked uneasy and was shifting from one foot to the other.

"Hi, Emma. I'm so sorry to come around so late, but I really had nowhere else to go."

She spoke slowly and tried not to slur her words. "What do you mean you had nowhere else to go? You can't just waltz back into my house and my life after what you said."

"I know what I said, and I'm sorry, Em. I've made a mistake, been an idiot. I know that now."

"It was you who left. Your choice to go."

"I was wrong. I can't stop thinking about you, and about us. I just need somewhere to crash for the night. Perhaps we can talk? Come on, Em. Please – just for one night."

Emma shut the door and hesitated, wondering what to do. Keeping the door on the chain, she opened it again and said, "Just for one night? On the sofa?"

"Yes, I promise, it's just the one night. If you still want

me to leave in the morning, I'll go. I can sleep on the floor or on the sofa. I just need somewhere. I'm really sorry to be doing this to you."

She sighed deeply.

Don't let him in. You'll regret it.

"Stay there. Give me a few minutes to think." She closed the door again. Her eyes scanned the room – what a mess. She ran about tidying, dropping the remnants of her meal-for-one in the bin, putting away the case files and the remaining red wine. Cushions plumped and kitchen worktop wiped. She took one last look.

Satisfied, she ran upstairs to her bedroom.

Quick, quick, quick... Roll-on deodorant, change of top, brush teeth, brush hair, a light lipstick. Mascara? No, too much. One last mirror check. Not great, but good enough.

Only slightly out of breath, she opened the front door once more.

"Come in. One night only. You can sleep on the sofa. I want you gone by lunchtime tomorrow."

"It's really good of you, Em. I know I've been a total idiot. I wouldn't have blamed you if you'd told me where to go."

He looks good, Emma thought. *His brown eyes are concerned. He's had his hair cut. He smells nice. New shirt?*

Don't be stupid. Make coffee, find a blanket for the sofa. Don't get sucked in, not tonight.

Dave went on. "I realise now, Em, I made a terrible mistake. I'm not expecting anything from you. I just want to say how sorry I am."

"You hurt me. I'm not going to lie. What you did was unforgivable."

The pair of them stood in silence for a moment.

Emma said, "Put your bag down. I was about to make coffee. Want one?"

"I can make it," said Dave.

She said, a little too quickly, "No. No, I'll do it."

Dave looked away sheepishly.

Emma opened the fridge. "The milk is old. Is black coffee okay?"

"Yes, perfect. Thank you."

She filled the kettle in silence and put coffee in two mugs. In her mind, she'd underlined with a big fat marker pen that Dave couldn't just walk back into her life, that they could not just pick up where they'd left off.

Was she dealing with this correctly? She'd been only months away from marrying this man, hoping to have babies together. She'd really wanted Dave's babies. They'd been just months away from spending the rest of the lives together, and now he felt like a stranger. She knew she should feel angrier, but, secretly, relief was all she felt.

They sat down together, an awkward silence between them. Two hot coffees steamed on the glass coffee table.

The obvious question was "How have you been?" But neither of them wanted to ask it.

"You still have my bottle of whisky under the stairs?" asked Dave.

Emma went to the cupboard under the stairs, opened the door and pulled out a bottle of single malt. "This one?" She set the bottle down on the coffee table and fetched them each a Royal Doulton cut-crystal whisky glass.

"You got me this bottle for my birthday," said Dave.

"Christmas. I got it for you for Christmas. The glasses too." She watched as Dave poured them both a double.

He raised his glass "To you, Emma Cotton. The world's hottest cop. By day she'll arrest you with her badge and powers of deduction. By night she'll seduce you with soft curves and Victoria's Secret."

He hadn't used that line in a while. In the early days, when they couldn't get enough of each other, they'd rented a beautiful stone cottage in the country. Somewhere, she didn't remember where. At the time it didn't matter; it could have been on the moon, as long as they were alone together. They never saw any of the countryside; instead, they'd spent the weekend fooling around, drinking, getting Chinese food and pizza delivered and fooling around some more.

Emma couldn't help but smile now and let out a little laugh. She raised her glass and said, "Cheers. But you can't get back in my good books that easily. So don't even try."

Dave drank down his whisky and Emma matched him. He poured them both another.

It felt good to laugh. To hear Dave's laugh.

CHAPTER TWENTY-SEVEN

Emma woke to the sound of movement in the kitchen. She looked at the clock. It was 2:30 p.m.

Her head pounded. Her mind raced back to the previous evening. "Dave," she said to herself. "You didn't." Her eyes widened. "Damn. You did."

Emma climbed out of bed and looked around for her underwear. Unable to find her clothes, she put on her dressing gown.

Feeling more than a little hungover, she opened the bedroom door. Dave was flicking through her collection of vinyl records. "Good morning. Afternoon, I mean. Why'd you let me sleep so late? My mouth... Urgh... I need water."

Dave looked up, surprise and happiness on his face. "You made me jump."

He stopped what he was doing and sidled over. He put his arms around her and gave her a few quick kisses, then slipped his hands inside her dressing gown and held her.

"Why don't you go and take a relaxing shower?" he said. "I'll make us both a late lunch and a gallon of tea."

"Dave, about last night…"

"It was amazing. You're amazing."

Emma pushed away his wandering hands. "David, it was a mistake. It shouldn't have happened."

"What do you mean, it shouldn't have happened?" He looked hurt.

"I had too much to drink. We both did. I wasn't thinking straight. If there is going to be an us, then we need to take it slow. Okay? Slow. Everything changed when you left."

"You are joking, aren't you? Last night was like the old days. You and me, Em. Why overcomplicate everything? Let's just pick up where we left off."

Emma closed her dressing gown and tightened the belt. "Really? You think it's that easy? You think you can walk out on me and just as easily walk back in?"

Dave put his hands out to hold her. "It only needs to be as difficult as we choose to make it."

She took a step back.

"I think it's best if you just leave, David. Maybe we can talk later? I just don't know right now. I have a lot on my plate, and I feel like shit. My bloody head. Look, I'll send you a text tomorrow. We can get a bite to eat and talk."

Emma was looking Dave straight in the eye. Something didn't feel right. He looked uneasy.

She tried to look around him and over his shoulder. He playfully tried to stop her. She pushed past, brushing him off as she moved. She walked through the lounge, looking around and looking at Dave. She peered into the hallway, went into the kitchen, turned around and came back out again.

His body language made it plain to her he was up to something. She wasn't sure she wanted to know what it was. At the same time, she had to know. Emma looked left and right, then at Dave. His eyes flicked towards the front door.

Emma opened the frosted-glass interior door. Her heart sank. His bag and a box full of his things were sitting in the porch.

"I can explain," he said. "I just needed to get a few things. You said yourself I could only stay one night. I wasn't planning on just walking out. It looks more than it is."

"Leave. Just get your stuff and go."

"Look, Em, it isn't what you think. You're overreacting."

"Just get the fuck out. I never want to see your lying face again. Go back to whoever it is you're screwing. I really couldn't care less. The poor bitch can have you."

"Fine. Screw you. Oh, I did. Last night. And you know what, Emma? You really are a piece of work. You really are one uptight, boring bitch. And that's the truth. Ever heard of fun?"

"Really? So that's what you really think of me. The truth is out."

"You want to know another truth? It's Rebecca. Yes, I've been screwing Rebecca Wild behind your back for months. She might be a mistake – I don't know yet – but at least she knows how to have a good time, in and out of the sack. You wouldn't know how to have a good time if it hit you in the face and screamed 'Good time!'"

In the background, Emma's phone started ringing.

"Just wait there one second, Dave," she hissed.

"Got to get your phone, have you? Christ almighty, we can't even have an argument without being interrupted by your work."

"Forget the phone," said Emma, rounding on him.

"You were telling me that while you and I were planning our wedding, you were sleeping with another woman."

He swallowed hard, took a step back and looked for the front door.

"Do you remember, David, that your golf clubs are under the stairs? Just wait there one second while I go get one. An eight iron can do a lot of damage to the human body." Emma had no intention of using a golf club on him, but the words had the impact she was hoping for.

Dave scrambled for the door. He jammed bags and boxes under his arms and ran for his car. He opened the boot, threw in the bags and boxes and jumped into the front seat.

Emma came marching out with a golf club over her shoulder.

"Goodbye, Emma," he panted. "I'll let you get back to playing cops and robbers. I know it's all you're interested in."

He rammed the car into gear and peeled away.

CHAPTER TWENTY-EIGHT

Unable to sleep, I left the house before anyone was up. Lyle was keeping me awake at night. She had forced me to get involved in her game, yet I had no idea why. Was it just for kicks? Was it a challenge? Or was there a motive at play I didn't see yet?

I wasn't surprised to see Cotton's car already in the carpark when I arrived. I'd heard from Etheridge that she had a reputation for being first in and last out.

I got buzzed in and made my way along the beige corridors. The sights, smell and sounds took me back to Scotland Yard.

I leaned in through Cotton's open door. "Knock, knock," I said. I held up two cups of Costa coffee and a bag of pastries. "Supplies?"

"Great to see you, come in. Anyone bearing pastries is welcome in my office." Cotton looked tired, but she managed a smile.

I passed her a coffee and the whole bag of pastries. "I like what you've done with the place."

She leaned back in her creaky chair and looked around

as though for the first time in a long time. I noticed a photo frame face down on Cotton's desk. When she thought I wasn't looking, she slid it into a drawer.

"I think I got put in here to keep me out of the way. It's nothing special, but it's my home away from home. I put in for some chintz curtains but I'm still waiting, and as for the crystal chandelier, it turns out there's a waiting list."

"Shame," I said. "Chintz and a crystal chandelier always add an air of romance to any investigation."

Cotton laughed, and her mood lightened. She had a pretty smile. Etheridge had told me she was a bit of a loner in the office. She was well liked, but she kept herself to herself and focused on her work. I'd seen it before, and my guess was Cotton felt she had a lot to prove. In time, I hoped that would change for her.

"They're working on getting us a bigger office," she said, "one we can both work in."

I looked around the cramped workspace. "Good idea."

"Where would you like to start?" she asked.

I took a sip of coffee. "I read through all the files you left me over the past few months. I'll need access to everything else. I couldn't identify a pattern with the victims," I said.

She got to her feet. "The only thing that connects these victims is Lyle and a Scrabble piece. They're different ages, ethnicity, backgrounds, sexual orientation and genders. Ages range from nineteen to fifty-eight. All either had an accompanying Scrabble piece left at the scene or inserted into them. Six victims. Six letters."

Cotton spread out well-worn photographs showing the letters T, C, H, I, R, R.

Thinking out loud, I said, "With Lyle as our prime suspect we need to ask: Why did she choose them? What do they signify to her? What's motivating her? Who are they to her?"

Cotton pointed to photos on her whiteboard. Next to each picture was a Scrabble letter.

"Letter I, Justin Grant, twenty years old. Letter H, Rachel Ellis, nineteen years old. They were thrown off a bridge with nooses around their necks. They had just met. A banner at the scene read— "

"I know what it said."

I'd seen pictures in the newspaper, and now the photographs were pinned to Cotton's wall. I thought about the huge letters on the banner: HONK for Hardy & Cotton.

Passing commuters had had no idea what the message meant or even who Hardy and Cotton were, but it hadn't stopped them honking their car horns with enthusiasm.

"You know about letter T, Martin Burke, and letter C, Dylan Durrant. Tied under piers and left to either drown with the incoming tide or bleed to death, their stomachs cut open and the contents pulled out."

Cotton squeezed the bridge of her nose. Filled her lungs and expelled the air loudly. Processing it all was draining her.

We kept going.

I asked, "How about Etheridge? Why wasn't his Scrabble piece left at the scene?"

"His Scrabble piece wasn't with the body. Lyle must have worried it'd be destroyed in the explosion and fire. The only interesting thing is the watch. Which, if you are right, ties Lyle to Etheridge's murder and you directly to her." She looked up quickly. "I'm sorry. That sounded…"

"It's fine. I know what you meant," I said. There was no point denying a truth I could no longer escape: I was inextricably linked to Kelly Lyle and all these deaths.

Cotton moved on and pointed to a new photo. "Now there is also the letter R, Lee Nunn."

Officers had established Nunn was last seen with a prostitute, although they hadn't been able to determine whether he'd used girls in the past or whether the prostitute had had anything to do with his death.

Cotton added, "Nunn was killed on his birthday. My current thinking is that he went with a prostitute as a birthday treat to himself. It's possible it was his first time."

Solemnly, I said, "He wouldn't be the first and won't be the last, I'm sure."

I pushed a photo of Etheridge front and centre now. "So why him?"

I could feel the weight of the investigation bearing down on my shoulders. But I couldn't deny a part of me felt a little exhilarated at being back in the game. The chase was on.

"I was thinking about that overnight," said Cotton.

Does this woman ever sleep? I thought.

"His death leaves the team without a leader, a void at the top." She passed me an almond croissant.

I said, "Lyle must know I cannot take over Etheridge's role in any official capacity."

We sipped our coffees and stared at the photos in silence. I took a bite of my croissant and chewed thoughtfully. At length, I said, "I know I'm reaching, but could Etheridge have stumbled onto something important?"

"Like what? Lyle hasn't hidden the fact she's the killer. Quite the contrary – it feels like from the very beginning she was letting us know it was her. We just couldn't join the dots until you pointed them out to us."

Cotton pushed Etheridge's photo to the top and lined up the other five victims in a row beneath. She said confidently, "Lyle's intention was for Etheridge's death to be the final push you needed to get involved."

I wasn't happy at that explanation, but it seemed the most logical. Lyle knew I wouldn't be able to let her campaign of terror continue.

CHAPTER TWENTY-NINE

The next day, I called Cotton at the office and left her a voice message. I was glad when she didn't pick up. I wasn't ready to start explaining my thinking. Instead, I let her know I was going to Somerset to pursue a fresh line of enquiry.

The truth was, I could see all efforts to date had got us no closer to finding and stopping Lyle. If I were to assist Cotton in any meaningful way, I'd need to approach the investigation from a different angle. It was time to try something new.

This tactic wasn't what Cotton had anticipated when she contacted me, however, and she might not sign off on it. But my gut was telling me we needed a fresh approach. Lyle had always stayed several steps ahead of pretty much everyone she knew her whole life. She was incredibly smart and intuitive, and we needed to understand her better. Understanding the real Kelly Lyle might help us catch a break.

I reached the Somerset borders around midday, just as the rain that had pursued me finally eased off. I forced myself to take a break and eat some lunch. I stopped at a pub called the Barley Mow Inn. Taking in the craftsmanship of its newly thatched roof, I made my way to a small back garden dotted with picnic benches. As I sat and watched people at other tables, leading seemingly ordinary lives, I started thinking about home. I was keen to avoid repeating mistakes I'd made in the past. I decided to call Monica. She picked up on the third ring and sounded in good spirits.

"I was thinking about you," I said.

"Nothing naughty, I hope. You're meant to be working. Are you okay? You sound down."

"I'm good. You know how it is – a few doubts."

"Listen. You don't need to do this," insisted Monica.

I loved the way she got straight to the heart of the matter. There was never any fluff or bullshit.

"Just walk away if you want to, James. We'll find another way. If we have to, we'll move as far away from Lyle as we can, somewhere she'll never find us. You don't owe anyone a damn thing. Only you can decide what has to be done here. Whether you attack this head-on or don't, I'm behind you one hundred percent, whatever you decide. You know that. Just be careful, that's all I ask."

"I love you," I said, forcing cheer into my voice. "You know how I get at the start of an investigation. It feels like I'm standing at the foot of Everest, ill-equipped to climb it."

"Take that first step. It's all you can do."

"What would I do without you?" I said. I closed my eyes and pictured her standing barefoot in the kitchen clutching the phone, Sandy looking up at her side, tail wagging.

"I'll get the girls to call you tonight."

"That'd be lovely. Thank you."

"That's better. That's my Jamie. I love you too. Stay safe and don't be gone too long. The bed feels very empty without my man in it."

Just over an hour later I arrived at the home of retired detective Richard Oatridge. His wife, Flo, was in the front garden of their cottage tying back some tall flowers, which she informed me were delphiniums. She was forcing bamboo canes into the ground and deftly running string between them.

"Do you have a garden, detective?" she said, straightening up and brushing dirt from her gloves.

"Nothing as beautiful as yours," I said, admiring the riot of colour. "A few shrubs and some pots. Seeing this, I think I could be converted. What are these plants? The bees love them."

Flo had a kind smile, and I could see she was delighted to share her knowledge. "These are echinacea. Beautiful, aren't they? They're one of my favourites. They're also used in herbal remedies to relieve symptoms of colds and flu."

I said, "I'm not sure I've seen a garden quite like this before."

"Before we bought the cottage it had been owned by an elderly lady. The gardens were her life. They're a very traditional English cottage garden style. In truth, the gardens are a large part of what made me fall in love with the place, and I suppose I felt a duty to continue her work. Before moving here, I'd never had any experience with gardening, but I soon realised that all I really had to do was care for the plants. Nature did the rest."

"Well, it's truly impressive," I said.

Flo took off her gloves and tucked them in her back pocket. "I could talk about the gardens for hours, but I know you didn't come all this way to hear me rattling on.

Let me call Richard. As usual, he's with his girlfriends. They seem to get more of his time than I do. Lately, though, Rose has been rather poorly, so he's been spending even more time seeing to her needs. Between you and me, I'm starting to wonder whether she puts it on so she gets extra attention – you know how old girls can be. I don't mind, though. It keeps him young and active and, most importantly, it keeps him out from under my feet for most of the day. We've always had our own interests. They say it's one of the ingredients that makes a strong marriage. What do you think?"

"I suppose so," I said, unsure how to answer.

The look on my face made Flo laugh. I soon learned that despite Flo's wholesome appearance, she had a wicked sense of humour, and Richard's 'girlfriends' were three rare-breed pigs named Molly, Rose and Delilah.

CHAPTER THIRTY

Richard showered and joined Flo and me in the garden for a light dinner. As he approached from the house, I got to my feet and put out my hand to shake his. He walked slowly with the aid of a walking stick and appeared to be in considerable pain.

"I'm fine, I'm fine," he whispered to Flo as she offered to help him to his seat.

He winked at me and smiled. "Cancer," he said.

Flo flinched like she'd received a small electric shock as he spat the word.

"I'll just take some painkillers. It'll ease off in a bit. They told me a week before Christmas that I had cancer." He laughed mirthlessly. "They told me it started in the prostate and had spread like wildfire. Nothing they can do. I'd left it too long before getting myself checked. Should have listened to Flo. She nagged and nagged, but did I listen? Of course not. Soon as you get back, go see your doctor. Get yourself checked, you hear me? It's no joke. Get yourself checked."

"I'm sorry," I said. "I had no idea. I wouldn't have come if I'd known."

"Nonsense," he barked. "Nobody knows. And why should they? I wanted you to come. What you said on the phone interests me. If it wasn't for my beautiful Flo, and those damn pigs, taking my mind off what's coming, I'd have gone crazy by now. Probably blown my brains out."

Flo said, "For pity's sake, Richard. Stop it."

In an effort to get comfortable, he shifted in his seat. "My pigs belong to Frank, our neighbour. He's got some land. He's nutty as a fruitcake but the nicest guy I ever met. Frank and his pigs have taught me a lot about life. I'll take you over there in the morning. We've assumed you're going to stay for the night."

"Well, I hadn't intended to. I couldn't impose."

"Rubbish. You're not imposing," insisted Richard.

I looked at Flo, who nodded in agreement.

"Now, take off that bloody jacket and tie, undo that top button and roll up your shirt sleeves and relax," said Richard. "The sun is out. We're in Flo's Garden of Eden, which is a work of wonder, and she's no doubt prepared some great food."

"It's only chicken and vegetables," she said modestly.

I did as Richard suggested. We talked about this and that while Flo prepared dinner.

During dinner, there was no talk surrounding the reason for my visit. Instead, we spent the evening listening to stories about Richard's past as a detective, how he and Flo had first met, their children, and the adventures they'd had together over the years. They asked about my family, and I told them about Alice and Faith and Monica. They insisted I come back and bring them with me next time, and I promised I would. We talked until 10 p.m., when Richard got too cold and tired to continue. Full of apologies and resentment, he reluctantly retired to his room.

At breakfast, he looked like a new man and was ready to get to work.

"Eat your breakfast, James. The sausages and bacon are from Frank's farm. Flo needs to pick up some bits in the village, and she is going to drive. We can talk on the way."

Thirty minutes later, on our way to the nearest pharmacy and supermarket, we were driving past the farm where Lyle had grown up.

"Close your ears, Flo," said Richard. "I need to talk police business with my friend James here."

Flo raised her eyebrows in a manner suggesting she'd heard the line many times before.

Full of enthusiasm, Richard said to me, "No doubt you passed the Lyle farm on your way in?" I nodded. "Kelly Lyle's father, Edwin, turned a modest dairy farm, inherited from his father, into one of the first large-scale industrial dairy farms in the UK, capable of producing large-volume and low-cost yields.

"It came at a time when supermarkets were beginning to take hold, and demand exceeded supply. Edwin Lyle was in the right place at the right time.

"With the profits from the farm, some property investments, some other 'behind-closed-door' deals and some clever accounting, Edwin Lyle became very wealthy. There is no doubt he was a smart businessman.

"The other thing there is no doubt about is that he was a mean bastard. A tyrant. An abusive bully who was prone to violent outbursts and furious rages. Rages that his wife and daughter bore the brunt of for many years.

"I have boxes of files on Kelly Lyle, and I've managed to gather medical records that show bone fractures and breaks on both Kelly and her mother, Theresa. I'm assured by experts the injuries sustained are consistent with serious violent assaults. In other words, he beat his wife and, from a young age, his daughter too. God only knows what else went on in that house behind closed doors. I don't need to spell it out; you've seen enough cases to know."

Flo parked the car. Richard and I walked to a small tea shop where he could keep warm and we could talk. I found us a table by the window and ordered two cream teas.

"You understand that I have no sympathy for Edwin Lyle," he continued. "Once I discovered what the man was like I was glad he was dead. At the time, I was the lead detective, and I still had a job to do."

I said, "I understand completely. We're all in the same boat. We gather evidence. The court then decides justice."

"Exactly, James. You know what I'm talking about; I don't need to spell it out. Anyway, finally Theresa had had enough. She tried to get them both away from the old man. That failed, and Theresa was forced to abandon young Kelly. For close to a year the girl was alone with her father. The increasingly desperate mother eventually managed to grab Kelly while Edwin was away from the farm. For a short while, they were safe.

"It didn't take long for Edwin, with all his connections, to track them down. The next thing you knew, Theresa was found to be an unfit mother and told if she ever wanted to see her daughter again, she must seek treatment for her mental health problems. This left Kelly, who's twelve at this point, nearly thirteen, to fend for herself against her bully of a father. Poor child."

I waited for Richard to take his pills and sip his tea before I encouraged him to continue. "Did you think a twelve-year-old girl was capable of what you're suggesting she did to her father?"

"Not immediately. Like everyone else, I assumed Edwin's death was an accident. Deaths like his are commonplace on farms. It's a dangerous occupation. What I've learned subsequently leaves me without the slightest doubt it was premeditated murder. Patricide, made to look like an accident by a young girl."

CHAPTER THIRTY-ONE

I couldn't help wondering how Lyle's life might have looked like had she grown up in different circumstances. Was killing her father the catalyst for what was to come? Had her father's brutality triggered something in her? Was she a product of her early environment or was she born to kill? Did she have her father's wickedness flowing through her veins – like father, like daughter?

Richard had no appetite and couldn't eat. He pushed his plate away and sipped at his tea feebly. He closed his eyes and rested. I watched his fingers tremble as he dozed, the backs of his hands bruised and blotchy.

I took the opportunity to send some text messages and read the news on my phone. When I looked up, Richard was awake and watching me. He smiled apologetically.

Dabbing the corners of his mouth with a tissue, he said, "Looking back, I remember arriving at the farm and seeing a child in complete control of her emotions. I assumed she was in shock, and the grief of what had happened to her father hadn't sunk in.

"She was confident, and she quickly explained the

events that had led to her father's death. She did it without a moment's hesitation or deviation. Each time, her explanation was repeated word for word. I stood back and watched her explain to fellow detectives how the farm worked, the hazards of a working farm and the steps leading up to the accident.

"I realise now that she had orchestrated everything. She was manipulating us, and because she was a child, and we couldn't imagine a child doing such a thing, we gave her the space to do so. I know it's an odd thing to say of a child, but that's what I now see."

I said, "Back then, I guess it was almost unthinkable. Sadly, times have changed."

"Damn right they've changed. I don't think I could be a detective today," he said. I knew he didn't mean it. He'd give almost anything to be young, fit and healthy. Back on the beat, chasing down bad guys. I bet he was one hell of a detective back in the day.

"I know she's smart," I said. "What can you tell me about her education?"

"What do you want to know? She was off the charts. Teachers told me she would turn up for class and breeze through lessons. The general consensus was that teachers felt what they taught was of little interest to her – because she already knew it.

"One teacher explained to me that Kelly was self-taught. She read and studied on her own time, all the time. She'd sit in lessons and read her own stuff. Advanced stuff. It was clear to the teacher that she had an insatiable appetite for knowledge, and school just didn't offer enough.

"Occasionally, Kelly would challenge a teacher on a topic or fact, mainly for the sport of it. Maybe she did so because she wanted to show off to classmates or because she was bored. Teachers soon learned Kelly was correct pretty much all the time or at least had a well-thought-out argument on most subjects."

From our table in the tea shop, we looked across the street and could see Flo waving and pointing to another shop she wanted to visit. Richard waved back and nodded agreement.

I was eager for Richard to keep going with his insights.

"There were lots of ways she could have killed her father. She deliberately chose a way that didn't kill him outright.

"Young Kelly waited until her father's attention was elsewhere, then she put the farm tractor into motion. When paramedics and police arrived, he was found pinned to the concrete wall of a barn by one of the tractor's forks.

"Do you think she ignored his pleas for help? To this day, I still wonder whether she spoke to him while he writhed in agony before eventually dying from multiple organ failure and massive internal bleeding. What do you think the young Kelly might have said to her abusive father?"

Despite what I knew of her I was still finding it hard to make the leap from abused child to murderer.

"Do you have any proof she did it?" I asked politely.

Richard scratched the side of his head with his thumb. He scrunched his nose. "Good question. Everything I have is circumstantial. Kelly claimed she was helping her father and that what happened to him was an accident. Who would argue otherwise? It was only over time that my interest in her grew. As time passed, I got calls from other forces asking for background information on her. That's when I started keeping records. I thought one day someone would come knocking on my door. And here you are."

Lucky me, I thought.

"What happened to her next?" I asked.

"Kelly stayed with her aunt, her mother's sister, in London. Theresa left the hospital she was working at and joined them. The farm passed to Theresa and continued to be run by a management team. It was eventually swallowed up by an investment company owned by Kelly. She then expanded the farm business overseas. Her investment company is global and has many interests. Its portfolio ranges from pharmaceutical research to property development."

"That answers the question of wealth. She seems to have no limitations when it comes to lifestyle."

"She made sure she has no financial limitations. She's a shrewd and tough businesswoman. Anyone working for her soon learns not to challenge her authority. Years ago, after a botched merger caused a downturn in profits, the CFO and COO made a move to oust her from the board. Before the takeover gathered momentum, both the CFO and COO died in a helicopter crash."

"Helicopter crashes aren't uncommon," I suggested. I knew very well what Lyle was and what she was capable of, but I didn't want my head filled with rumour and hearsay; I wanted as accurate a picture of her as possible, so I had to challenge Richard a little.

To prove his point, he swiftly continued. "A project manager for her property development company, a guy called Alan Wilson, mysteriously disappeared after some financial irregularities were discovered.

"Only Wilson's hand was ever found. The hand had been sawn off and sent by UPS courier to the company's accounting department. Word soon spread among management and staff that Wilson's hand was a message to anyone else who might consider dipping their fingers into the Lyle cash register.

"Once again, however, she could not be tied to the

disappearance. As a smokescreen, she even put up a million-pound reward for information leading to his whereabouts or the arrest of the perpetrators. As I said, she's a smart lady. As well as a dangerous one."

Flo took us home and Richard slept for a couple of hours. Flo showed me to the attic, and I pulled out some boxes of files and started looking through them.

Flo pulled a dust sheet off another pile of boxes. "It's done him a lot of good talking to you," she said. "I see glimmers of my old Richie. He spent years gathering all this. Little by little, piece by piece. He wants you to have them now. He hopes you can finish what he started."

"I hope so too. He's a good man. He doesn't deserve what he's going through. Neither of you do."

The pressure I was feeling to stop Lyle had just got more intense.

I loaded the boxes of files into my car and returned to the house to find Richard up and taking another round of tablets.

"I'm surprised I don't bloody rattle when I walk, the number of these I take," he grumbled.

As he walked me to my car, he grabbed my arm. "There is a lot of information in those boxes," he said quietly. "It could take weeks if not months to go through it all. My advice is to start with her time at university. She was young and full of ambition and somewhat vulnerable. It was the time before she got smart enough to properly cover her tracks. I never quite got time to fully look into that time of her life. You might just get lucky."

Saying goodbye to Richard and Flo was emotional. I'd grown fond of them in the two days I'd spent with them. Although he was a tough old sod, I wasn't sure how much fight Richard had left in him. I promised I'd stay in touch.

CHAPTER THIRTY-TWO

After leaving Flo and Richard's home, I decided to stay at a hotel overnight. I couldn't face the drive back to Dorset, and, in truth, I was keen to delve into the case files piled up in the back of my car. I sent Cotton a text message to let her know I was okay and making some progress. At least I hoped I was.

I ordered room service, settled down with a notebook and spread Richard's reports out over the bed.

I started with the case files Richard had suggested I look at first. It didn't take long before I understood my next move. I was about to call home when my phone rang.

"Where are you, Daddy?" It was Faith, and she sounded excited. "I was hoping you'd be home by now. I wanted to tell you about my test at school."

"I'm sorry, baby. I'm working, and I'll be a few more days. You can tell me now if you want."

"Okay. So, it was a spelling test. You know how I need to work on my spelling, don't you? I practised and practised with Monica and Nana Hardy, and do you know what I got? It was out of twenty. Guess, Daddy. How many do you think?"

"I don't know. You say you practised them a lot."

"Uh-huh, over and over. Just guess."

"Eight out of twenty?" I joked.

"No way. Really? Are you kidding? Eight? Daddy thinks I only got eight."

I heard Monica in the background say, "He's messing around. You surprise him. Tell him what you got, sweetheart."

"I got twenty out of twenty," Faith said with pride.

"Wowee! No way. Really? Well done. That is fantastic! Twenty, you say?"

"Yep. Not one wrong. The hardest word was 'consequential.'" Faith diligently spelt it out for me over the phone.

I then spoke to Alice, who was in the middle of messaging a friend on her phone to arrange a sleepover and didn't chat for long. She passed me to Monica.

"It went well today," I said. "I'll be away another day, two days max. How are you? You sound different. Like you have something on your mind."

"Really? Nothing in particular." I could tell Monica was holding back, but I didn't press her. She'd tell me when the time was right. "Your parents send their love. They popped in earlier."

"Thank you. I love you and miss you. Are you sure there's nothing wrong?"

"It'll wait. I love you too. I'd better go. Let you get on. Look after yourself."

"You too."

The call ended, and I found myself rubbing the phone on my chin, thinking about Monica's tone. I'd not heard her sound that way before. I put the thought to one side and carried on reading.

I sipped single malt from a teacup and read as fast I could. I had questions and wanted to phone Richard, but it was late. I knew he wouldn't mind – he'd probably welcome the excitement – but I knew it wasn't the right thing to do. I'd call him in the morning, perhaps.

From what I could tell, Lyle had been the victim of a serious assault while at university. It had led to an arrest, and a young man had been charged. The phone rang again. This time it was Cotton.

"Evening, James. I got your text."

"Emma, before you ask, I'm going to be a few more days. Tomorrow I'm heading to Lyle's old university to speak to them about an incident that took place during her time there. How are things your end?"

"Shit. But I won't go over it now. I'm too tired. I'll wait until you get back here. There's no point burdening you with it. Stupid as it sounds, I just needed a little reassurance that you're making headway. No matter how small."

"I feel surer than ever that the only way to get out in front of her is to think like her. The only way we do that is if we understand her. We do that by digging into her past and speaking to people who knew her." I hoped I sounded more confident than I felt.

I could hear Cotton stifling a yawn. "Okay. I'm going to try to get some sleep. Tomorrow's going to be a long day. Again. Please stay in touch. Call me if you get anything."

"I will," I said. The bedside clock showed it was just past midnight. "I won't be far behind you. Just one thing."

"What?"

"I need you to call the university and get me in front of the person in charge, probably the chancellor."

"Anything else?"

"Tell them it's a murder enquiry. I need to see all they have on Kelly Lyle and another former student..." I flicked through the papers strewn on the bed. "Here it is: Jacob Gregory. If they put up resistance, threaten them with a warrant. And if you have to, you could suggest you'll make their life hell by arriving with a team of detectives to turn the place upside down."

"Goodnight, Hardy."

"Does that mean you'll do it?"

"Yes, I'll do it. Goodnight," she said with exasperation.

The call ended, and I punched the air.

CHAPTER THIRTY-THREE

I arrived on campus early and headed straight to the office building. I was quickly informed I wouldn't be able to see the chancellor but that the vice-chancellor, Sir Martin Arnez, was expecting me.

"Come in, detective," said Arnez. He put out his thin hand, which I shook. "Take a seat. I've asked Julia McKiernan to join us," he said. "Julia is our head of HR. She'll be taking notes of our conversation. I'm sure you understand."

McKiernan smiled and turned to the first page of a new notepad. I guessed she was in her early sixties. She wore navy trousers and a jacket that looked tailored. Her hair was short and dark and flattered her petite features.

Speaking to both McKiernan and Arnez, I said, "Of course. You understand the conversation can go no further than the three of us. My being here is part of an ongoing murder investigation."

"My lips are sealed," said Arnez. He pretended to zip his lips closed with finger and thumb the way a child might.

McKiernan studied my reaction. I had a feeling she missed very little of what went on within these grounds.

"I'm not entirely sure how I can help," Arnez went on. "You see, this 'incident' between Miss Allerton and Master Gregory was before my time."

I'd learned from Richard's case files that Lyle had taken her mother's maiden name of Allerton while at university.

"It was also before the time of the current chancellor," Arnez continued. "Unfortunately, the very person who might have known a little more, my predecessor, has, sadly, passed away.

"The whole misunderstanding between the couple in question was, of course, handled most professionally and delicately by the police. They understood the need for discretion in this distasteful matter and acted accordingly. You see, the university itself had very little to do with the events that took place. Events that eventually became something of a tragedy for all involved but have long since been resolved to everyone's satisfaction. It seems you're rather late to the party, as it were. It appears, therefore, you've had a rather wasted journey. We've really put the whole sorry matter behind us and moved on. It's sometimes best to let sleeping dogs lie. Don't you think?"

I let his words hang in the air and waited until McKiernan finished scratching with her pen. I was more than a little angry at his attitude. I was used to uncooperative witnesses, but this guy took the biscuit.

McKiernan coughed gently and shifted in her seat, her eyes moving between Arnez and me like a boxing referee's.

"Mr Arnez, let me see if I understand you correctly," I said coldly. "Am I right in thinking, Mr Arnez, that the university's position is that it would rather not discuss the rape of one of its female students?"

Arnez placed the expensive-looking fountain pen he'd been playing with down on his desk. He cleared his throat and then blurted, "This is not kindergarten. We cannot monitor and are not responsible for everything that goes on here between students."

I ignored him. "A gifted young woman was attacked, beaten and raped while on *your* campus. An aspiring student full of promise was left shattered and scarred while on *your* grounds. Betrayed by a fellow student."

"You've got this all wrong," insisted Arnez.

I steamed on. "And your position is that it wasn't the university's responsibility to ensure adequate precautions were taken to ensure every student's safety."

"That isn't what I said at all. It wasn't like that," insisted Arnez. "You're misinterpreting events——"

I spoke over top of him. "A student at your institution was scarred both physically and mentally. Scars that she'll carry with her for life. Scars that will dictate the course of her life."

"You don't know that," protested Arnez.

"I do know that. And you want to bury what happened. Is that what you're saying?"

"I think you're being more than a little unreasonable. I mean to say——" Arnez raised his voice and repeatedly tapped his finger on the desk. "Kelly Allerton was a problem before she ever arrived here. We should never have accepted her. But we did. We offered her a place, despite having reservations, and look what happened."

McKiernan stopped writing.

I waited for Arnez to calm himself. I spoke soothingly now. "She's to blame?"

"Not entirely, of course."

"Are there any members of staff who were here at the

time of the assault? The truth, please. I'd rather not find out later and have to come back."

Arnez sipped a glass of water. His slender hands were trembling. "That's what I'm saying to you, detective. There is no one here from that far back. It was over twenty years ago." He stretched his neck and cleared his throat. His discomfort was plain to see. We both now knew the university's position on what had happened. He looked between McKiernan and me, wondering whether to say more.

"Well, it seems you are correct: I've had a wasted trip," I said abruptly. "I apologise for taking up your time."

I got to my feet, shook Arnez's moist hand and waited for him to show me out. McKiernan closed her notebook and got to her feet.

"I am truly sorry we couldn't assist more," said Arnez. "We take all crime very seriously. Especially crimes of this nature. It's just that it happened so long ago."

"You've been more helpful than you realise. Just one more thing before I go," I said, as if it had just occurred to me.

Arnez flinched.

"A large donation was made to the university at the time of the assault. The university's financial records show a gift of seventy-five thousand pounds from Charles Gregory."

"I would have to check that," muttered Arnez.

I pulled out a sheet of paper showing the transaction and held it towards him. He smiled weakly as he put on his reading glasses and examined the printout.

"Ah, yes. From what I understand, Mr Gregory was a very generous donor – we have many donors who contribute to the university's welfare. It's not unusual to receive large sums such as this."

I said, "Considering the timing of this donation, can you see how the payment might be construed as an incentive to sweep the allegations against his son under the carpet?"

Arnez spoke calmly. "I see what you're getting at. The timing is a little unfortunate. You'd have to speak to Charles Gregory to be sure, but I think at the time he expected the whole debacle to blow over. That it was nothing more than a lovers' tiff. The gift was a kind of compensation for any inconvenience caused to the university."

McKiernan stiffened at these words.

"A lovers' tiff, you say," I repeated.

This appeared to be another example of Lyle bearing the brunt of the abuse of male power. It was more likely the money was to ensure the allegations were dropped. I'd need to check to be sure.

McKiernan showed me out. She seemed in a hurry. At first, I thought she was keen to get me far away from the bumbling Arnez, but then she asked me to wait while she checked her computer. I took a seat outside her office. She returned a few minutes later.

"Goodbye, Detective Hardy," she whispered as she discreetly passed me a folded slip of paper.

Once in my car, I unfolded the note. It was an address in Majorca, Spain, for Mr and Mrs Charles Gregory, the parents of the young man charged with beating and raping Kelly Lyle.

It looked like I was going to need to pack a few things and catch a flight.

CHAPTER THIRTY-FOUR

Emma sat alone at her desk checking notes, cross-referencing names, facts and interview notes and catching up with her correspondence. It was dark outside, and she should have gone home hours ago.

She forked a large portion of chicken chow mein into her mouth before running her finger along the seal of an envelope and pulling out a letter. She read it through then stopped chewing and reread it.

Dearest Emma,

It appears you're going around in circles, round and round like a child's brightly coloured windmill.

If you really want to play my game, you need to first look at what happened to Hardy's wife. I need you to see the big picture. James deserves to know the truth. Only then can we take this game to a whole new level.

All my love, Kelly L.

P.S. Do you dream at night of being held by Hardy? Who could blame you? He's a handsome man. If only he were single…

Emma turned the letter over and read the back. She

jotted the numbers and letters down on a legal pad: GU851PH52.

The loud ring of the desk phone startled her.

"Yes?" barked Emma.

"Bad time?" It was Hardy.

"I'm okay." Emma put the letter down on the desk and covered it. "Tired, I suppose. I feel like I'm going around in circles." She blinked. *That's what Kelly Lyle thinks too.*

"That's what these cases are like – you know that. We find a thread that takes us nowhere, so we pick another thread and follow it. If that thread also leads nowhere, we simply pick up another. We keep going one thread at a time."

Emma tucked the phone under her chin and tied up her hair. She asked, "Where are you?"

"Hotel room. In the morning I'm boarding a flight to Palma, Majorca. I need to speak to a father about his dead son. It's a long story. I'm following the thread."

Emma was a little surprised Hardy had chosen not to discuss his next move with her but she didn't comment on it. Instead, she said, "Don't get used to the climate. I don't want you staying out there."

She looked out the window at the cold, dark night and the spots of rain on the glass.

"I won't. I had better go. I've got another call that I must take – someone is calling me back. Are you sure you're okay?"

"Yes. Go. Go take your call. I'm fine."

The line went dead.

Emma picked up the letter again and considered what was being said. Lyle sure had a way of getting under your skin.

…I need you to see the big picture. James deserves to know the truth…

She started rooting around in her desk but couldn't find what she was looking for. She went to her filing cabinet and began pulling out the drawers one at a time. "It's got to be here somewhere."

She slammed the last drawer shut.

Hands on hips, she stood in the middle of her office.

"I know…"

Emma pulled her chair up in front of her PC and, after a few minutes' digging around on the internet, found what she wanted. She leaned back in her chair and reached back across her desk for her phone. She punched in the number and left a message. "This is Detective Inspector Emma Cotton. I'd like to leave a message for a Detective Rayner. I need him to call me back urgently."

She left a direct number and her mobile number and once again emphasised how important it was that Rayner call her back as soon as possible.

She then did another search online for articles associated with the death of Hardy's wife. She knew a lot about his career and his success tracking down serial killers but realised she knew very little about what had happened to Helena.

The news articles she was able to find online gave a sensationalised perspective of her murder. The press at the time was focused on the number of street crimes and a sharp rise in violent crime overall.

It was apparent the media's focus was on the fact that if the wife of a detective chief inspector wasn't safe, only a relatively short distance from her home, then crime on the streets of London must be out of control. And the British police force must have lost their grip.

Later articles focused on the man who was eventually found guilty of her murder. He was a drug addict who the press named as Tony Horn. He had been sentenced to life and was to serve a minimum of fifteen years.

Emma leaned back in her chair and absently forked another huge portion of chow mein into her mouth. It was stone cold and greasy. She chewed and she thought.

She picked up the phone again, punched in a number and chewed hard to get rid of what she had in her mouth. The phone was answered more quickly than she'd expected, and she had to swallow hard so she could talk.

"Hello, this is Detective Inspector Emma Cotton. I need to see a prisoner." After a bit of back-and-forth, she put the phone down.

Satisfied, she finished the cold chow mein and washed it down with an even colder cup of tea. She needed to look into Helena's death quietly. She wasn't sure how Hardy would react if he knew she was digging into his past. Yet, it was he who, only a few minutes ago, had told her to pick up a thread and follow it.

What troubled her was that the thread was being handed to her by the killer herself.

CHAPTER THIRTY-FIVE

I felt out of place among the holiday-makers at Palma de Mallorca Airport. With my passport checked and no suitcase to collect, I moved quickly through arrivals.

Seeing excited children and exhausted parents brought back memories of a two-week family holiday in Majorca when Alice and Faith were just toddlers. Where had the time gone? I made a mental note to look into bringing the girls back there as soon as possible.

I was to be met by a driver at the airport. Outside arrivals I soon spotted Felipe holding up a piece of paper with my name on it. He was tall, casually dressed, welcoming and full of smiles.

In a few minutes, my bag was in the boot of the car, and we were in his air-conditioned taxi heading towards the home of Charles Gregory. Outside it was hot and sunny. I put on my sunglasses, sat back and gathered my thoughts.

"Do you know Mr Gregory well?" I asked Felipe.

"*Sí*. Yes. I know Mr Gregory well. Mr and Mrs Gregory have met all my family. He make my children laugh and dance. My wife cook for them; she like to cook. He ask for me to drive him. I drive him. He sometime call at my home to talk and drink."

"It sounds like you're good friends."

"I think we are friends, yes. He sometime come fishing with me on my small boat. He's not so keen on fishing. Eating fish, yes. Fishing, not so much." Felipe laughed and appeared to be about to launch into a story when his mobile phone rang. He started speaking Spanish to a woman who I guessed to be his wife. By the time he had finished his animated conversation, the taxi was heading up a narrow and winding road to the Gregorys' villa.

A Spanish woman who introduced herself as the housekeeper showed me to my room on arrival. I showered and changed my shirt.

Having freshened up, I made my way through the house to the sun terrace. The house, with its long windows and large open rooms, sat on a hillside overlooking the Mediterranean Sea. The bright blue water below looked inviting as I stood admiring the view.

"Please come in out of the afternoon heat, inspector. I have assumed you would be thirsty and hungry, so Maria, who met you at the door, has prepared a cold lunch for us both."

Charles Gregory passed me a glass of iced tea and shook my hand firmly. He was friendly but didn't smile. He was expensively dressed and well groomed. His bright blue eyes fixed on mine as he gestured towards a pair of antique leather armchairs.

In the middle of the room sat a magnificent wooden dining table, its centrepiece an ornate flowerpot holding several large flowering orchids. We sat beside wooden doors in a cool and shaded part of the dining area.

Wishing to get our conversation moving, I said, "You have a beautiful home, Mr Gregory."

Gregory looked around and nodded. "Call me Charles. Thank you. I chose the location, designed and developed the property, but my wife is the one who made it a home. She has good taste. If I were to be perfectly honest, I wouldn't know where to start when it comes to interior design."

Charles's hesitant and fleeting smile suggested he was keen to know the reason behind my visit.

"We get very few visitors," he said, "and we like it that way. Naturally, I'm intrigued when a former Scotland Yard detective chief inspector leaves his family and endures a nearly two-hour flight to speak to me. I assume the reason must be extremely important."

"I don't recall mentioning I was a detective chief inspector."

"I still have a few contacts back in the UK. We also have internet. I Googled you. You've worked on a lot of high-profile cases. I am, therefore, even more intrigued that, having retired, you've come all this way to speak to me. Have we met before? Is that it? Or do I owe you money?"

We both laughed at his joke. I said, "You don't owe me money. It does seem, though, that the investigating detective has been investigated."

I looked around the room.

"We're alone," said Charles. "My wife is shopping and will not be back for some time. Maria, the housekeeper, has finished for the day. I gave her the rest of the afternoon off. You can speak freely."

"I am assisting a colleague with her investigation," I said.

"Surely, Inspector Hardy, you could have picked up the phone?"

"Perhaps. My questions are of a delicate nature. I wanted to speak to you face to face."

Charles sipped his water and said nothing.

"I'm here about your son, Jacob."

Silence.

I continued. "I am sorry to bring it up. I know it must be difficult."

"Of course you're here about my son," said Charles. "I know what happened will never go away. My son knew that too. Which is why he took his life. Although it could be argued he had his life taken from him because of what happened. And in turn, ours were taken from us the day he killed himself.

"This might look like paradise to everyone else, but for my wife and me, it feels like a prison and every day is a living hell. Ask your questions. I'll help if I can."

"I've read the case files, but I'd like to hear your version of events. More accurately, I'd like to hear your son's version."

"Are you opening up the case again? I don't think we want that."

"No. It's a separate investigation, but I think what happened to your son could help."

"Jacob was our only child. He was our miracle baby. Doctors told us we couldn't have children and yet one day, out of the blue, Patti told me she was pregnant. Happiest day of my life.

"Jacob was a shy boy, perhaps because he was an only child. He was very bright but socially awkward. A little too caring for his own good, you could say. He often found himself being taken advantage of.

"Growing up, he was bullied quite a bit. He had a

tough time at school. He got through it and got his place at his chosen university. He loved it and was doing exceptionally well. He started to flourish and come out of himself.

"In his second year, he met a girl. He was very inexperienced, you understand, and he was soon telling us how he'd fallen in love. He would talk to his mother on the phone about how smart this girl was and how beautiful and kind and thoughtful. We were delighted but, as a lot of parents would, we urged caution. Though, in truth, we were over the moon. For us, the relationship was the icing on the cake. Somebody saw the beautiful boy we saw, and they were making him happy.

"One weekend at the beginning of his third year he came home for a few days, and we could see a change in him. Patti and I tried to speak with him, to find out what was going on, but he was distant and didn't want to talk about it.

"We hoped it would pass and gave him the space he wanted. Then, a few weeks later he phoned to say he'd broken off the relationship. We were surprised but supportive. At first, he didn't say why it had ended. It was a while before he told us what had been really going on between them."

CHAPTER THIRTY-SIX

Charles leaned forward and poured us both a glass of iced water. He took a sip then looked at me, his eyes hard and unforgiving. "The young woman had become obsessed with him. She'd become manipulative and violent towards him. The day he called us she'd threatened to kill him."

"How did Jacob sound when you spoke?"

"How do you think he sounded? Scared, confused, upset, emotional… He was scared for himself and, Jacob being Jacob, he was worried for her too."

"Were the police involved?"

"Not at this point. Jacob didn't want that. He told us he'd spoken to the university's chaplain and things had been resolved diplomatically. Had we known what was to come we'd have done things differently. Hindsight and all that." I could see the sadness in Charles's face.

"Go on," I urged him gently.

"Things were quiet for a while. It seemed the young woman was keeping her distance and that Jacob and the university had managed to resolve the situation. We all moved on with our lives.

"At the end-of-term party, the two of them got talking. She apologised for her prior behaviour. She told Jacob she'd had family problems and that had caused her to act out of character. They agreed to be friends and spent the evening talking.

"Foolishly, after a few drinks, they returned to his room and spent the night together. The young fool had sex with her. Anyway, the next morning, he woke up alone. He was disappointed but thought nothing more of it.

"Later that day police officers arrived at his door. At first, Jacob thought it was a prank. He very quickly realised it was no joke. He was cautioned and very publicly taken in for questioning. He was quizzed for hours about the young woman and their relationship and the events of the previous night. He was shown pictures of her injuries; the bruises and cuts and blood-stained clothes. Of course, they also had DNA evidence. He was told he would be charged with rape."

"What happened next?"

Charles looked drawn and pale. Recounting the story was taking its toll, but he fought on.

"I know what you're thinking: too many drinks. Maybe some drugs. Young man who didn't want to hear 'no.' Jacob forced himself on her."

"What do you think happened?"

"We know what happened," he said sharply. "The only witness, another student in an adjoining room, was too scared to speak out. She knows what happened. She saw the girl inflict her own injuries. The witness feared for her life. She would only speak to us privately and would not make a formal statement no matter how hard we, or the police, insisted."

Charles had tears in his eyes. He got to his feet and paced around the room like a caged tiger, frustration and fury charging through his body as if all this had happened only yesterday.

Finally, he stood behind his armchair and said, "Do you have children, inspector?"

"Two daughters. The eldest is about to become a teenager."

"If you know your daughters as well as I know – knew – my son, then I don't need to explain how I knew he was innocent."

I'd heard similar words, a hundred times before, from parents who would sooner die than believe their child capable of committing a serious crime.

"Before we go any further," I said, "I must ask you about the money. You donated a considerable sum to the university."

"It was foolish. Arrogant. Regrettable. A rash decision that, in retrospect, was plainly misguided. It's true what they say: hindsight is twenty-twenty. I had this notion at the time the girl was after money. Money isn't something I've ever been short of, and I simply wanted to help my son.

"The university was to act as an intermediary. I was desperate to see the whole thing go away, and I am ashamed to say I instructed them to make her an offer. Jacob knew nothing of this, of course. Neither did Patti. Patti would have been dead against it."

I knew how it would look and play out in court if it was discovered Charles had offered hush money to the victim.

I could also see how Charles, in such a desperate situation, might have acted irrationally.

I asked, "Did the offer of money have the result you were hoping for?"

"For a short time. I'd hoped the money had worked and that an understanding had been reached. That she'd drop the false allegations. However, it soon became clear she was out for blood, and I'd merely made things worse. There was a trial, of course. The scandal was horrendous. The shame, unbearable. The helplessness, heartbreaking. Friends and family turned their backs on us.

"We supported and believed in Jacob, and he knew that. We told ourselves that by staying strong as a family, we would get through it all, somehow. We assumed that despite it all the truth would come out and Jacob would be found innocent and the whole sham exposed.

"Instead, it was one of those terrible situations that you read about in the newspapers, where the accused is found guilty before ever stepping inside a courtroom. Jacob's spirit was broken. He stopped talking. The strain got too much. We tried to reach him, talk to him, tell him we believed in him and that, ultimately, he'd be found innocent.

"Every day we told him how much we loved him, but it wasn't enough. The evening of the fifteenth of May, while in police custody awaiting sentencing, he took his own life. Our miracle baby, our gentle boy, was found hanging in his cell."

Charles wiped a tear from his cheek with the back of his hand and cleared his throat. He gripped the armchair and said, "As far as I am concerned, the bitch murdered him. She might not have put a gun to his head and pulled a trigger. Nevertheless, she murdered my son."

"I'm sorry. Truly sorry."

Gregory got up and walked to the window. He stared out to sea. "I'm sure you are, inspector. Unfortunately, those words sound hollow to me these days."

"Did you ever hear from the woman after Jacob's death?"

"Why?" Gregory turned on me with hurt in his eyes. "Where is all this leading? Why does all this matter now?"

"I'm simply trying to understand what went on," I said softly. "I'm trying to build a picture."

A woman's voice from behind me said, "Yes, we did."

Patti Gregory had returned and now walked across the room to kiss her husband. Her elegance, glamour and confidence belied the eyes of a mother who had suffered and cried until there was nothing left to give.

Patti said, "She sent us photos of Jacob and herself. Happy, smiling photos. There was also a note."

"Do you have the note? Do you recall what it said?"

"No, I burned it," she said, "along with the photos."

Charles reached out and held his wife's hand. "I don't need the note. I'll never forget. It read, 'What a shame. Jacob beat me to it.'"

Patti added, "She's evil. She couldn't resist twisting the knife once more. I know exactly what that note implied."

"Did you go to the police? Start building a case to clear his name?"

"There was no point," replied Charles bitterly. "He was gone. He was the centre of our world, and he was gone. Nothing could change that. Although we might not be able to prove it, we knew the truth. We've always known the truth. And that's all that matters."

Said Patti, "Unlike me, my husband still holds out hope we'll one day see justice. So, tell me, inspector: why are you dragging this up again? Haven't we suffered enough?"

I owed the Gregorys an explanation. I had listened to their story, and it was time I laid my cards on the table. I just hoped I didn't damage their already devastated lives any more.

I looked from Charles to Patti as I explained. I spoke slowly and clearly. "I'm investigating a woman named Kelly Lyle. She is the prime suspect in a series of murders that date back a great many years. I'm looking into her background to build a picture of who she is and what motivates her to kill. My hope is that it if we understand her, it will help us catch her."

"Then you've had a wasted trip, inspector. As you'd well know, if you'd done your homework, the woman responsible was named Kelly Allerton."

I paused before replying gently, "Kelly Lyle's mother's maiden name is Allerton. She took the name while at university. The woman I am pursuing is the same woman who drove Jacob to commit suicide. Kelly Lyle, or Kelly Allerton as you knew her, is wanted in at least four countries in connection with a string of murders. We also believe there are countless other cases where she aided and incited others to commit murder. I must stop her."

Charles Gregory's eyes brimmed with tears and his body trembled. He pulled his wife to him, and they held each other. I couldn't return their son to them, but I had managed to throw light on some of the questions that had haunted them for years.

Only Lyle knew the truth about what had really happened between Jacob Gregory and herself. Maybe one day, once she was behind bars, I would be able to ask her.

CHAPTER THIRTY-SEVEN

A bead of perspiration ran down the guard's neck. Prison Officer Terry Farley tugged his collar with a finger. He watched as she mingled among visitors, most of them friends and family of the inmates.

Farley looked her over as she casually chatted and joked with one of the regular visitors – a wife he recognised whose husband was back in again for dealing – as though she'd been visiting every month for years.

She looked different from the last time they'd met. Her hair was unwashed and unbrushed, and she wore no make-up. The fancy, expensive-looking designer clothes were gone, replaced by faded jeans, a sports sweatshirt and battered tennis shoes.

She didn't stand out, grabbed nobody's interest and didn't look out of place at all. If Farley didn't know better, he'd think she was the wife or sister or girlfriend of one of the cons – which was just what she wanted.

As the visitors were shown through to the visiting room, Farley made sure he stood next to her. He whispered, "You promise that after this you'll leave my family and me alone?"

She didn't look at him. She looked straight ahead and said, "I'm going to need your help for one more visit. After that, you'll never hear from me again."

Farley swallowed hard and pushed out his chin. Rubbing the back of his sweaty neck, he said, "You said nothing about a second visit. We had a deal. I can't do this again."

"Circumstances have changed, and I'll need your help one last time. I'll be in touch. And one more thing."

Farley sucked in air and said, "What?"

"Stop sweating, Farley. You look like you're doing something illegal." Kelly Lyle winked and left him looking anxiously around the room.

She moved through the room full of visitors and prisoners to sit down opposite inmate Tony Horn.

"Look at me, Tony," she ordered. "Stop looking around. I need you to settle down. We don't need any undue attention. You're as bad as Farley. You look like you're going to piss your pants."

Horn whispered loudly, "What if someone recognises you?"

"Even my own mother wouldn't recognise me."

"What if someone does?"

"Well, let's hope they don't. Stop looking so nervous."

"How the fuck do you expect me to react? You being here could bring all sorts of shit down on me."

"Mind your language, Tony," Lyle snapped. "Take a deep breath. Act like we know each other. Smile."

"Where's Tina?"

"Tina isn't coming today. She'll be along again next time."

He looked around the room. He could see inmates looking; he could feel their eyes on him.

"If someone here figures out who you are they're going to wonder why Kelly Lyle wants to see me. They're either going to think I'm an associate of yours or that you want information from me. Pretty much everyone in here knows my background, so it's unlikely they're going to think I'm an associate. Which makes me a snitch, and that pretty much makes me a dead man."

"Stop being so melodramatic. Nobody gives a damn about you. You're a nobody. And in a place like this, if you're smart, that can work to your advantage. Just keep your mouth shut, your head down, and you'll be fine."

Horn looked over Lyle's shoulder at the officer. Farley was watching them. Horn felt uneasy about a screw being involved. His head kept telling him this was a bad situation. Very bad. Very effing bad, indeed.

"Don't look at Farley. Look at me," said Lyle. "He has no interest in our conversation. He's got huge problems of his own."

Horn turned to Lyle. Did she really have prison guards in her pocket?

She leaned towards him. "Do you know why I'm here?"

Horn shrugged then decided not to piss Lyle off any more than he already had, so he blurted, "The detective's wife? Helena Hardy?"

Her cold eyes fixed on his, and she said, "Before you answer the next question, Tony, I need you to remember that it's me you need to be afraid of. Nobody else. I need you to give me the name of the man who sent you to kill Helena Hardy."

Horn smiled uneasily and said, "You know who it was. Everyone does."

"I need to hear you say it."

"Richter. It was a guy called Edward Richter who paid me. He told me he'd pay well. I wasn't meant to kill her. He told me to scare her, threaten her, make it clear that if her husband didn't back off with his investigation into him, she or her kids would get hurt. But I fucked it up. Fucked it up big time. I stabbed the bitch. Can't tell you why I did it. I'm a piece-of-shit junkie. My whole life is a fuck-up. I talked to her, then she ran, then I chased her, then I stabbed her. If she hadn't run—" Horn began wringing his hands. "When I told Richter what I'd done, he was furious. He went nuts. Then when he'd calmed down he said he'd help me get out of the country. He said everything would be okay. But he screwed me. He never had a plan to help me. Before I knew it the police were all over me. He had set me up. The only way they'd have found me that quickly was if Richter had tipped them off. He knew I'd never grass on him or cut a deal. I was scared of him."

"It's me you need to be afraid of, not Richter," hissed Lyle. "He's a dead man. He just doesn't know it yet."

"What do you want from me?" Horn's eyes began to dance around the room again.

"I want you to tell the police exactly what you just told me. Tell them it was Edward Richter. Not too obvious – I just need you to point them in his direction. Do you think you can do that?"

"Police? I don't want them visiting me. What about the screws? Do you think they won't let Richter know I spoke to the police? Of course they bloody well will. Someone always talks. Always. This is too much. I can't. You need to leave me alone. Find someone else."

Lyle ignored his protests and pushed back. "The police will visit you very soon, I guarantee it. Don't worry about the guards. I have an agreement with our friend back there." She nodded towards Farley.

Horn rubbed his unshaven face. "I don't know. Can you protect me in here? I need protection. You must know some people."

"Tony, look at me. I don't want to threaten you to do it, but you know what will happen to you if you don't do what I ask. Think about this instead: if I can walk in and out of one of Her Majesty's prisons, how hard do you think it is for me to make sure no one lays a finger on you? Of course you'll be protected."

"I guess so." Horn began tugging at his ear and tapping the table. *Tap-tap-tap*, like hitting a tiny drum. "I just tell the police what I told you, but subtle-like? I can do that. You promise I'll be okay?"

Lyle pointed to her disguise. "I did all this for you. I've also bribed and threatened the necessary officials to get me in front of you. I've gone to great lengths to ensure nobody in this prison recognises me. And no screw, other than Farley, knows I'm here today. Would I do all that if I wanted any harm to befall you?"

"S'pose not."

"You have my word. You do this for me, and I'll make sure you get looked after. You also get the satisfaction of knowing the man who put you here is going to pay for it."

Lyle got to her feet and turned to walk away. "Time for me to go. This place reeks of losers and testosterone."

Horn looked up at her. "Why do you hate Richter so much? I mean, what did he do to piss you off so much?"

"It's better you don't know. If you did know, you and I wouldn't be having this conversation."

"Why is that?"

He could feel Lyle's hot breath on his face as she leaned in close. "Let's just say the other men who were with Richter when he crossed me were taken apart piece by piece with a filleting knife. Toe by toe, finger by finger, ear by ear, eye by eye, tooth by tooth, hand by hand, foot by foot." She smiled. "You get the picture. I kept them alive for days just to hear their screams. When they begged me to kill them and end their suffering, I kept them alive longer."

Horn didn't blink. He'd heard stories about Lyle, and as her face hovered inches from his, with absolute hate in her eyes, he suddenly believed every word he'd ever heard.

He agreed he was happier not knowing what Richter had done.

CHAPTER THIRTY-EIGHT

I arrived home from Spain exhausted, emotional and desperately in need of some family time. It was my family that grounded me and reminded me what real life was about. I was glad to be back. I needed time to listen, share, relax, laugh and love. I was keen to spend quality time with those who were truly important in my life.

Moving from London to live on the south coast in Dorset and walking away from my career at Scotland Yard were two of the biggest decisions of my life. One of the toughest things about the move was knowing I'd be leaving my parents behind. So, it was the icing on the cake when they said that, if I agreed, they'd like to join us in Dorset.

I can recall how Mum had taken my hand and said, "We'd like to join you down south. Neither your father nor I want to miss a second of our granddaughters growing up. You know they mean the world to us."

I didn't hesitate for a second. "Of course I want you with us. I just didn't know if I should ask."

With her tongue firmly planted in her cheek, she'd added, "Also, Monica and I have spoken, and we are in agreement that it will take both of us to keep you on the straight and narrow."

"Is that right?" I'd said, delight still on my face. "Scheming behind my back? I'll have to watch myself."

Mum and Dad had settled into a lovely home just down the road from us. And every day without fail, they visited us. Sometimes it was just a quick hello; sometimes they popped in to help out or share a meal. Occasionally, they came by just to check up on me and make sure I wasn't considering going back to taking the kind of risks I'd taken back at Scotland Yard.

Everyone was at the house when I arrived back from Spain. I'd received my welcome-home hugs and kisses, unpacked my travel bag and showered off the dirt of travelling. Now, happy and clean and smelling of soap, I was putting the kettle on to make tea when Mum took me to one side.

Never one to dance around a question, she asked, "How are things between you and Monica? You two look so perfect together. Are things working out?"

"Incredible – she's the most amazing woman. I'm completely in love. And the girls are over the moon that Monica and I have finally made things permanent between us."

"I don't need to tell you how close you were to losing her. I'm so glad you came to your senses."

"There isn't a day goes by I don't think of Helena," I said. "I miss her – of course, I do. I remember all the good times we had together. My memories are happy ones. They're not tainted by regret, anger and grief like they had been."

"And tell me truthfully, Jamie, how are the girls adjusting to life on the coast? They seem happy – are they?"

"They love it here. The new house, living by the beach, new friends, new school. They adjusted easily, the way children do. The move was what we all needed. I just wish it hadn't taken me so long to see it."

Mum said, "Well, you mustn't beat yourself up about it. Sometimes things happen when they're meant to. You're here now, and I haven't seen you look so happy in a very long time."

"And here is my beautiful Monica," she said as my love came into the kitchen, "radiant as ever. Is this son of mine looking after you? He'd better be; otherwise, he'll have me to answer to."

"I think so," said Monica with a cheeky grin. "There's always room for improvement, but with a little time I'll whip him into shape."

"I hope you're listening, son. I just hope you'll soon be putting a ring on this poor girl's finger."

"Mum, for God's sake, do you ever stop?" I said awkwardly.

"I brought you up to always do the right thing and to speak your mind. If I'm not speaking the truth, you just let me know." When she didn't think I was looking, she winked at Monica. They both had a little laugh at my expense.

Alice appeared at the back door, her face pale and her eyes wide with fear. I could see something wasn't right.

We all stopped our laughing.

"What is it, Alice? What's wrong?" I asked.

"It's Grandad. He's fallen over. He's holding his chest."

"Oh, my dear God, no," said Mum.

Monica took her hand and put an arm around her to keep her steady.

"Show me," I said. "Where is he?" I grabbed my phone and followed Alice.

We ran to the back garden and found Faith with her small hands holding her grandad's head as he lay on the grass

Faith said, "We were playing hide and seek. We were having fun." She looked up at me, her eyes full of fear and questions, her lips trembling. "Is Grandad going to be okay?"

Mum stepped forward. Crouching beside her husband, she placed a hand on his cheek. "Henry, can you hear me, darling?" She looked up at Monica. "Aspirin – do you have any aspirin? Quickly, Monica, quick as you can."

Monica ran to the house in search of aspirin.

I phoned for an ambulance. As I spoke, the words felt like they weren't coming from me, that none of this was real, that this was a nightmare I was desperate to wake from.

"It's my father," I told the dispatcher. "I need an ambulance right now, please. I think he's had a heart attack."

CHAPTER THIRTY-NINE

I found the ward, and the nurse pointed me in the direction of Dad's bed. Behind a privacy curtain, Mum was clutching his hand as he slept. He looked like he'd aged twenty years. He looked pale, frail and vulnerable, not at all like the strong, tireless man I knew.

Who was this man in front of me?

It was hard to comprehend what I was seeing. My dad, the man I always thought of as invincible, was lying in a hospital bed connected to a heart-rate monitor. The tough, uncompromising, retired and highly decorated chief superintendent, known at New Scotland Yard for his straight talk and zero tolerance on crime, had just gone toe to toe with death and, for the time being, come out on top. We needed to make sure it stayed that way.

I spoke to Mum in a hushed voice. "What did the doctors say?"

"It was a heart attack. They're doing tests. He'll need an operation to put one of those stent things in. Right now, they're stabilising him, and he's on thinning medication for his blood."

"Where's the doctor now? I want to speak to him."

"The doctor said she'll be back as soon as she has more news. Don't make a fuss, Jamie. Your dad's stable and they'll let us know as soon as their tests are completed. Come and sit here beside me."

"Do you want me to phone Brad?" I hadn't spoken to my brother in a few months. He's a Royal Marine who, when I spoke to him last, was heading out on operations off the coast of Africa. I wasn't sure how I intended to get hold of him, but I felt like I needed to do something.

"No, not yet. No point worrying Bradley until we know more."

I said, "Dad will be fine. He's as tough as they come." I wasn't sure whether I was reassuring Mum or myself.

I stared at the heart-rate monitor. It was hard to think, and harder to find the right words, so Mum and I sat quietly for a while. We hoped Dad knew we were there, supporting him and praying for him.

CHAPTER FORTY

Emma waited.

Her eyes felt heavy, and she was fighting sleep. It was nearly 11 p.m., and it had been a long day.

She sat at home in silence and in near darkness. The only light in the room came from her laptop, perched on the coffee table in front of her, and a table lamp on the far side of the room. A moth circled the table lamp; it bashed into the lampshade before resting on a nearby curtain.

Emma waited and listened.

Watson looked up at her. He rolled over onto his back, lifting a front paw, hoping for a belly rub. Emma didn't notice. She was deep in thought.

Lyle's letter circled her brain, going around and around in her mind. Emma had memorised the words, but the same line still stood out.

...I need you to see the big picture. James deserves to know the truth...

She picked up a copy of the letter. The original was at the lab being tested by the techies – even though it was unlikely anything useful would come of it. She looked down at the laptop, willing it to notify her of an incoming email.

Once again, she read the letters and numbers on the back of the letter: GU851PH52.

What did they signify?

Perhaps the letters and numbers were some sort of code, the numbers representing a letter's position in the alphabet – number 1 being the letter A and number 5 being the letter E, etcetera. Maybe it was an anagram. Emma spent some time moving the letters about but couldn't form them into anything useful.

Maybe the code was a map co-ordinate. Was it the location of another body?

She messed around with the code in her mind for a little while longer before closing her eyes and waiting.

Be patient, she told herself. *Let Vince work his magic.*

Vincent Constantine rarely left his home; to Emma, and anyone else even remotely acquainted with him, it seemed he lived online. His first language wasn't English or Spanish or French or German. No; Vince's first language was computer code, those seemingly random letters, numerals and characters that, when arranged in the right order, created the language that gave your computer instructions. To the untrained eye, computer code made no sense at all, but to Vince, those letters, numerals and characters were the gateways to a whole other world.

He had worked for a while for Government Communications Headquarters, commonly known as GCHQ, until his resignation. He had then worked on surveillance and clandestine operations with the National Security Agency and had also helped set up the platform for the National Cyber Security Centre. Until his sudden resignation, his desk had been in a soundproof office in a building that had no name. The sort of building where even the cleaner needed the highest security clearance just to be able to refill the soap dispenser.

After a bitter disagreement over the sharing of sensitive information with foreign agencies, Vince had had enough and just up and walked away. He had set up shop on his own and now worked freelance.

Four minutes ago, Emma had sent him an email with Kelly Lyle's code. If anyone could figure out what it meant, Vince could.

Emma closed her eyes.

Come on, Vince.

The laptop chimed. The sound of an email reply.

It was from Vince. *Please be good news.*

Emma read the message.

Subject: Too Easy

Message: Hi Emma,

Your code is a UK address – reversed! Too easy. Next time, I want a challenge.

GU851PH52 to 25HP15 8UG.

It's an address. House number 25. Post code HP15 8UG.

You can find it on Google Maps.

I'm still single and holding out hope there will be a you and me one day. You'll always be the only girl for me. Hope you're doing okay?

. . .

Vince ended his message by signing off (backwards) with *evoL ecniV,* which he no doubt considered hilarious.

Emma opened Google Maps and tapped in the address: house number 25, post code HP15 8UG. If Vince was right, and he always was, the house was in the town of High Wycombe, Buckinghamshire.

Further online searches showed the property had once been managed by a letting agency called Majestic Lettings.

It was a long shot she'd reach anyone now, but she made a call to Majestic Lettings. No one answered. She left a voicemail message.

She then called the nearby police station and requested officers wake up whoever needed waking to get keys to the property.

No longer feeling tired, she looked at the time. 11.37 p.m. High Wycombe was a two-hour drive. At this time of night, with little traffic, she'd get there quicker.

Emma grabbed what she needed and headed up the M27 motorway. As she drove, she spoke to officers who had woken the somewhat-bewildered owner of Majestic Lettings, Bobby Singh. She rang off, called Singh, and insisted she must get into the property tonight.

Singh wasn't happy at being woken in the middle of the night or the idea of police officers entering a property he managed without a warrant. Emma quickly mentioned she was investigating multiple murders. He was more receptive when she suggested he might be seen as impeding the investigation by not cooperating. But also, should visiting the property lead to an arrest, she would be sure to mention his public-spirited contribution at a future press hearing. Singh agreed to assist.

After she rang off, she wondered whether she should have told Hardy what she was doing. The address had come from Lyle, and she wasn't entirely sure what she was looking for or what she might find.

Why was Lyle interested in Hardy's late wife anyway? Maybe she wanted to screw up his life again just as he was getting it back together.

Emma decided to keep her investigations to herself for now.

CHAPTER FORTY-ONE

Just before 2 a.m., Emma arrived at the office of Majestic Lettings. She peered through the glass in the front door and noticed a light on out the back. She knocked a couple of times. Singh made his way from the back office to the front door and let her in.

He was a short man with bloodshot eyes and a high-pitched voice. He greeted her and said, "This is all very unusual. I hope you understand, I wouldn't be doing this if it wasn't for a murder investigation. My clients—"

Emma interrupted what was sure to become a monologue on the quality of his service. She was too tired and too keen to see inside the property. She also knew Singh lived upstairs in the flat over the office, and she didn't consider his coming downstairs and handing over a key to a police officer as the inconvenience of the century. Deciding she might need his assistance later, however, she felt it best to proceed with politeness.

"I appreciate your cooperation. I'm sorry for the inconvenience."

"I really should be coming with you, but my wife has

had to fly home to Scotland to see her parents and I'm here supervising the children." His eyes flicked upstairs.

"I don't need to inconvenience you further. I'll just take the keys and take a look around the property. I'll push the keys back through your letterbox when I'm done."

"That would be ideal. Now, you have to understand that nobody has lived in the property for a very long time. We had some squatters living there for a while, but that was all dealt with. Since then we've had no tenants. The rent is paid, anonymously, every month, and the owner of the property has decided they would rather keep it empty. It's beyond me, but it makes my life a lot easier, so I don't complain. What I'm saying is, we do our best, but I haven't visited the property myself in a while, so I can't vouch for how it looks. Someone pops in from time to time to check there aren't any burst water pipes, but beyond that I don't know."

Stifling her impatience, Emma nodded that she understood. "I don't want to keep you from your family any longer. If I could take the keys, I'll be on my way."

The little man shifted uneasily and reluctantly handed over the keys. "Please be careful. Don't damage anything."

Key in hand, Emma headed to the car without looking back.

A few minutes later she was outside the property. She pulled into the driveway. The light from her car headlights showed the building to be well maintained – on the outside at least. The lawn was short; the small patch of garden and the driveway were weed-free.

She reached into the glovebox and pulled out a torch. She flicked the switch, gave it a shake and a tap, and the light came on.

CHAPTER FORTY-TWO

Emma shut the front door behind her. She flicked the switch to turn on the hallway light. It clicked, but no light came on. *Shit. The fuse must have tripped*, she thought.

The house smelled damp and felt cold. Stepping carefully, she shone the torch into each downstairs room. There were no furnishings to speak of. The rooms were empty except for carpets and the occasional set of curtains.

The only exception was the dining room, which had a dining table and four ornate high-back chairs.

Emma shone her light into the kitchen. There were no electrical appliances, and all the cupboards were empty. A single upturned glass sat beside the kitchen sink.

Back up the hallway, she shone the torch into the under-stairs cupboard, which was also empty except for an off-cut of carpet and the household fuse box.

Leaning inside, she flicked the only switch that was down. No light came on. She tried the main switch, pushing up, then down, then up. Nothing. *I guess Mr Singh is skimping by not paying for electricity. I bet his customer wouldn't like that.*

She made her way upstairs, each step creaking and springy like it might give way beneath her. The air became thicker and damper as she moved further up.

The upstairs landing had four doors. She shone the torch left and right and over her head. Every door was open, and she peered inside each one. Nothing of note.

Overhead in the hallway was a loft hatch. She went back downstairs to get one of the dining chairs. She placed the chair just below the hatch, stood on it and pulled down the ladder. Torch in hand, she climbed the ladder and shone its light around the empty loft.

After about an hour of fruitless searching, Emma sat at the table in the dining room with Lyle's note in her hand.

GU851PH52, or 25HP158UG.

What if Vince was wrong? Perhaps it wasn't an address. Did it mean something else? Why was she allowing herself to be led by Lyle? Was Lyle getting her to chase her tail, just for the fun of it?

No. There had to be something here that she'd missed. It was too much of a coincidence that this property was empty and the owner was paying the rent without looking for a new tenant. Emma had no doubt that if she looked hard enough, she would find that Lyle, or one of Lyle's companies, owned the property she was sitting in. Why had Lyle sent her here?

She got up and moved slowly around the house again. She stood in the kitchen doorway and shone light on a mouse making its way along the worktop before disappearing down behind the sink. She needed to check on top, behind, and beneath every cupboard, drawer and door. There was something here Lyle wanted her to find.

An unexpected breakthrough came on her second search of the upstairs. Emma noticed that two of the bedrooms had very small walk-in wardrobes. Just big enough to stand in.

For some reason, the one in the master bedroom had a lower ceiling, which also appeared to be separated into two parts. Emma pushed on it and felt some movement on one side. Pressing at the edge, she heard a latch click then felt it release. One half of the ceiling opened. She lowered the panel, revealing a hidden space that she guessed was some sort of security space. Perhaps the previous owners had put their valuables and important documents in there in case of burglary.

Shining the torch up into the space, Emma could see something inside. Adrenaline pumping, she dragged out the items – papers and a handbag. After running her hand around the hidden area to check there was nothing more, she took the items downstairs and put them on the dining table.

She spread out the papers and could see they were cuttings of newspaper articles. *This is it*, she thought, her heart pounding. Lyle had wanted her to find this. The articles were reports on Helena's murder.

Apprehensively, she turned her attention to the handbag. She realised it had likely belonged to Helena.

Deep breath.

Emma opened the handbag and started taking out its contents, placing them one by one on the table. A small hairbrush, a couple of pens, a mobile phone, children's hairbands, plasters, tissues, a shopping list and a coin purse.

She unzipped the coin purse, and the first thing she saw was a photograph of Hardy and his family. It was unmistakable. They all looked so young and happy. Helena had been beautiful.

She couldn't tell where the photo had been taken, but

it looked like a family farm park. In the background were small goats looking through a fence. Alice and Faith were holding ice creams. Emma suddenly felt like she was intruding on memories that belonged to Hardy. She wanted to feel jubilant, but she felt only sadness.

She looked at the newspaper articles again. Circled in black pen was the name Tony Horn. Horn was the man who'd killed Helena and was serving a life sentence. Lyle had left a trail of breadcrumbs, and, despite wanting to resist, Emma knew she had no choice but to follow them. For the time being at least.

Her inspection of the property complete, she closed and locked the front door behind her. She drove around to Majestic Lettings and pushed the keys back through the letterbox door. Singh was very likely upstairs getting his children ready for school.

The air felt fresh and cold on her lungs. It was nearly 7 a.m., and the roads were filling up. It had been raining, and the streets glistened in the morning light.

She needed to find a hotel to crash out and steal a few hours' sleep. Things were moving fast, and later that day she had two appointments booked, one of which was with Detective Rayner. Rayner was the nearest thing Hardy had had to a partner during his time at New Scotland Yard. Emma knew they were close, like brothers. If anyone could tell her more about what had happened to Helena, then it was him. She'd found it impossible to ask Hardy, so if she wanted answers, his best friend Rayner was the one to ask.

CHAPTER FORTY-THREE

Sienna poured Lyle and herself a glass of Chardonnay then joined her on the balcony. She handed Lyle her glass and they stood together and took in the view.

"This really is a beautiful spot," said Lyle. "Perhaps, in another life, you and I could stay here forever." She put her arm around Sienna and moved close.

The rich red evening sun was low in the sky, and most people had left the beach. Dog walkers and those wishing to enjoy an evening stroll peppered the water's edge. Only a few families remained, soon to be replaced by groups of teenagers preparing to party into the small hours. Seagulls patrolled the sand for leftovers, occasionally breaking into squawking fights at the discovery of a partially eaten sandwich or discarded chips.

"If you could go anywhere in the world, where would you go?" asked Sienna.

Lyle laughed with affection at the child-like question.

"I've been to most European countries, and they're all special in their own way. I'd love to take you to Paris, of course, and Venice, Barcelona and Prague. There's also the

United States and Canada once we've visited the cities of Europe. And Asia – well, that's out of this world."

"I've always thought Australia would be a great place to explore and lose yourself. Thailand too."

"That sounds like an excellent idea, somewhere you can go unnoticed for a very long time. I have some wonderful memories of my time travelling. For a long time, I was a very different person."

Sienna took a large gulp of wine. "She must have meant a lot to you. The woman who broke your heart, I mean."

"Yes, she did. She was the first person I trusted who didn't go on to disappoint me. She never let me down, ever."

"I don't understand."

"She didn't leave me, if that's what you're thinking. She was taken from me. Murdered. I wasn't there to protect her. She was in the wrong place at the wrong time. It should have been me that died."

"I'm sorry. You mustn't blame yourself," said Sienna.

Lyle looked at Sienna in a way she didn't understand. Sienna added, "Did they catch the person who did it?"

"Eventually. I know exactly where he is. At some point, I'm going to pay him a visit."

"You're braver than me, that's for sure. I don't think I could do that. In fact, I know I couldn't do it. Confront a killer, I mean. No matter how much I might want to."

"You might surprise yourself," said Lyle. "We are all capable of much more than we realise. It's often just a case of setting your mind to it. You seem to have a way of getting what you want." She nudged Sienna, and they laughed.

Lyle watched as Sienna went inside to fetch the bottle

of wine, returned, set it on the balcony table and put her hair up in a bun.

Sienna could feel Lyle's eyes on her; she liked it. She topped up their glasses. "It must be painful to know she's gone and he's still…" She let the sentence trail off. "It makes you think that prison just isn't enough."

"There are times I've wished I could get hold of him. I'd hand out my own form of justice. I'd be sure he truly pays for what he's done. I can think of a million ways to make him suffer. After I'd finished with him, he'd think hell was summer camp."

Sienna shuddered at the icy way Lyle spoke. She smiled uncertainly. "I know what you mean," she said.

CHAPTER FORTY-FOUR

Emma was taken to the office of prison governor Lloyd Trent.

Governor Trent didn't look up from signing documents as he said, "Come in, Detective Inspector, come in. I'll be with you in a moment. Officer Farley, please stay with us. This won't take long."

"Yes, sir," said Farley. He closed the door and remained standing behind Emma.

Emma took in her surroundings. There were trophies for soccer and rugby in a glass cabinet as well as photos of Trent shaking hands with politicians and celebrities lining the wall. There was also a considerable number of photos of him holding fish. She didn't know much about fishing, but she could see that one fish, in particular, was huge; she thought it might be a marlin.

On the wall behind Trent was a photo of the Queen, and above that a quarter-size Union Jack flag. Emma's eyes returned to the governor, who was now watching her. He took the wire-rimmed reading glasses off his long, thin nose and put them down on his desk. He was a gaunt-looking man who, beneath his shirt and tie, appeared to be nothing but skin and bone. She thought about the huge marlin and considered the strength and determination it would have taken to haul it in.

"Detective Inspector Cotton, I spoke to your new superior this morning." A thin, wet smile spread across the governor's face. He'd immediately put her on the back foot.

"I was curious to know why you, Detective Inspector Cotton, were interested in seeing one of my prisoners. Unfortunately, and surprisingly, your superior couldn't shed much light on it. It would seem the head doesn't know what the tail is doing. Wouldn't you say?"

The governor waited for an explanation.

Emma tried to remain courteous. "My hope is Tony Horn can clear up a few questions that have arisen during a current investigation. Naturally, I can't elaborate due to it being an ongoing investigation."

"Can't say or won't say? What do you think, Officer Farley? Do you think the inspector here thinks we were born yesterday?"

"I wouldn't like to say, sir." Farley kept his eyes forward and remained expressionless.

"Officer Farley is far too polite for his own good, Inspector Cotton. I, on the other hand, have learned to question everyone and everything while understanding that the nature of most people is to never, ever tell you the whole truth.

"Take your Mr Tony Horn, for example. Horn gets hardly any visitors and has no idea that he's a compulsive liar; he's just lied for so long it's become a natural response to any question.

"On rare occasions, his girlfriend Tina visits. It's rare

because she's usually either high or busy turning tricks in some godforsaken squat to pay for her drug habit.

"Tony Horn does not make friends easily. He can't help himself. You could say he has a way of rubbing people up the wrong way."

The governor looked Emma up and down. His smile widened to reveal large teeth. "Perhaps, Inspector Cotton, he'll rub you up the wrong way too. He's a nasty little man. It might be prudent for me to be there while you interview him."

Emma turned to see that Officer Farley was looking down at the floor.

"I think I'll be fine. I'd just as soon speak to Tony Horn privately and be on my way. I don't wish to inconvenience you further. I can see you're a busy man."

Governor Trent stroked his earlobe and tilted his head thoughtfully. "This morning, I read through your list of questions. I can see you gave them some thought. I appreciate that. They all appear acceptable."

Emma knew the sorts of questions the governor would agree to. She didn't want any delay getting to see Horn, so she had kept them mundane.

Trent looked at the papers on his desk again. He waved Emma away with his hand.

"If you don't need my assistance, you're welcome to go. Just remember, these prisoners are starved of attractive women. You'd be advised to button that blouse right up to that delicate little chinny-chin-chin of yours. Between walls confining over five hundred frustrated men, a glimpse of lacy bosom can wreak all kinds of havoc. I know you wouldn't want that, Inspector Cotton. Officer Farley will take over from here. Goodbye, detective."

CHAPTER FORTY-FIVE

Emma followed Officer Farley through gate after gate. Buzzers sounded, keys rattled and doors crashed shut.

"I'll be with you at all times," said Farley. "He has his funny ways – the governor, I mean. Don't mind him. I've met quite a few in top jobs, and he's far from the worst. I sometimes think to get to the top you need to behave a bit differently from the rest of us."

Farley nodded at a colleague who handed Emma some forms to sign. "I've served in the armed forces and worked in business and now the prison service. They have their differences, but they also have their similarities. I don't need to tell you that the behaviour of those with power can seem alien to those without it, just as choices made by a powerless man can seem strange to others. Human nature, I guess."

He looked at Emma's chest. "I'm sorry if he embarrassed you, but the governor was right to mention the top button. You and I know there is nothing inappropriate about your blouse, but the point he was making was that things we take for granted on the outside can be blown out of all proportion in here."

Horn was slouched in a chair daydreaming when Emma and Farley walked into the room. On seeing Emma, he sat up straight and briefly smiled before leaning forward with his arms on the table.

Emma dragged a chair out from under the desk and sat opposite him. Farley took a second chair beside her.

"Now, Horn, remember our chat earlier?" said Farley.

Horn nodded. "Yes, I do," he said keenly. "I remember every word. Yes, I do."

Farley continued. "This is Detective Inspector Emma Cotton. She's going to ask you some questions. I want you to answer her truthfully and thoroughly. You remember how I told you that this conversation is utterly confidential? Just the three of us, right?"

"Y-y-y-yep, yes I do," said Horn.

He moved like a little bird. His head tilted and bobbed from side to side as he tried to evaluate the situation. His gaze moved from Emma to Farley and back again, then down at the papers on the table in front of Emma, his beak-like mouth opening and shutting the whole time. He was finding it hard to sit still.

"Can we remove his handcuffs?" said Emma.

"That is not something I am permitted to do. Governor's orders. It's for your own safety."

"I see." She looked at Farley in a way that suggested she and Horn needed some space.

Farley looked at Horn, who was picking at a fingernail, then at Emma. He got to his feet and moved to the corner of the room and sat down.

She smiled at Horn and tried to put him at ease. "Tony – do you mind if I call you Tony? As Officer Farley has explained, I'm here to ask a few questions. Is that okay?"

"What sort of questions? I do like questions. I'd like to know what sort they are before I say yes. I will say yes, but I'd like to know first."

She looked at his arm; the forearm was covered in scars.

Horn followed her glance. "I have a destructive addictive personality. I used to cut myself. Not anymore. The doctors say I was born this way. I think they're right. I've been addicted to lots of things. Right now, I'm trying really hard to stop. It's not easy. I find I can be addicted to anything. Drugs, of course, plus gambling, smoking, sex, alcohol, harming myself, harming others, masturbation, exercise, religion, even mundane things like reading. I once stayed awake a whole week just reading. I read book after book after book without sleeping or eating."

He leaned forward and said conspiratorially, "The doctor here is very kind; she's given me some medication that helps me control it. She's nice. Pretty, like you."

Emma smiled. "Tony, I'd like to ask you about Helena Hardy. And what happened."

Horn blew out his cheeks, then loudly forced air out through his lips. He put his head down on the table and looked up sideways at her.

"I regret hurting her. I was in a nasty place at the time with my addictions. If I could go back and change anything, it would be that. And I don't just mean because I ended up here. I mean because I was weak. I'm stronger now. I was doing heroin at the time; nothing else mattered except my next fix. I was really low; I wasn't thinking straight. I never did anything like that before. I used to break into houses and steal stuff. I did that, but I never hurt nobody. Not that I know of. I think I'd remember if I did."

Emma tried to appear sympathetic. "What was different this time? Why did you kill Helena Hardy?"

Horn's eyes flicked over at Farley again. "Like I said, I was on drugs. All sorts. Mainly smack, but I was drinking too."

"I need you to help me understand what happened that day. Why did you decide to snatch a purse in the street when you'd been breaking into houses all the years before that? Why the change in behaviour? I've seen your record. Up until the day you killed Mrs Hardy, you had no record of violence."

Horn scoffed and rolled his eyes. "You make it sound like I was able to make rational choices. I was a junkie. Why does anyone do anything? I don't know. Perhaps I just wanted a change from doing break-ins. I was desperate for my next fix. I saw an opportunity. End of…"

Horn was trembling now and looking anywhere but at her. Emma could feel he was holding back.

"You were a long way from the squat you were reported to have been staying in. Can you explain that? What were you doing on the same street as Helena Hardy?"

"I moved around a lot. I never liked to be in the same place too long."

Emma turned and looked at Farley. "Would it be possible to get a couple of cups of water, one for Tony and one for me, please?"

Farley looked at the pair of them and shook his head. He slowly got to his feet and tapped on the door. He said, "For your own safety, Inspector, I can't leave you. Someone will be along with water in a few minutes." He sat back down.

Emma tried once more. "I find it hard to believe, Tony, that you just happened to be on that street at the very same time that the wife of a senior Scotland Yard detective was there. A senior Scotland Yard detective who was leading the most-talked-about investigation of the day. And you also expect me to believe that the very day you decide to take a day off burglary you're on the same street as this detective's wife. A street which is a long way from your home. To do a bag snatch and not a break-in."

"I know. Weird, innit?" Horn leaned back in his chair and ran his fingers through his hair.

"Did someone put you up to it?"

"Nah."

"Why were you on that street?"

"I don't know what you mean."

"You're a bad liar, Tony."

"I can't—"

"You can't what? You can't tell me who put you up to it? Perhaps I can find some way to make your stay here easier. I just need to know why you chose Helena."

"There's this prisoner I know, Jimmy Whip. He gets comics sent to him. I'd like some comics."

A little confused, Emma smiled and said, "I'll make sure you get some comics. A lot of comics."

Horn's finger was tapping like a beak on the table. *Tap, tap, tap, tap, tap.* "All I heard was the detective was getting too close. All right? Look, if you don't want the shit storm you get from killing a copper, well, the next best thing is to threaten his wife. Or his family. You get me? It was a job. I was doing a job. The wife wasn't meant to die."

Horn gave a look that said she *needed* to understand.

She could see Horn knew he'd said too much and was

going to clam up. This was the breakthrough she was hoping for, but she needed more. "A job for who? Which detective was getting too close? Too close to what? Who hired you?"

"Let's just say I was under *seismic* pressure at the time. You get me?"

The door behind them opened and a guard came in with one cup of water. He put it down in front of Horn and remained standing beside them. "That's it, Horn," he said." Governor wants you back in your cell. Let's go."

Officer Farley looked surprised but got to his feet. "You heard the man. That's it for today, Horn. It's time to wrap this up. If the inspector has any more questions, I'm sure she can return another time."

"I've got lots more questions I need to ask today," said Emma. "I've barely even started."

Farley shrugged. "I'm sorry. I've got my orders."

"You won't forget my comics, will you? The comics are very important. Very important." Horn got to his feet, and the two officers led him away.

Emma sat in her car and thumped the steering wheel. She went over the interview in her mind. Nothing was making any sense. Was Horn full of shit like the governor said? Why would Horn lie? He had nothing to gain. Even if someone had put him up to it, the fact still remained: he had murdered Helena Hardy.

And if someone did put him up to it, then who was it?

She slammed the car into gear and blew out a breath. She'd wasted precious time. She should have been looking into the most recent victims and not into a case that had already been solved. What the hell had she been thinking? This was a wild goose chase. Lyle had her blindfolded, jumping backwards through hoops with her hands tied behind her back.

You're an idiot, she told herself angrily, *letting Lyle play you like that*. If another person died because of her stupidity she'd never forgive herself.

CHAPTER FORTY-SIX

Emma pulled off the M3 motorway and into a service station. The car park was nearly full. After circling it twice, she found a parking spot, grabbed her leather bag and headed inside.

It was Saturday morning, and the service station was busy with families getting breakfast and taking a bathroom break before continuing their journey.

She quickly checked her appearance in her smartphone camera and brushed a hand over her jacket as she approached the entrance to Starbucks. She looked around the coffeehouse and caught sight of a big man sitting alone reading the morning paper and nursing a cappuccino. He looked up and immediately shot up his hand, got to his feet and walked over.

"DI Cotton?" He put out his hand. Emma's hand was swallowed up in his as they shook.

"And you must be Rayner?" she said, looking up into his eyes.

"That's me, for my sins." His warm greeting immediately put her at ease.

Rayner was a giant of a man. Not fat. He was tall, fit and strong-looking, like a rugby player. Emma could see he would be great to have in your corner under certain circumstances. He had a tan, and his hair had bleached a little in the summer sun. His eyes were kind and warm. She could see instantly how Hardy and Rayner might be friends. They both had a relaxed, calm aura about them, despite the work they both did.

"I'm getting a fresh coffee. What can I get you? Coffee or tea or something else?"

"A decaffeinated black coffee would be great. Thank you."

Rayner's table was in the corner, and with his back to the wall he could see everyone in the room and anyone who came and went. Emma and Rayner settled in for a long chat after introductions and small-talk were out of the way.

"So, Hardy couldn't stay away? He's back doing what Hardy does best, is he?" Rayner took a large bite of his blueberry muffin. "Hardy got me into these; they're addictive." He held up what little was left of his muffin and laughed.

Emma watched him hoovering crumbs off his sleeves with his mouth. "I'm not sure how much you know. But yes, he's back in on a temporary basis. Not by choice."

"It's never choice. If you're one of those people, then catching bad guys is what fuels you. If that's how you are, then you're just never going to stop. How can you?" Rayner was talking about Hardy, himself and, although he didn't know it, Emma as well.

"As I said on the phone, this is about Kelly Lyle. She's playing a twisted game, and Hardy seems to be an integral part of it. We're trying to figure out why."

Rayner sat back and ran his fingers through his sun-bleached hair.

"I see. You got all the stuff I sent you? It's everything we have on Lyle. Not much there, I know, considering."

Emma nodded.

"What is it?" Rayner was leaning forward.

"Take a look at this." She passed him the letter from Lyle. "What do you make of this?"

Rayner read the letter and got to his feet. He finished his cappuccino and said, "Let's take a walk."

They didn't walk far – just outside to a patch of green with a few picnic benches. Rayner wanted a change of scenery, and walking helped him think. He felt uncomfortable sitting in a coffee shop discussing his ex-partner's past life.

"Don't ever repeat any of this. Especially to Hardy. He's a very private man. I'm only talking to you now because I can see you need to figure out what in hell's name is going on."

"You have my word, of course. Go on," said Emma.

"Hardy and I grew up together; we've known each other since we were kids. We got into some scrapes but never anything serious, just boys being boys. He's a complicated guy in some respects, and in other ways he's pretty straightforward. You get what you see. For example, when he fell in love. That was straightforward. There was never any question in his mind once he'd met Helena that she was the one for him. I got to know her and watched how he fell truly, deeply, in love. I couldn't have been happier for him. They were perfect together. She understood him, and he understood her. And I loved them both."

The way Rayner spoke, and from his body language,

Emma could feel his pain. "What really happened? I've only read the press stories."

"You can ignore that shit. The press says what it wants to say to sell stories. You know that."

She nodded. "I've had my share of run-ins with the press. I'm just trying to understand what's going on here and what Lyle wants me to know. I think it must be important."

Rayner was finding it difficult to know where to start. "Hardy and I were working crazy hours. A multiple-murder case, as usual. I remember it was particularly nasty. I'm trying to think of the guy's name Richter, Edward Richter. That's the guy. Real sick bastard.

"Anyway, this guy had us working all hours. Richter was really going to town on his victims. Hardy and I just couldn't find enough hours in the day. We were desperate to stop him. He just seemed to be one step ahead of us the whole time. It was as though Richter knew what we were thinking. We wondered at the time if he had someone inside the department feeding him information. You know, giving him the heads-up on our progress.

"We thought we might never get a break in the case. We felt like we were getting close, but not close enough. We'd been working a few days back to back, and Hardy was ready to drop. We both decided to take a break. Go get some sleep. Spend some time with family. We agreed we'd take a couple of days off. Hardy was going to surprise Helena and the girls."

CHAPTER FORTY-SEVEN

Rayner smiled as he recalled the moment.

"Hardy and I both decided it was best to ease off a little and let the information we'd gathered sink in. Recharge our batteries, then continue.

"Hardy's kids were young back then. I think Alice had been at school a couple of years and Faith was just getting ready to start. I love those girls. It still hurts to remember what they went through, losing their mother the way they did.

"I can remember it like it happened only yesterday. We were just packing up to leave when out of the blue Hardy gets a phone call. I can still see his face and the fear in his eyes. I feel sick to my stomach just thinking about it.

"We rush over there and find Helena in the street. I'm pushing everybody back. Hardy is ahead of me, and I tell everyone to get back, get back. Hardy is down beside her, holding her. Holding her so tightly. Comforting her. Screaming for an ambulance. Helena was down, pressing on her wound. Hardy's hand was over hers. He was talking to her. Telling her, 'Everything is okay. It'll be okay.'

"The tone of his voice changed as he realised she couldn't hold on. I remember him saying, 'No, don't leave me. Please, Helena, don't leave me.'

"All I could do was stand and watch as she slipped away. My best friend's world came crashing down right in front of my eyes, and there was nothing I could do. It broke him. I'll never forget the look he gave me. He wanted to die. He wanted to go with her. It was the worst day of my life."

Rayner's eyes were full of tears. He was quiet while he composed himself, putting away all the information he had unpacked so he could continue.

Emma put out a hand and stroked Rayner's arm. "I'm sorry. Truly I am. It wasn't just Hardy's life that changed that day."

Rayner forced a smile. He wiped away his tears with bear-like hands. His voice breaking, he said, "Isn't it strange how memories can stay so vivid? You think you've got your emotions under control, but of course they're still there, just below the surface."

He blew his nose with a tissue and continued. "Hardy was left a widower, and Alice and Faith were left without a mother. He needed Helena. We all did. When I think of Helena and Hardy, I understand what it means to be soulmates. That's what they were: soulmates. For a long time, Hardy wasn't himself. How could he be?"

"How did he change?"

"He threw himself into his work, working day and night. We caught the filth that killed Helena, a piece of crap called Tony Horn. It wasn't hard to track him down. It brought Hardy no comfort, of course.

"Eventually, after an anonymous tipoff, we took down Edward Richter and put him away. And I thought Hardy was going to slow down. Take some time to mourn and be with Alice and Faith. But he jumped straight back into another case, then another. He didn't give himself time to adjust after each case. No downtime. He was full on. Fortunately, his parents were around, and for a while they picked up the pieces. They stepped up and helped with Alice and Faith. Alongside Monica, of course, whom you must have met?"

Rayner smiled at the thought of Monica and added, "If Helena was Hardy's soulmate, then who says lightning never strikes twice? Monica was an angel sent straight from heaven. I know it sounds twee, but with Monica by his side, he found his way back to the land of the living. I truly believe that."

"Tell me about Tony Horn."

Rayner's eyes went cold. "He's a junkie lowlife and first-rate liar. Do not believe a word that comes out his mouth. He says whatever he has to say in order to save his own neck. He has convictions for burglary, aggravated assault, theft, robbery, dealing – a list as long as your arm. Always looking for cash for his next fix. The day he ran into Helena she was in the wrong place at the wrong time. He tried to snatch Helena's bag, but she wasn't having any of it. She held onto it and refused to give it up, so he pulled a knife. She fought back, and the piece of shit stabbed her. He's now serving life in prison. I hope he's having a hard time. I really mean that."

"Is there anything else you know about Horn or Helena that you think I should know? I don't see how any of this relates to Lyle. Did she have any connection to Tony Horn?" asked Emma.

"She could just be messing with your mind. She's one crazy bitch. My advice is to go speak to Horn but take everything he says with a pinch of salt. The guy is a loser. A dead end."

She decided not to tell Rayner she had already visited Tony Horn in prison.

They talked for a while longer. Rayner was interested in how Hardy was getting on. He felt bad he hadn't visited his old friend, even though he knew Hardy wanted space. A chance to find himself, a chance to settle into his new life. But he knew once he and Hardy got chatting, the conversation would inevitably turn to talk of Scotland Yard and his ongoing investigations. Rayner, being a friend, hadn't wanted that. He'd wanted his buddy to enjoy his new life without thoughts of murder investigations.

But now Rayner knew Hardy was back on a homicide case of his own.

"I'll be down in Dorset soon," he told Emma. "I need to visit Hardy Senior. I hear his heart attack was nasty. It's also about time I visited Hardy and the girls. How are they all holding up? I spoke to Monica very briefly and passed on my love. She said Hardy Senior was making good progress."

"James is shaken up, of course. Everyone is. From what I know, he's doing okay. He will probably open up to you more than me. If I'm honest, I still feel like a bit of an outsider."

"He'll get used to you. Give him time. He has a hard time letting people in, but he'll come around. From the way you handle yourself and from what you've told me, I get the feeling he trusts you – although you can't see it yet.

"Look, if there's anything you need, call me, day or night. If Hardy trusts you, I trust you."

CHAPTER FORTY-EIGHT

Lyle found her parking space beneath a large green magnolia tree whose blossoms had long since fallen. She checked her hair in the rear-view mirror. She was a redhead with blue eyes today; she was always a redhead when visiting Mother.

She introduced herself to the receptionist as Kelly Allerton and waited in the seating area a few minutes before being taken to her mother's room, where she found her in distress about someone or something that Lyle didn't quite understand.

In a soothing voice, Lyle comforted her, shushing her the way one would calm a child.

"Your mother is a real sweetheart," said the nurse. "We love her dearly. She does get like this from time to time. It seems she's hoping her husband, your father, will visit her soon and whisk her away for their honeymoon."

Lyle continued to stroke her mother's hand. "He's dead. Thank God," she said. Without looking up, she said, "You can go now, nurse."

The nurse shrugged, pulled a face, mouthed the word "Bitch" and left the room.

Lyle called after her, "Shut the door behind you."

For the next long while, she sat with her mother. She read to her, brushed her hair and told her stories about what she was doing, how well the business was doing. She asked her mother how well she was being treated, but it became clear her mother thought she was at boarding school, not a care facility.

Lyle got out the photo album and they flicked through pictures together. She pointed out photos of herself as a young girl and her mum and dad holding hands and smiling.

"There were some good times too," she said, as much to herself as to her mother. "I remember this day; do you remember it? We went to the shops together and we both bought new dresses for the summer fair. That was a hot day – I remember you bought us both ice creams and they were melting all over our hands before we could eat them – we had to rush to finish them. Do you remember, Mum?"

Her mother smiled and nodded. "I don't like Melvyn. Not Melvyn," she whispered.

Lyle wrinkled her brow. Who was Melvyn, and why didn't her mother like him? She leaned in closer to ask the question, but her mother had drifted off again.

She sat and watched her mother as she slept. She was no longer the woman in the photos, the young mother full of joy. Things should have been different, for both of them.

A big man carrying dinner swung open the door; his presence filled the room.

"Wake up, Mrs Allerton!" he boomed. "Your din-dins is here. Come on, wake up." Then, not having noticed Lyle in the chair, he muttered, "You don't want to sleep away what little time you have left, now, do you?" He stepped forward and gave a start as he noticed Lyle. "Hello there. Nobody told me Mrs Allerton had a visitor today. Who might you be?"

"Her daughter. I'm guessing you're Melvyn."

"Has someone been talking about me?" He tapped his name badge, which read *Melvyn Barclay*. "That's me, in the flesh. All of it – one too many pizzas." He chuckled heartily at his own joke.

Theresa Allerton was awake now, and Lyle watched as her eyes followed Melvyn around the room. Her mother recoiled slightly as he put down the dinner tray and pushed it in front of her.

"Here you go, Mrs Allerton. You've got fish and vegetables tonight." His eyes flicked towards Lyle. "It's your favourite, isn't it?"

Her mother didn't say anything. She watched Melvyn.

"All right, well, I'll leave you to it. I'll be back in a little while to collect the tray and bring you a nice hot cup of tea. We've got apple pie for dessert as well. You'll like that. I'll put a little scoop of vanilla ice cream on the side for you. See you in a bit."

Lyle got her mother comfortable and helped her start her dinner. "I will have to go very soon, Mother," she said as she sliced up the piece of fish. "There is someone I need to go and see."

"Where's your husband? I haven't seen him in ages. Where are your children? My grandchildren – where are my grandchildren?"

"I'm not married, Mother. You know that."

Her mother's brow creased with sudden anger. "Who would have you? Who would have a useless bitch like you?"

Lyle felt herself tense; those were the words she'd

heard her father use about her mother. The screaming filled her head. The sound of the punches, the sound of a chair screeching across the kitchen floor as Mother tried to get away.

"I love you, Mother. I've really got to go. But I'm going to come back again very soon." She leaned over and gave her mother a kiss.

On her way out, Lyle took a look around. There was someone she wanted to have a word with before leaving. It didn't take long before she spotted Melvyn and a skinny young woman smoking outside a set of glass doors in the recreation area.

Melvyn saw Lyle and leaned in towards the young woman to say something, a half-smile on his face. The young woman sniggered and nodded. They watched as Lyle came closer, both feigning disinterest and wearing smug smiles, as if they had some sort of upper hand.

Lyle pushed open the glass door. She marched up to Melvyn and got her face up close to his. His back was up against the wall. She took another step and pressed her chest against his. Now toe to toe, he could feel her hot breath on his neck. As his bravado evaporated, he found himself forced to look away.

After an uncomfortably long silence, Lyle turned her head and looked at the skinny girl. "Samantha Dickson."

The skinny girl touched her name badge and nodded. "Yes?"

"You and I will have words another time – that, I promise you. Right now, though, you can go." Lyle turned and looked at Melvyn again, then addressed Samantha once more. "I need a serious conversation with your friend Melvyn."

Samantha looked at Melvyn and then at Lyle. She dropped her cigarette, crushed it out with her foot and scuttled off as quickly as she could.

Lyle pressed herself even closer to Melvyn. "You so much as lay a finger on my mother again and I will cut you up into chunks. I will cut you into pieces and put you through a meat grinder. Then, I'll bag you up and send you to Battersea-fucking-Dogs' Home, where those sorry-looking dogs will eat you up and shit you out. Do you understand? Nod your head for me if you understand."

Melvyn nodded.

She pressed a finger into his fleshy cheek until his lips puckered and said, "Good. And if I hear your girlfriend, Samantha, or anyone else, has laid a finger on my mother or even says anything I think might upset her, I will go after them, and then I'll come after you too. Do you understand? Nod for me if you understand."

Melvyn nodded again. He could feel himself sweating uncontrollably.

"Good boy. From now on you're going to be my mother's guardian angel."

Lyle reached into Melvyn's trouser pocket and pulled out his packet of cigarettes and cigarette lighter. Keeping her face next to his she put the cigarette in her mouth and lit it. Melvyn squirmed and tried to turn his face further away. He could feel the flame of the lighter and pictured the hot tip of the cigarette next to his face. She inhaled deeply, then blew the cigarette smoke directly into his face. "Not a finger, Melvyn."

He nodded once more. "I understand."

She took a few steps back and watched as he stood up straight. Pathetic.

"From now on, Melvyn, you're to be the poster child for every member of staff. If they step out of line, I'm coming after you. I want you to start taking a regular bath as well. You stink."

Melvyn nodded again and whispered, "Whatever you say."

"Open your mouth for me, Melvyn."

He looked at Lyle and, with only a moment's hesitation, did as he was told.

Lyle took the cigarette from her mouth and turned it before placing it in his mouth.

"Good boy. Now finish your cigarette and enjoy the rest of your break."

CHAPTER FORTY-NINE

Dave Howes was feeling pleased with himself. He hated confrontation and was happy with the way he'd stood up to Emma.

Getting her back in the sack had been a bit of luck. His only concern now was whether Rebecca would find out. He thought it very unlikely that the two women would ever speak, so he quickly put it to the back of his mind.

With little traffic on the A31 New Forest dual carriageway, Dave kept his foot pressed on the accelerator. It would be at least an hour's drive to Rebecca's house in Southampton, and he wanted to get there as soon as possible. He thought he should let her know he was on his way. Recalling his night with Emma had put him in a playful mood, and he wanted to remind Rebecca how much he loved her.

He reached into his jacket pocket and pulled out his mobile phone. Balancing it on his thigh, he found Rebecca's number and hit *Call*. He picked up the phone and put it to his ear.

Rebecca didn't answer, so he left a message. "Hi, Becks, it's me. I'm on my way. Sorry it's all taken so long. You know how Emma can be. She made things *really* difficult. It got so late that, rather than drive back at night and disturb you, I ended up sleeping on a mate's sofa. Anyway, Emma and I straightened things out. I'm all sorted. I got all the stuff I wanted, and I'm on my way over. I never need to see her again. Love you. Did you miss me? I've been thinking about you. A lot."

A silver Volvo came up close behind Dave's car. He didn't notice the car until it pulled around him and came up alongside with its blue lights flashing.

He dropped his mobile phone onto the passenger seat. He was well over the speed limit and immediately took his foot off the accelerator.

"Damn it. Shit."

Shock and fear surged through his body. The police car remained level, and Dave turned to look at the officer at the wheel. She waved a hand to indicate he should pull over.

He pulled over onto the hard shoulder and slowed to a stop. The unmarked car pulled in behind him, its blue lights still flashing.

Reaching across to the passenger seat, he switched off his mobile phone. He opened the glovebox and tossed it inside.

In his mirrors, he watched the police officer making notes. Then the officer got out of the Volvo and walked up to the passenger side of his car. He opened the window.

The traffic officer leaned over and looked in. "Good evening, sir," she said.

Dave replied casually. "Good evening, Officer. Did I do something wrong? Is everything okay?"

"You were recorded driving in excess of the national speed limit. You were also driving while using your mobile phone. Licence and insurance, please."

He passed the officer his driver's licence and explained that his insurance was at home.

"Come with me," she instructed him. "I need to run some checks. We need to fill out some paperwork. Step this way."

He followed the officer to her car. She motioned him into the passenger seat.

"This shouldn't take long," she said. "I just need to run through some paperwork and then you can be on your way. You will, of course, receive a fine and six penalty points on your licence. If it were up to me, it would be an instant disqualification, but there you are. It's not up to me."

Dave sighed resignedly. He knew that police cars have cameras and that he had very likely been filmed using his phone. The situation would only be made worse if he tried to contest the truth of the matter.

The officer examined his licence. "Please confirm your name."

Dave picked at his fingernail. "David Alexander Howes."

"And your permanent address?"

He gave Rebecca's address. The last thing he wanted was the police contacting Emma.

He watched the officer fill in the space for his address. He looked at her fingernails. They looked well-manicured. His eyes moved to her hands, her uniform, her face and her hair. He leaned forward to look at her shoes.

New uniform and new shoes, thought Dave. *Hair and fingernails like she's come straight out of a salon.*

Dave looked around the car at the dashboard and the

dash cam. Something seemed wrong. He couldn't put his finger on it, but something felt out of place.

The police officer looked at him, and he looked away. He looked back and said, "I know this is going sound silly, but can I see some identification, please?"

"I showed it to you."

"I'd like to see it again. Please." He sat up a little straighter.

The officer looked mildly amused. "Of course you can. You are entitled to see my identification. Better to be safe than sorry. One moment."

Dave felt pleased with himself. He heard the rip of Velcro as the officer opened a jacket pocket. His eyes followed her as she first looked ahead and then turned in her seat to look behind.

He turned his head to see what she was looking for. The officer appeared to be looking to see whether any cars were approaching. Dave could see the road was empty.

"Here we go," she said.

He put out his hand and took the warrant card. Studying the card, he didn't notice the officer's other hand as it suddenly pressed a taser into his chest. The taser's 1,200 volts seared through his body.

Rigid from the shock, he was unable to prevent the hand holding a cloth covered in chloroform from covering his nose and mouth.

Lyle pulled the seatbelt across Dave's body and fastened it. She took off her police hat, wig and jacket and dropped them in the footwell behind his seat. She got out of the Volvo and walked back to Dave's car, where she hunted around for his mobile phone. She finally located it in the glovebox, tucked it in her pocket and returned to the unmarked police car.

Satisfied that Dave looked like a sleeping passenger, she

pulled back onto the dual carriageway and made her way to the workshop.

CHAPTER FIFTY

Emma was closing the front door behind her when the call came in. She dropped her shopping bag on the worktop and answered the phone. It was a woman's voice, one she didn't recognise.

"Is he with you? If he is with you, tell him he can go screw himself."

Emma had a good idea who this was and who she was talking about. "Rebecca? If you're talking about Dave, he's not here. I did tell him to get out, and I assumed he went straight back to you."

She could hear Rebecca breathing on the other end of the phone. She started unpacking her shopping. She opened the fridge and tucked a carton of milk inside. She took the loaf of bread and dropped it on top of the bread bin, the bread bin being full of biscuits. She folded up the shopping bag and stuffed it into a drawer.

"Dave was here," she said. "I threw him out. Between you and me, Dave isn't the man I thought he was."

Rebecca said, "I'm sorry. By the time I found out about

you, it was already too late. I was already in love with him."

Emma knew she was lying. Dave had mentioned Rebecca Wild, a co-worker, on many occasions. She'd been so busy with the Lyle investigation over the last few months that she hadn't given it much thought.

Looking back, she realised it had probably started out as Dave using Rebecca's name as a way to gain her attention. Perhaps he'd thought she might feel a little jealous and give him some attention rather than focusing full-time on her investigations. She could only presume that, after he didn't get the response he hoped for, he'd taken it a step further. Then another step, until…

"I tried calling his mobile," said Rebecca. "At first it went to voicemail. Now when I call his number, I get a message that says 'This phone might be switched off.'"

Well, that's odd. Emma wondered whether Dave might have more than one relationship on the go. It seemed unlikely, but then again, until recently, the thought of him with any other woman had seemed impossible to her. She now realised Dave was full of surprises. She wondered whether she could delicately ask Rebecca whether she thought he might be seeing someone else. She decided there was no easy way to ask.

"Is there anywhere else you think Dave might go?" she asked.

"No; I assumed he was with you. He told me his parents live in Cardiff. He left a message telling me he was on his way over to me. That he'd spent the night at a friend's place, that night he came to see you. I called all the friends of his I know, and they've not seen him. I don't understand what's going on."

Telling Rebecca that Dave had been in her bed and not

on a friend's sofa would benefit no one, Emma decided. At least not at this particular moment.

"He is really close to his parents. Although I doubt he's gone to Cardiff without telling you. I shouldn't worry too much. He'll turn up. I can assure you he won't be coming back here any time soon. I feel sure he's been sidetracked in some way, the way blokes are. He'll be knocking on your door before you know it."

Rebecca didn't sound convinced, but Emma had had enough of playing nice. She ended the call as politely as she could then threw her phone onto the armchair and watched it bounce.

CHAPTER FIFTY-ONE

Emma had been polite to Rebecca and told herself she no longer cared what Dave was doing, but it didn't stop her feeling hurt and angry. Emotions clawed their way through her body. His betrayal had winded her; it was like a punch to the stomach.

She fed Watson and then they sat together on the sofa while she ate a microwave curry and drank white wine.

It was just after 11.30 p.m. when her mobile phone, still on the armchair, woke her.

"Hello?" She knew she sounded sleepy. She cleared her throat and tried again. "Emma speaking."

"It's lovely to speak with you finally. I'm a big fan of yours, Emma. Why wouldn't I be? You're a strong, independent, beautiful woman. This is really exciting."

It was a woman's voice. Emma was confused. Was this a prank call?

"Who is this? I didn't catch your name."

"You'll figure that out soon enough, darling. I've been watching you. You're a fascinating little thing. Buzzing here, there and everywhere. You're like a pretty little bumblebee buzzing in circles around the garden. Hopping from one flower to another; round and round you go. And then, after bumbling around for hours and hours, you go home to your pussycat. Meow. Emma, all alone with her cat. How's that working out for you? What do you think Dave's up to right now? Right this minute? I bet you one million pounds you can't guess."

Emma could feel her breathing speeding up. She was awake now and on high alert.

Instinctively she looked behind her. She got to her feet, walked quickly and quietly to her front door and checked that the security chain was on. She went to the window and looked out. She looked up and down the street but could see very little; the only light came from streetlights.

She found a scrap of paper and a pen to record exactly what the woman was saying. She sat down on the couch, set the paper on the coffee table, pulled up her sleeves and began to write. At the top of the page she marked the time, and in capital letters "KELLY LYLE."

"Why are you calling me?" she asked, keeping her voice level. "I'm pleased you are calling me – of course I am. I just wondered why now?"

"I felt now was the right time."

"When can we meet?"

"I don't think that's a good idea. You've seen what I do to people who disappoint me. For the time being, I think it's better we don't meet. For now, I find you more interesting alive than dead. Dave, on the other hand…"

Emma's eyes widened. She put a hand over her mouth to cover her gasp. What did Lyle know of Dave? Her brain started putting all sorts of connections together. She felt her heart pounding.

She asked hesitantly, "What do you mean?" She

thought she knew what Lyle meant, but she prayed she was wrong. *Please be wrong. Please God – no, not David.*

"I have a little surprise for you. I suppose you'd call it a gift. I've been watching you, watching Hardy. I've also been watching Dave. I could see what he was doing. He isn't good for you."

Emma noticed Lyle had said "isn't," not "wasn't."

"I could see what Dave was doing long before you ever turned a blind eye to it. Love really is blind." She chuckled at her own joke. "Dave won't be breaking any more hearts. He's a distraction, and I need you to focus. You're a smart woman, Detective Inspector Emma Cotton, and you can do a lot better than him. You have a bright and shining future ahead of you.

"To fulfil our potential, there are those we need to leave behind. For you, Dave is one of those.

"We women need to stick together, look out for one another. So, I had a very long talk with Dave, and he agreed that he'd mistreated you and you should move on with your life without him. By the end of our conversation, he also agreed that he deserved to be punished. I will admit he is unaware of the full extent of the punishment I intend for him. Let's just say sometimes I get a little bit carried away. You know how it is; we both find satisfaction in our work – just in different ways."

Emma was shaking uncontrollably now. She could hear her voice trembling as she pleaded. "Please, no. I don't need you to do anything on my behalf. Dave is a good man. He and I are history, yes, but he's a good man. I'm fully focused on the investigation. I'm giving you all my attention. Just let him go. Please, let me know where he is and that he's safe. There's no need to hurt him. He's no threat to you."

"Oh, Emma, you're such a sweetie. Dave is history. Of

that, you can be sure. He was selfish and caused you pain. I think in the long run you will thank me for what I've done."

Past tense, Emma noticed: "what I've done."

"Myself, I have a love-hate relationship with men. I think it's one of the things that define who I am. I used to think it was a problem. Now I see it as a blessing.

"It's been lovely talking to you, Emma, but I really must go now. Dave has regained consciousness, and I need to strike while the iron is hot, as they say. One last thing: this is a freebie, just for you. No Scrabble piece this time."

"Kelly, let me speak to—"

The call ended.

Emma felt the room spinning. Her body tingled. She got to her feet and began pacing up and down. She thought she might vomit. She went to the window and opened it. She needed air, lungs full of cold air. She couldn't think. She needed to think. She was just about to call Hardy when her phone beeped.

It was a message from Lyle.

She clicked on it.

An address.

It must be Dave's location. It had to be.

Emma searched around for her keys. She snatched them up from the kitchen worktop and sprinted out the front door.

Even though her head was telling her she was too late, her heart was urging her to hurry. She prayed there was still a chance.

CHAPTER FIFTY-TWO

An anonymous tipoff had led officers to a workshop on a small industrial estate. It was after 12.30 a.m. when I arrived. The desk sergeant who had called me told me the attending officers had insisted I would want to see the crime scene. Whether I liked it or not, I was being dragged deeper and deeper into my old routine.

A young officer was outside the workshop throwing up. He had one hand on the wall as his legs buckled beneath him. His partner, Officer Franklin, came to the door and said, "It's this way, sir. I hope you've got a stronger stomach than Grantham. We're lucky he didn't puke all over the crime scene."

The workshop was used by a printing business. Along one side was a guillotine and a collating machine. The back wall had racks piled high with paper of all descriptions. On the right side of the workshop was a modern-looking printing press. In the centre of the room was a long white-topped bench.

Stairs led to the second floor; there were offices and a graphic design studio on a mezzanine floor. A walkway at the top of the stairs gave access to the offices. A handrail ran along the edge of the mezzanine floor for the safety of those using the walkway. A rope was tied to one of the handrail posts.

At the end of the rope, hanging upside down by his feet, was the naked body of a man. His head and hands had been removed, and his stomach had been sliced from left to right, its contents spilling out over what remained of him.

Franklin looked at me. "This was on the bench. We haven't touched it." He pointed to a glass jar on the bench. I squatted down to look at the contents.

"It's his tongue," I said.

"Yeah. It wasn't enough to do all that to him." He gestured at the mutilated body. "They also needed to cut out his tongue and stick it in a jar. I hope I never see anything like this again."

I remembered saying something similar when I was a young detective constable. Since then, I'd seen many scenes like this – and many much worse.

I heard raised voices behind me and turned to see Cotton rushing in through the front door.

"Is it him? Is it David?"

I looked at what was left of the body suspended from the ceiling. I watched as she ran and stumbled towards the body. As she got close, she fell to her knees and let out a mournful cry.

"I'm sorry, Cotton," I said without knowing why. "I don't understand. Do you know this person?"

"He was my fiancé." She looked at me with tears pouring down her face.

I looked at the headless body. "How can you be sure?"

"There on his arm – the tattoos."

His blood-soaked right arm and shoulder were extensively tattooed.

Cotton looked at me and then behind me at the bench and the glass jar.

I needed to get her out of there. I helped her to her feet and, putting my arm around her to keep her up and keep her moving, took her outside.

CHAPTER FIFTY-THREE

Cotton leaned against the front of her car. I stood beside her, unable to fathom what was going through her mind. Her face and eyes were puffy. She blew her nose and wiped it.

"I'm okay. He was my ex-fiancé. We'd just broken up." She tried to laugh. "I'd just found out he was sleeping with someone else. The trouble is, I still loved him. I probably would have taken him back if we'd had a chance to work it through."

She rooted around in a pocket and found another tiny piece of tissue to wipe her nose.

"I wish you hadn't seen that." I looked back towards the horror show in the workshop then took off my jacket and put it around her.

I realised how little I knew about her life beyond this investigation. I felt helpless seeing her this way. She looked so vulnerable and so alone. I wanted to put my arm around her and tell her everything would be okay, but I stopped myself. I knew the Emma I recognised, the fierce and tenacious Detective Inspector Cotton, would soon be ready to hunt down the bastard who had done this unspeakable crime. She'd make them pay. That was the reason I didn't comfort her.

She brushed herself off and cleared her throat. She looked at me and struggled to find the words. "Lyle did this."

I said nothing. I waited, giving her time to compose her thoughts.

"Lyle called me a couple of hours ago... to tell me she had David... She wanted me to know she had him. That I could do nothing... nothing to stop her punishing him... Her killing him this way was a gift, she said, for me."

In her eyes, I could see she was holding onto the blame for Dave's death.

"You couldn't have stopped this, Emma. You're not to blame in any way. She killed him several hours ago. She's playing with you. Whatever she told you, it was a lie. You couldn't have got here in time. There was nothing you could have done to stop this."

She took off my jacket, passed it back to me and said, "Thank you." After a moment, she asked, "What's this about a recording? I heard someone say there was a video. I want to see it. Don't look at me like that."

The fighter is back, I thought.

"It's on a smartphone left on what remained of Dave's clothes, the clothes she cut from his body.

"There is only one phone number on the phone, which we now know is your number. I haven't watched the whole recording, but what I have seen is disturbing. It's very graphic. I'm not sure you should see it. Or at least, not right now. You should give yourself a little time."

"Time is something we don't have. Don't you dare sideline me on this. It's my investigation, and no matter how far it goes, I'm in all the way. Show me the damn recording."

Her eyes were full of fire; I could tell she was going to watch the recording whether I thought it was a good idea or not.

The recording bounced around at first. It showed the floor moving past and the sound of someone walking. The picture panned left and right then all over the place.

"Fast-forward a few minutes," I said. "We can analyse the full recording another time."

Suddenly the video showed Dave's face. I turned to Emma, who showed no emotion. The frame pulled back to reveal Dave's naked body. I could see no blood, but his face was red from exertion, and he was crying.

In a soothing tone, Lyle was shushing him and asking him to hush.

The picture moved again, and as it panned back it became apparent Dave was hanging upside down, his arms tied behind his back.

"Please, just let me go. I won't tell anyone. It's not too late to let me go. You seem like a nice lady. What's your name? Let's talk. My name's David Howes. Let's work this out. If I upset you in any way, I'm sorry. It's not too late — just let me go. I can pay you. Do you want money? How much do you want?"

Not wanting to see, yet unable to stop himself, Dave's eyes followed Lyle as she moved about the room. Full of fear, he didn't stop watching her for a second.

Then his expression changed. Momentarily, his mouth and eyes widened before he squeezed them shut. Whatever was about to happen, he no longer wanted to see.

He started screaming, "Dear God, no. Oh, dear God, no."

Lyle's voice was angry. "Open your eyes, Dave. Open your eyes now, or I'll cut off your eyelids."

As best he could, Dave obeyed.

Lyle walked around him as she spoke. "I know you like games. You think you're a big man…"

"No, I don't. You have the wrong person," he spluttered.

"Interrupt again, Dave, and I'll cut your head off, right here, right now. You think you can trample over women? That you can play games with women? I'm a woman. Shall we see how much you like my games?"

Dave began screaming, an inhuman scream. Spots of blood and streaks of blood appeared on his face as his body buckled and rocked from the pain.

The screaming changed to a deep, pitiful murmur.

The camera zoomed out again and showed where Dave's lower body had been cut and slashed.

Lyle appeared in front of the camera again. She crouched in front of him and said, "Open your mouth, Dave."

He screamed and whined. His body moved like a fish out of water as Lyle worked on him.

The screaming stopped, and there was silence. Dave had passed out, his body and mind unable to take any more.

Lyle's blood-covered hand appeared briefly in front of the camera, and then the bloody horror of Dave's butchered and bloodied face was revealed.

The sound of Lyle's footsteps. The clink of metal as the instrument used to cut him was put down. The sound of a lid closing.

The camera was picked up then and approached

Dave's body. Lyle filmed him from all sides then angled the camera down at the pool of blood gathering below his swaying body.

We watched as Lyle washed and dried her hands in the workshop's sink then walked back towards Dave's limp body. As she walked, she turned the camera on herself and began to speak.

CHAPTER FIFTY-FOUR

"I hope, given time, you'll appreciate what I've done for you, Emma. But right now, we're running out of time. So much still to come and so little time. There's another big surprise coming up very soon. I need everyone's attention on this. That means you too, Hardy. Are you there, James? Of course you are; I know you can't stay away from something like this. You and I are similar in so many ways.

"I still have very fond memories of the very first time we met. Do you remember? We sat beneath the stars, and you reassured me. Are you comforting Emma the way you comforted me? I bet you are. He's such a gentleman, isn't he, Emma?

"Back to Dave. I've nearly finished with him. I'm going to remove his hands and head now. Then he'll be ready for you.

"Before I go, I want you to know everything is in place for the next part of the game. James, I'll see you then."

The phone moved around again. Lyle set it down and angled it so that she could film herself. We watched a few more seconds as she brought Dave around from unconsciousness. Then, as the screaming started again, Emma switched off the phone. I gave her some space as she walked around for a while, getting herself together.

Lyle's words about there being another surprise worried me. The fact she was announcing it suggested she had something even more terrifying planned. Until we could figure out what that might be, I wanted to keep Emma close.

When she finally walked back over to me, I said quietly, "You've been through a hell of a lot tonight, and I would consider it a personal favour if you would come and stay at my house. I don't want you alone right now, so unless you have someone you can go and stay with, I want you to stay close to me. We have room."

"I don't need a bloody babysitter."

"I'm not suggesting that. I think the smart thing is that we play safe. That means we look out for each other. I want to know you've got my back, and you to know that right now I've got yours."

I could see she didn't want to look weak, so I made it easier for her.

"We need to get ahead of this, which means we need to put in more hours. Why waste time going back and forth to the office when we can work from my study? I have a guest room, freshly decorated and never used. We can work smarter and try and find a way to stop Lyle once and for all."

Reluctantly, she agreed. "I need to go back to my place and get a few things."

"I'll come with you. For the time being, we stick together as much as possible."

CHAPTER FIFTY-FIVE

Having found her way to the kitchen for breakfast, I think it would be fair to say Emma must have been a little surprised at how noisy and busy the house was.

Sandy immediately started barking with excitement at seeing her – a new face in the house.

Mum had popped in for before visiting Dad, who was still in the hospital and would soon undergo a further heart operation. She and Monica were deep in conversation as they prepared a healthy breakfast for everyone. Since Dad's heart scare, mealtimes consisted of a lot more fruit and vegetables. I was going along with it for the time being. I suspected the new regime wouldn't last long.

Alice had an exam coming up and was in the next room practising the violin.

Faith was on the family iPad laughing and talking to friends. She was explaining to them that she'd had a woman detective inspector staying at her house overnight. I had no doubt that as soon as she got the chance, Faith would be interrogating Emma.

Handing a cup of coffee to Emma, I said, "Good

morning. Sorry about the noise. How are you feeling? How did you sleep?"

"I'm okay, thank you. I slept surprisingly well."

She looked around at what I could only imagine she considered pandemonium.

Tongue in cheek, I said, "It can get a little chaotic in the Hardy household. You should see it on a busy morning."

She laughed, and I introduced her to everyone while we all sat down for breakfast.

Mum gave Emma a discreet hug and a kiss and said how sorry she was. I'd explained the situation to Mum and Monica. Naturally, Alice and Faith had no idea about the terrifying events of the previous night.

While my eldest, Alice, was playing the perfect hostess by helping Monica serve breakfast, Faith made sure she was sat next to Emma so she could observe her while taking mental notes. It didn't take long before she began her interrogation.

"Do you come from a big family? Emma, are you married? You're not wearing a wedding ring. How long have you been a detective inspector? Do you have any brothers or sisters? What's your middle name?"

I looked at Emma apologetically. "Please don't quiz our guest, Faith."

"You always ask such personal questions," added Alice.

"Daddy says there's no point beating about the bush. If you've got a question, ask it outright. Isn't that right, Daddy?"

Had he been there, I could imagine my dad finding this conversation hilarious. It was a bit of advice he'd given me when I was a child.

Mum jumped in and tried to help. "Asking direct questions is fine if you grow up to become a detective,

Faith. Until then, such direct questions to someone you barely know can seem a little impolite. It's lovely you're so inquisitive, but maybe try asking a question that's a little less direct."

"It's fine," said Emma. "Honestly, I don't mind." She gave Faith a warm smile.

Faith thought about her questions and tried again. "Are you divorced? Is that why you're not wearing a wedding ring?"

Emma started laughing.

Monica gave Faith a wide-eyed look of disbelief. "Faith, what are we going to do with you?"

Still laughing, Emma said, "No, I'm not married. I was engaged for a while, but that didn't work out." She looked at me in a way that said she was okay.

There was a bit of awkward silence between the adults for a split second before Faith continued. "Is it because you haven't met Prince Charming yet? Monica says men are beasts; you just need to find the least beastly one. Isn't that right, Monica?"

Now it was my turn in the firing line. "Is that right?" I said, looking between Monica and Faith and Alice. "So that's what you're all saying behind my back, is it?"

"Absolutely," laughed Monica. She winked at the girls. "I think it's important these two young women understand that beastly boys grow up to become beastly men."

"Hear, hear," said Mum. "And they eventually become beastly grandads."

"Well, that's just charming," I said. "And all this time there was me thinking I was your dream come true."

Mum said, "You are, dear. You are her dream come true." She added in a whisper from behind her hand, loud enough for everyone to hear, "Bless him."

Breakfast went on this way for a good hour or so. Lots

of good-natured fun and heartfelt laughter. It was great therapy. Every one of us around the table was hurting in their own way.

Emma looked relaxed and in good spirits. There was no doubt she was feeling pain, and she would need time to grieve. But right then she was putting that to one side and getting on with dealing with the here and now.

After we'd all helped with the clearing up and the packing away of breakfast, Emma and I went to my office to spend some time going over the case. It was time to decide our next move.

CHAPTER FIFTY-SIX

I'd lost track of time while going over the case files with Emma, and visiting hours at the hospital were over. I pressed the buzzer and peered through the window of the ward's secure doors.

To my surprise, I was welcomed with a big smile from the ward sister. She'd been told who I was and that I was working the murder investigation they'd all heard about on the news. I was allowed in under strict instructions that I shouldn't stay more than half an hour and to be "as quiet as a church mouse."

"Your dad talks about you a lot. He's so proud," said Nurse Gillespie. "He's a lovely man. He makes us all laugh. Tells us stories about his granddaughters."

"Thank you for looking after him. It sounds like he's in good form."

"Yes, he is. His operation got pushed back because an emergency came in, but we're monitoring him, and the doctor will reschedule at the earliest opportunity."

I found Dad sitting up in bed reading the *Daily Echo*. On seeing me, he folded the newspaper and put it to one side. His face still looked pale and the rims of his eyes were red, but he was smiling and appeared stable.

"Stop your gawping and sit yourself down," he ordered. "You're looking tired, James. Have you been sleeping?"

"I'm okay," I fibbed. The last thing he needed to hear was how the Lyle case had escalated.

"How are my granddaughters? I'm looking forward to seeing them and Monica. She promised to smuggle in some of that carrot cake of hers." Suddenly his eyes filled with tears.

"What is it, Dad?"

"Ah, nothing. Just being a dope."

"Come on," I insisted. "Talk to me."

He picked up his paper, unnecessarily folded it one more time and put it back down on his lap. "You know, for a moment there, when I was on the floor, staring up at the sky, I thought it was all over. I kept telling myself 'I'm not ready to go,' but there was nothing I could do about it. Now I'm feeling like I'm on borrowed time.

"Something like this makes you realise how our time here can be all over in the blink of an eye and how precious each second is. It also makes you reassess what's truly important. Don't get me wrong – I've always known what's important. Yet, something like this really focuses the mind."

Dad wiped away a tear. "I want to get out of here. I don't want to waste another second in this hospital bed." He looked anxious and scared in a way I'd never seen him before.

"You need the op, Dad. Wait and see the doctor in the morning. Get the operation over with, and you'll feel like a new man. I guarantee it."

"If anything happens to me…"

"Listen, nothing's going happen. You've had a scare, that's all. A message from your body. Fixing a condition like yours is routine stuff for doctors these days. You'll be fine."

He ignored me. "If anything happens to me, your mother will be okay financially. I need you to promise me you'll look after her. I know you will, but I just need to hear you say it, for my own peace of mind. She puts on the air of a strong, independent woman. Inside, I still see the young woman I met all those years ago. She acts tough, and she is in many ways – she certainly knows her mind – but that big generous heart of hers is easily broken."

"I promise, I will. But we shouldn't be having this conversation. You've both got years ahead of you."

Dad smiled weakly. I could see he didn't believe me. I guessed he was still in shock and feeling tired and vulnerable.

Suddenly, he brightened up. He sat up straight, put his paper to one side and said, "I might have told you the story, many times, of how your mother and I met at a dance. She was there with her girlfriends, and as soon as I saw her, I knew. The way she looked, moved and laughed. She was the only girl in the room I wanted to talk to. For me, it was love at first sight.

"We danced a few times that evening. We talked and talked, and I told her I was a police officer with big plans for my future. I thought it would impress her.

"What I didn't ever tell you was what your mother said to me that evening. She told me she'd had a nice time but that a second date wasn't in the cards. She turned me down."

Dad laughed to himself as he pictured the moment in his mind.

"I was full of myself back then. A hot-headed young

man. What I didn't see was that, to your mother, my confidence and my stories of wanting to be a detective came across as arrogance. She told me years later I had spent the whole dance talking about myself and had wanted to know very little about her. Being naive, and keen as mustard, I thought the way to win her was to do all I could to impress her with my achievements and ambition. I'd messed up.

"What it meant was I'd made it harder for myself to win her over. In time, she saw who I really was and realised that the way I behaved that first evening was just for show."

Dad put his hand on mine.

"The truth is, I didn't know how to behave around girls back then, and I was putting on an act. As you get older, son, you realise that being something you're not is harder than being who you really are. And for your own peace of mind you must accept who you are. Those who care about you will accept that. Be true to yourself, son. We only get one shot at this life, so whatever happens, be true to who you are."

He wrinkled his nose and brushed away a tear. It looked like storm clouds were gathering in his mind, and I wanted to keep him upbeat. I said, "Well, you won her over in the end. And the two of you have been together, *ahem*, many years." I coughed jokingly to cover the number of years.

Dad laughed a little too loudly, and we looked at each other like naughty schoolboys as we noticed Nurse Gillespie giving us a stern look. We continued to chuckle quietly.

"You'd better get out of here before you get thrown out," he said at last. "Thanks for coming, son. You've cheered me up. Give Monica, Alice and Faith a kiss from me. I'd better get some sleep now. No doubt your mother will be here at the crack of dawn to fuss over me."

"You love it, really. All this attention."

"You bet I do. I'm making the most of this. Go on, get out of here. Go and see that beautiful family of yours."

I thanked Nurse Gillespie on my way out and headed home.

CHAPTER FIFTY-SEVEN

Edward Richter sat back in his chair and folded his arms. He looked across the table at the woman opposite him, his eyes unblinking, as he tried to read her face.

"So you're my new psychologist? What makes you think you're smart enough to poke around inside my head and tell me why I do what I do? How long have you held a psychology degree? Nice wig, by the way. Though I prefer brunettes, if you know what I mean."

"We both know why I'm here, Richter."

"Isn't it risky of you coming here? What's to stop me calling the guards right now and turning you in?"

"That's not your style."

"Prison can change a man."

"So I've heard."

Richter scoffed. "I'm not going to pretend I don't know it was you who slaughtered those women and framed me for it."

He shifted uneasily in his seat. "This visit can't be about your girlfriend. That was years ago. Don't tell me you're still whining about that? If you are, it's just a pretence. I don't believe you are capable of love. I've often wondered whether, hidden deep inside you, there might be a heart. I concluded that if there is, it's ugly, twisted and cold. Let's face it – try as you might, you'll never find peace. So, come on, tell me, why are you really here?"

Lyle showed no emotion. She had been straightening her badge, which read "Criminal Psychologist," as she waited for Richter to finish.

"I'm here because I want you to know that I'm the one who decides your future. And I wanted to take another look at you before I decide how that's going to unfold."

"You're so full of shit, Lyle. If you could get to me, I'd be dead already. Then again, maybe you think you have more clout than you actually do. Delusional, they call that. Look it up." Richter laughed and slapped the table with a tattooed hand.

"You can sit there and act all cocky. I really don't care. I'm out there living life. Drinking wine, eating great food, travelling the world and getting laid. You, on the other hand, are lucky if you get an hour in the yard. Made any new friends in the showers? How's that working out for you?"

Richter appeared unimpressed by Lyle's little speech. "Little overdramatic, don't you think? We both know you can't touch me. We both also know her death was unintentional. What's the *real* reason you're here? Is it that you're bored with me? I mean, if life's so good on the outside and you have your freedom, then why waste your time visiting me? The difference between you and me, Lyle, is I know who I am. I accept it. I know where I fit in. You, on the other hand, well, you're still a lost little girl who's angry at Daddy. Maybe it's time you got over it. Perhaps it's time to take a long, hard look at yourself and move on. Perhaps you're suffering from never having had a *real* man in your life?"

He paused and placed a finger on his lips, pretending to think. "Something just occurred to me. Why didn't I think of it before? Ooh, Kelly, perhaps you're still looking for a *real* man. Is that what it is? You're confused about your sexuality. Is that why you're here? How about I show you how a *real* man feels, then you can decide?"

Richter gave a filthy, guttural laugh as he leaned back in his chair and pretended to unzip his trousers.

Lyle closed the fake folder of notes in front of her and placed her clasped hands on top of them.

"Richter, you can act with as much bravado as you like but your time is coming. You'll never know it's coming. But I guarantee it is, and from a most unexpected hand."

"Blah, blah, blah, blah, blah, blah." He jumped to his feet and tried to grab Lyle from across the table. She took a step back to avoid his grasp. He grabbed the fake file and paperwork and threw it across the room.

"You want to know what your *real* problem is, Lyle?" He grabbed his crotch. "You wish you had a pair of these. When I get out of here, I'm going to pay you a visit. And this time I won't miss, I can promise you that. You're a fucking dead woman. Dead – you hear me?"

Richter ran his finger slowly across his throat. "Dead."

CHAPTER FIFTY-EIGHT

Emma and I had been working out of my home office since the early hours, challenging assumptions and making calls. We decided to take a break, get out and go for a walk.

"How are you holding up?" I asked.

"You need to stop asking me that. If the same had happened to your old partner Rayner, would you be asking him the same question?"

"As a matter of fact, I would. Partners look out for each other."

"Is that what we are? Partners?"

"So long as we can trust one another. Agree not to hide anything from each other. And look out for each other. Then I'd say yes, we're partners."

Emma turned to look at me. I could see she was wondering whether I knew. To her credit, she opened up about going to see Horn. When I showed no surprise, she narrowed her eyes at me. "Rayner told you?" Her voice was accusing.

"As I said, partners don't hide things."

She looked annoyed and embarrassed, like a child

who'd been caught cheating a friend. "I wasn't hiding anything. I wanted to understand before speaking to you. I didn't want you distracted from your own line of enquiry with what might amount to nothing."

I wasn't angry, only mildly annoyed. Annoyed that Emma had chosen to speak to Horn without consulting me. What had happened to Helena would always be very personal for me, and it felt as though she'd stepped over the line.

"I really believe the tipoff is connected to this current case. It makes sense to look into it," said Emma.

"You believe there is some sort of connection between what's happening now and what happened to Helena? Lyle told you that?"

"You make it sound like that's impossible."

"You could have got yourself killed. Lyle's toying with you. It what she does. All it's done is get Tony Horn killed."

Emma stopped in her tracks and looked at me as if she hadn't heard me correctly. With shock on her face, she said, "What? Is he dead? How? When?"

"He was found dead in his cell. In truth, I'm surprised it hadn't happened before this. He had a way of pissing people off, from what I heard. What did he say to you, exactly?"

"Nothing, really. I got the impression he was trying to change. Trying to get his life back on track. He was obviously a troubled individual."

I didn't like the way Emma spoke about Horn. As far as I was concerned, he had no right to a life. I really didn't care to hear that Horn had been trying to improve his life. I knew I shouldn't be, but I was glad he was dead.

"Do you think Lyle got to him?" she asked.

Now it was my turn to be shocked.

"I have no idea. I don't see why Lyle would want Horn dead. As far as I know, they have nothing connecting them."

"Lyle wants me to look at Helena's murder. All these recent murders are all very close to home."

I nodded in agreement. "Most recently with Etheridge's murder, Dave's and now Horn's."

Emma added, "It feels like every step of the way, she's corralling us towards an endgame. We need to ask why. And we need to ask how it all fits together."

We walked for some time in silence, both of us thinking and wondering what we were missing.

"Something Horn said has been going around and around in my head," said Emma. "He said the detective had been getting too close. What do you think he meant?"

I shook my head. "My guess is it didn't mean anything. Either he told you what you wanted to hear, or he was concocting a story ready for when he was eligible for parole."

Emma stopped walking and said, "I'm going back to the office. The station office. I'll drop by my house first, grab a few things and start working from there. I've slept on my office sofa more times than I care to admit."

I didn't like it, but I could see from her manner there was no point arguing with her.

"You're welcome to stay in our guest room for as long as you want; you know that."

"Thank you. If the sofa becomes too uncomfortable, I may take you up on it. You have enough going on, with your father in the hospital. I'm also thinking I can't let Lyle drive me out of my home. I really should go back there. And sooner rather than later. And there's one more thing."

"What?"

"You're not going to like it."

"Try me."

"I want to speak to the killer you were investigating with Rayner when Helena was murdered. I want to speak to Edward Richter."

We didn't speak on the walk back to the house. I couldn't stop her seeing Richter any more than I could insist she remain at my home.

As I watched her drive away, I wondered whether I should have confronted her and asked whether there was anything else she had neglected to tell me.

There was no doubt in my mind Emma was an excellent detective, and I decided that even though I liked to think I had all the answers, in truth I knew I didn't. Perhaps this investigation was too close to home and I was blinkered to what was really going on.

Giving Emma the space to investigate the way she saw fit might yield a breakthrough. As the saying goes, "Sometimes the secret to leadership is to step back and let others lead."

Since she had spoken to Rayner and to Horn, I guessed it was only a matter of time before she began digging deeper. I had nothing to hide, but I was concerned that she might get in over her head and not ask for help.

I decided to call in a few favours and make sure someone was looking out for her.

CHAPTER FIFTY-NINE

I answered the phone on the third ring. I sat up in bed as I felt my body go numb. Monica lightly touched my back and whispered, "What is it, James?"

I couldn't find the words. I switched on the bedside lamp and fumbled around for my clothes.

Monica sat up and looked at me. "James? What's going on?"

I gave up trying to find my sock and pulled on a fresh pair.

"That was Mum on the phone. She's at the hospital. Dad's had another heart attack. I need to get over to the hospital right away."

"Shall I come with you? Shall I get the girls up?"

I was looking under the bed, hunting for my shoes. I was having difficulty thinking where they would be.

"No, no," I said. "Would you stay here? There's no point worrying Faith and Alice. Let's wait until we know more. Is that okay? I'll call you."

"I'm so sorry, James. Of course. Your shoes are downstairs. You always leave them downstairs. Let me help you."

The drive to the hospital was a blur. I was filled with emotions and thoughts of what I might find when I got there. All I knew was I should have visited more often. I should have been there. I hated the thought Dad might have been without family when it had happened again. Had Mum been with him?

I ran across the car park and in through the emergency doors. I took the stairs two at a time and reached the ward.

Nurse Gillespie was on the phone and waved me in. I tried to read her face to understand the situation.

The ward seemed too calm and too quiet. This wasn't what I was expecting. I wasn't sure what I was expecting, but it wasn't calmness.

I started to conclude Dad must be okay. Perhaps it was a false alarm. If he'd suffered another heart attack, he was in a hospital and in the safest hands.

Perhaps I'd built the whole emergency up in my mind to be more than it was. I suddenly felt sure he was okay. He was probably sitting up in bed with a big smile on his face, joking with the nurses and apologising for being a troublesome patient.

I walked over to Nurse Gillespie's desk as she began to hang up the phone. As I approached, Mum came around the corner.

I smiled at her as I looked for reassurance that everything was okay.

She looked up at me and burst into tears. She threw out her arms and held onto me. "He's gone, Jamie. I'm sorry. Your dad has gone."

This must be a nightmare, and I have to wake up.

I wanted to break away from her hold on me. I didn't believe her. I needed to see Dad. But Mum was hugging me so tight I was unwilling to leave her. I stayed and held her. She needed me now, and I needed her.

This wasn't how it was supposed to be. Dad was meant to have had a routine operation and be coming home. *This can't be happening.*

I sat with Mum for a time, and we talked about Dad and how strong he was. We convinced ourselves that if he'd had to go, it was better this way than after some drawn-out and lengthy illness. I guess it was a way to make ourselves feel better when, in truth, all we could feel was the injustice of him being taken away so soon.

After a couple of hours talking with nurses and doctors, then summoning the courage to leave, Mum and I were ready to go home.

I drove Mum back to her empty house.

"Are you sure you don't want to stay with us? I think it would be better if you were with us right now."

She squeezed my hand. "Thank you, Jamie. I have things to do. You have your family, and they need you. Just now, I need my own space. You understand?"

"I'll see you in the morning," I said. "I'll come over first thing."

"Okay. Night, night."

I watched Mum walk up the path to her front door and enter the house they had shared. Never again would she hear Dad's voice call her and ask how she was. Where she'd been and if she was okay.

I waited until she turned and waved and switched on the house lights. I drove away with tears streaming down my face.

CHAPTER SIXTY

Lyle opened the fridge and felt the rush of cold air on her legs. After examining each shelf, she took out a punnet of strawberries. She ran them under the kitchen tap as she gazed out the kitchen window. She turned off the water and then, carrying the punnet with her, began to stroll through the house. Occasionally she popped a strawberry into her mouth.

The house, with all its unique smells, looked and felt homely. Lyle looked at the children's drawings and paintings and certificates that plastered one wall of the kitchen.

Walking from room to room, she felt at home and at ease. There was something about the place that made it feel how she imagined a family home should.

In the hallway sat a hairy, partly chewed dog's bed. There was no dog in it. Lyle had made sure the house was empty of people and animals. In fact, she'd sat for several hours waiting for everyone to leave.

The daughters were at school. Monica and the dog

were visiting the grieving mother again. Hardy was out looking for clues that didn't exist.

Lyle stepped past the dog's bed and went into the sitting room. On the coffee table were children's colouring books and an iPad. A doll's house sat on a low table beside the television, along with a pushchair that was crammed full of dolls. Lyle straightened a long-legged doll.

She went over to the fireplace and looked at the photos. Smiling faces of children, grandparents and Mum and Dad. She picked up a photo of the two girls and removed the picture from its frame. She tucked it into the back pocket of her jeans and popped another large strawberry into her mouth.

Lyle made her way upstairs, finishing off the last few strawberries as she went.

Peering into each of the rooms, she decided to go into Faith's room first. The room was light and airy, and the walls were painted a very pale pink. There were fairy lights along one wall and around a large mirror. The lampshade hanging from the ceiling in the middle of the room was multicoloured glass, and the bedspread and pillow were fairy themed. Lyle picked up the pillow and hugged it.

A small white desk caught her eye. She read through the homework, writing and drawings. Picking up a brightly coloured pen, she drew a heart on the corner of one of the pictures.

She picked up a little glass jar filled with a mixture of sweets, the sort that used to cost a penny. She gave it a shake to see all the different varieties.

Alice's room was decorated more maturely; it was undoubtedly a young girl's room, but certain things, like an alarm clock, the floral bedding and curtains – not fairy themed like Faith's – and the creamy-white walls, made it feel more grown up.

A few teddies and dolls at the end of the bed hinted that this was still a child's room, although they appeared more ornamental than used as toys.

Monica and Hardy's bedroom had very little in it. It looked as though it were being prepared for decorating. There were no carpets, and clothes were packed in boxes. There were no wardrobes. Besides the bedside table, with an alarm clock and the cable from a phone charger, there was a dining chair that had been brought up from downstairs. Lyle was a little disappointed there was no chest of drawers to go through or wardrobe to peer into.

She stuck her head into the bathroom, stepped in and ran her hand along the edge of the bath. She squeezed a green rubber bath toy and laughed out loud as it croaked. She smelled the soap, shampoo, body lotion and moisturisers.

Next, she opened a tall floor-standing cabinet and went through the shelves one by one.

Back downstairs in the sitting room, she went to a row of family photographs. Picking them up one by one, she studied them. At the end of the collection stood a school photograph of the two girls standing side by side in their school uniforms, Alice with her hair plaited and Faith with her ponytail slightly askew. *Such pretty girls,* Lyle said to herself. *Happy, pretty girls.*

Lyle folded the photograph, still in its cardboard photo frame, and slid it into an inside pocket of her jacket. *Okay, girls. You can come with me.*

She heard the sound of a car pulling into the driveaway, followed by the sound of car doors slamming and children's voices. Monica and the girls were home from school already.

As Monica opened the front door, allowing the children

and dog to rush noisily into the house, Lyle slipped out through the back.

CHAPTER SIXTY-ONE

Emma was back at the prison for the second time in a month. This time, she was visiting the man Hardy and his partner Rayner had been pursuing at the time of Helena's death.

On her arrival, Governor Trent had not mentioned the death of Tony Horn. Instead, it hung in the air unspoken, as if neither one of them felt any inclination to discuss it.

"You could say I was a little surprised to hear you were coming back so soon. And to see one of my star prisoners this time. You must have friends in high places to get a visitation with Edward Richter so quickly."

Emma was puzzled by the governor's tone. "Well, I don't know about that. I just put in a request through normal channels."

"Really? It doesn't matter now, though, does it? You're here."

There were a few moments of silence as the governor read through the visitation request. Emma felt sure he would have already done so.

"Edward Richter, real name is Edward Fischer, is a

special prisoner. You will not be in the same room as him. He will remain in his cell for the entire interview. Is that going to be a problem?"

"No, no problem at all."

Trent sat back in his chair and played with his tie. He patted it and stroked it flat. He deliberately let his eyes wander over her as he said, "He's kept apart from other prisoners. It's better that way."

"For his safety. I understand." She could have kicked herself for making an assumption.

Trent shook his head. "For their safety. I deemed it necessary to put Richter in solitary confinement after he killed three fellow inmates within his first week of being here. When asked why he killed them, he told me he was bored. I therefore deemed it necessary to remove him from the rest of the prison population. He's been in isolation ever since."

"I was informed that I would be allowed only one interview, and I wondered why that might be. It's likely I'll need to come back and ask Richter more questions. Is that going to be a problem?"

The governor's expression changed. He looked like he had a bad taste in his mouth.

"The powers that be, Detective Inspector Cotton, have decided that Richter should be moved. It would appear the facilities in another prison will more closely suit his particular needs. So, you see, I cannot make any assurances."

Emma wondered whether Richter's move was a result of Horn's death.

"When is he moving?" she asked.

"I don't have a date for the move yet."

"Do you know which prison he is being moved to?"

"Emma – I hope you don't mind me calling you

Emma. Security surrounding a prisoner move is critical and not something we broadcast." The governor rocked back and forth in his chair. "I'm sure you're keen to get today's visitation underway. Would you let me accompany you? As I've explained, Richter can be rather hostile at times. It might be a good idea if you are accompanied by somebody who understands his state of mind. I've spent a lot of time alongside men like him. There are ways that we can approach your questioning that will appeal to him and increase his willingness to cooperate."

"That is very kind of you," said Emma. "I think I'll be fine."

"Of course you will. Well, you know the drill. Stick to the questions that we have approved. Do not deviate. We will monitor the conversation at all times. If you deviate from the script you've provided, the interview ends. If his manner towards you becomes coercive, distasteful, inappropriate or threatening, the interview ends. If there is a prison emergency, the interview ends. If we decide the interview is over, the interview ends.

"Remember, for Richter, this interview is a privilege. He is kept in isolation twenty-three hours a day, seven days a week, three hundred and sixty-five days a year. Richter and prisoners like him are unpredictable. We don't know how he will behave towards you. Do you still wish to proceed?"

Emma nodded. "Yes." She cleared her throat and said more loudly, "Yes, I do. And I understand."

"Very well. Off you trot." He picked up his desk phone and began punching in a number. Then he decided he hadn't finished with her and added, "Inspector, I'm sorry about your fiancé. What happened must be quite painful for you."

"Thank you," said Emma.

"I would remind you, Inspector, never to give any of these prisoners, Richter in particular, personal information. Do not think for one second that you can appeal to his humanity. He can be quite charming, and that can be disarming. Never for one moment forget what he is."

"And what is that?"

"Why, a predatory animal, of course. He lacks compassion and will not think twice about using your female nature to his advantage. Under this roof, the feminine allure a woman might wield on the outside to advance her position will be twisted and used against her. Richter will smell your manipulation before you open your sweet little mouth. Tread carefully, Inspector."

The governor didn't wait for a response. He turned his back and continued with his phone call.

Emma stared at Trent for a moment before deciding she had nothing to say.

CHAPTER SIXTY-TWO

Richter sat on the edge of his bunk as Emma and Prison Officer Farley approached. By the time Emma was standing behind the red line, one metre from the cell door, Richter was on his feet and looking out at her in anticipation.

She looked down at her toes, which were just behind the line. She looked up to find Richter smiling broadly. The muscles in his tattooed arms flexed as he leaned against the bars of his cell.

Once introductions were over, he whistled and said, "Well, aren't you a sight for sore eyes. I'll be dreaming about you for nights on end, mm-hmm."

Over a speaker came the voice of a prison guard. "Any more of that, Richter, and the interview is over. You hear me?"

Richter shouted back, "Oh, come on, Officer Pearson, I'm just playing. Don't be such an old grump. Don't you know nothing about manners? I'm just paying the lady a compliment. You know what one of them is?"

Richter nodded his head towards the chair against the

wall behind Emma. "Why don't you take the weight off those pretty little legs of yours?"

Having considered how it would feel to have Richter standing over her, she said, "I'll stand, thank you."

"I would offer you tea and biscuits, but I'm all out at the moment," he quipped. He smiled and showed his nicotine-stained teeth. "Now, what brings a little darling like you to these palatial surroundings?"

"I've been told I'm wasting my time speaking to you, Mr Richter."

"Mr Richter? My bank manager used to call me Mr Richter, and I buried him in several shallow graves in a wood near Watford. If you don't call me Edward, or better still, Eddie, then we can't be friends, and I only have conversations with friends." He winked at her.

"Eddie, do you know a prisoner by the name of Tony Horn?"

"Straight to the point; I'm liking you." He shouted up the corridor, "I like her, Officer Pearson. She can move in." Turning back to Emma, he spoke in a hushed tone. "You know Officer Pearson's wife just left him. He's very sad. I do my best to cheer him up. I heard she had an affair with her Italian dentist. Do dentists have to abide by a code of ethics, like doctors? If they do, I reckon Officer Pearson could get that playboy dentist struck off. I mean, there's drilling your patients, and then there's *drilling your patients*."

Richter made a clicking sound out of the side of his mouth. "It won't bring his wife back. I mean, he's a dentist; he's going to be loaded. Nice house, nice car, nice holidays. She'd be stupid to walk away from all that.

"But getting one over on *il dentista di Casanova* would have to make Officer Pearson feel better. I reckon he'd appreciate me bringing my thoughts to his attention later. What do you think? I'm sorry, what were you saying?"

"Tony Horn. Do you know a prisoner by that name?"

"I heard what happened to Tony. God rest his soul. In a place like this, a death like his is an all-too-common occurrence. Tony had a big stupid mouth, you see. A big stupid mouth gets you trouble quicker than you can say 'I ain't said nothing.' So, someone shut him up. It happens. It had nothing to do with me. Look around. I'm not getting close to no one."

Emma paid close attention to Richter as she quickly moved on to the next question. "Do you know Kelly Lyle?"

Richter's expression didn't change. He pressed his face to the bars and said, "Should I?"

"It seems as though she knows you. I imagine your paths have crossed at some point." Emma was taking a gamble here. She had no idea whether Richter knew Lyle. All she knew was that Lyle had directed her towards Horn and Horn had steered her towards Richter.

Richter narrowed his eyes, clearly re-evaluating her. At length, he straightened his back and stepped away from the bars. She noted a curious and more respectful attitude as he said, "Is that right? And what makes you think that?"

She decided to use Horn's death to her advantage. "Tony Horn told me."

"Is that right? You're a smart woman. I can see that. Let me ask you a question: What made you want to become a detective? I'm sure you could have been anything you wanted – an accountant, doctor, dentist, teacher, or even a bloody lawyer. What made you want to be a detective? It's not the pay, and it's not the hours."

"Let's stick to the questions. Do you know Kelly Lyle?"

Richter paced back and forth like a caged tiger. "Was Daddy a policeman? Did you want to be like your brothers? What were you hoping being a detective would give you? Respect? Power? Were you powerless in some way as a child? Is that it, Detective Inspector Cotton? Why are you really here? Is there someone you're hoping to impress? Whose respect are you looking for now?"

"You're avoiding my question. Do you know Kelly Lyle?"

Richter looked down the corridor. "I'm calling Pearson. This meeting is over. If you're not willing to converse, Inspector, then you should leave. I'm finding you dull. You want to know about Lyle and me, then tell me about you. That's my price."

Richter turned his back and walked to end of his cell.

Emma picked up the chair, brought it closer to the bars and sat facing the cell. "When I was twelve years old, a classmate disappeared. She vanished while walking home from school. She used to cut across fields to get home. She did it every day, until one day she never arrived.

"There was a big search, with police and dogs and volunteers checking every inch of the area. I can still remember seeing the pictures on the news and wanting to be part of the search team.

"For a long time, it felt like everyone was holding their breath. As the days passed, I think there was an unspoken understanding she was dead.

"Eventually a body was found in a river just outside of town. My classmate had been tied up, raped and beaten to death.

"While other girls in my class were scared and crying, I was angry and full of questions and desperate to know who did it.

"A detective came to our school to talk to us all. He was accompanied by a woman, a female detective. She was smart and kind and was part of the team looking for the killer. I desperately wanted to be like her.

"I asked them how I could help. I asked questions, and

I told them I wanted to do something to help them catch the person who did it. They didn't laugh at me; they understood me. I answered all their questions about my classmate. They took the time to explain to me the kind of man that would commit the type of crime perpetrated against her. They told me the police force needed good detectives, and I should work hard and study hard."

Richter had returned to leaning on the bars of his cell. He listened intently, digesting every word. When Emma finished speaking, he asked, "Did they catch the man who murdered the girl?"

"It was so long ago I don't remember."

"You're lying. You were doing so well," said Richter.

"No. I don't think they ever did."

"You're lying. Why would you lie?" He turned his back on her. He walked the length of his cell then returned to face her. "You knew the man who did it."

CHAPTER SIXTY-THREE

Emma could feel her face burning. She felt the intensity of Richter's eyes scrutinising her. He was studying her like an entomologist studies a bug.

"It must have been someone you trusted. You felt betrayed. You realised it could quite easily have been you who he'd taken. It could have been your lifeless, ice-cold, naked body they pulled from the river.

"A teacher, father, brother, cousin, uncle, friend, neighbour."

Emma felt a tear swell in the corner of her eye. She brushed it away as she said, "You're very astute. It was a neighbour. A young man I had known my whole life. We had occasionally played games together when he was a boy. He lived just a few doors down from my house. He was eighteen years old, and because he had a slight facial disfigurement the local children teased him. It seems he decided he would make someone pay.

"There. You got your answer. That incident set me on the path that has led me here. Now it's your turn."

Richter took off his shirt. He was lean and muscular,

and tattoos covered his arms and most of his torso. He stood close to the bars. "You see this here?" He pointed to a burning heart in the centre of his chest. "I see this every day. I put it there as a constant reminder of Lyle's hatred for me. She and I go way back."

"Does she hate you enough to want you dead?"

Richter laughed uncontrollably. After a few moments, he regained his composure and said, "Only if I die a slow and painful death.

"Lyle is super rich. More money than she'll ever need. I had this bright idea of breaking into her home and taking a share for myself. My first mistake was not doing my homework and finding out who she really was.

"Anyway, I recruited a couple of lads. They weren't too sharp, but I trusted them, and I knew they'd do as they were told.

"My idea was we'd break in, tie her up, threaten her a bit and see what we could get out of her. She was bound to have a safe full of cash and jewels. Simple.

"Trouble was, and mistake number two, I hadn't really planned it much beyond that.

"We broke in at night and made our way upstairs. We found her alone in bed and fast asleep. We grabbed her, tied her to a chair and threatened her. We did all we could to scare the life out of her. All the while we demanded she tell us where the money, jewels and other valuables were. She didn't tell us a thing. No matter how much we beat her or threatened her. One of the lads beat her half to death, and she gave us nothing.

"Mistake number three was when one of the punches snapped her neck. All we could do was ransack the house and take what we thought might be valuable. It didn't amount to much once it was split three ways.

"What we didn't know was the woman we killed didn't

know anything about the safe, money, jewels or the art on the walls. The woman we beat to death wasn't Kelly Lyle. It seems our Kelly likes the ladies as well as the men, if you know what I mean. Worse than that, Kelly was in love with the woman we'd killed. I mean properly in love. We couldn't have fucked up worse if we'd tried."

"What happened?" asked Emma.

"She came after us with all the vengeance of the devil herself. She killed the two lads easily enough; took them apart piece by piece. Somehow, I managed to stay one step ahead. That is, until I wound up here. I'm thinking it's only a matter of time until she pays someone enough to cut my throat in the middle of the night." His voice dropped to a whisper. "That's the real reason I got myself out of the general population. I'm safer in isolation."

"Why do you think Lyle hasn't got to you yet?"

"That's a good question. I suppose she knows I can't go anywhere, and she's a patient woman. She put me here. You know that, don't you?"

"Detective Chief Inspector James Hardy put you here."

Richter pressed his face to the bars and hissed, "He might have put the cuffs on me, but Lyle served me up to him. She couldn't get close to me because of his investigation. The next best thing was to have me arrested and put away until she was ready for me."

Unconvinced, Emma said, "You make it sound so simple."

"Well, it's worked out for the best. It's not bad in here. It's warm. I get fed. I have a routine. And to be honest, I got sick of constantly moving around, so it's nice to be settled. That probably sounds crazy to you. But, if you learn to accept your circumstances, your mind and body can adjust."

He pressed a finger to his temple. "What's in here can transport you anywhere. It sets you free. Close my eyes and I can recall the taste of beer. I can transport myself to a time when I would sit in my car, across the street so she didn't see me, and watch my daughter walk to school. And if I try really hard, I can picture the little things, the everyday things you take for granted. The sound of a cutlery drawer, the ping of a microwave, a pizza delivery, the smell of cut grass, the sound of a motorbike or roadworks or a bus or a train or a supermarket announcement calling for assistance in aisle three. Switching on the telly. The smell of a woman and the feel of her soft body beneath me."

Emma looked around as the guard approached. A voice from behind her announced, "That's it, Richter. Time's up. Time to go, Inspector."

Richter began speaking rapidly, and Emma stepped close to the bars to hear what he was saying. She could smell him now. His breath, his body odour.

The guard's voice came over the speaker. "Step away from the bars, Inspector. For your own safety, step away."

"How is Detective James Hardy? You know Lyle is obsessed with him. You know that, don't you? That isn't a healthy position for anyone. He needs to watch out. How are his children? Two girls, right? Alison and Faith? Are they growing fast?"

"You know I can't answer that," said Emma. Where was Richter going with this?

Two prison officers came running. She could see Richter had more to say.

He spoke rapidly. "Hardy thinks he got a lucky break stopping me. He's wrong. Lyle planned all of this. Be quick. Ask the right question."

"How do we catch Kelly Lyle?"

"Wrong question. A better question is, 'What will Lyle do next?'"

A prison officer motioned with his baton for Emma to step away from the bars. She moved back, and the prison officer stepped between her and Richter.

Richter began shouting as Emma was led away. She turned, sidestepped the officer and ran back to stand in front of the bars.

He reached out and grabbed her. Pulling her to the bars, he whispered in her ear, "Lyle will want his progeny."

"Progeny?"

"If I really wanted to hurt him, I mean really hurt him, it's what I would do. It's what Lyle will do. Lyle thinks in terms of power and leverage. If she wants leverage over Hardy, then there is nothing he cares more about than his children. She will go after his daughters."

He let go of Emma and moved to the middle of his cell with his arms up in the air.

Fear surged through her body. She turned to the prison officer. "I need to get to a phone. I need to make a call, now. Get me out of here."

Richter was yelling from his cell as Emma ran.

No one was moving fast enough. She needed to get out. She needed to speak to Hardy.

Richter's voice echoed down the corridor after her. "Tell Hardy to watch over his kids. Tell him I'll see him soon. I'll be getting out one day. And when I do, I'll be going to pay him a visit. A visit he'll never forget."

CHAPTER SIXTY-FOUR

I arrived home and was greeted by Faith as she came running up to give me one of her super-squeezy hugs.

"Daddy, you're back. I missed you."

I picked her up and swung her around. "I missed you more."

"I missed you more," insisted Faith, and she filled me in on the day's events without pausing for breath. "Nana Hardy was here, but she's gone home now. Alice is still at a sleepover with her new friend. Monica said I can have my favourite tuna pasta for dinner and stay up late. Sandy dug up some more daffodil bulbs, and she chewed my Barbie's leg. Monica and I are in the garden – come and see. I've been painting her toenails, and she did my fingernails." Faith held up her hands and showed me her fingernails, which were bright pink with sparkles. "Can I do yours, Daddy?"

I couldn't help but laugh. "Your nails are beautiful, honey. Although I'm not so sure pink sparkly fingernails are a good idea for me. Maybe another time or a different colour. Let's go and see how Monica's toenails look."

Faith put her small hand in mine and took me through to the garden. Monica was in a garden recliner with her feet up on a chair. Beside her was an array of nail polishes and lipsticks.

Leaning over, I gave her a long, lingering kiss.

"Hello, stranger," she said. "You missed all the action, you know. We've had a busy day, haven't we, Faith?" She squeezed my hand. "How are you holding up?"

"I'm okay. I've missed you all." I wanted to stay upbeat, so I said, "Yes, Faith was just telling me all about it. It sounds like you've been having fun."

Monica looked radiant and happy. I could feel my body relaxing. Being home and around those I love was always good for my soul. I swooped in and gave Monica another kiss.

Faith's hands were on her hips, and she gave us both a look that said *No more mushy stuff.* She levered us apart and insisted I examine Monica's toenails. "That's enough kissing, Daddy. Look, I've done her toenails different colours. Each one is different."

Faith proudly lifted Monica's foot so I could see.

"I've been really pampered," said Monica with a smile.

I chuckled encouragingly. "They look wonderful. You know, now I've seen Monica's toenails, I'm not so sure I want to miss out. Maybe you should do mine. What do you think?"

I was about to ask whether there was any news on how Alice was getting on at her new friend's sleepover when there was a *knock-knock-knock* at the front door, followed by the doorbell ringing repeatedly. Monica looked at me quizzically.

"Who can that be?"

I opened the front door to a woman I'd never seen before. She looked pale and scared out of her wits. My first thought was that she was ill or had been in a traffic accident.

Monica pushed past me and looked behind the woman. "Janice, what is it?" she demanded, her voice full of concern. Then to my horror, she said, "Alice? Where's Alice?"

I wasn't sure what was going on, but I was catching up quickly. I knew Alice was at a sleepover and I guessed this was the mother of Alice's new school friend.

"Please tell me Alice is here," said Janice frantically. "My Chloe told me Alice went with a policewoman. The policewoman said she worked with Alice's father, so Alice went with her. Please tell me she's okay."

I felt the hairs on the back of my neck stand up. My whole body went cold. I took the woman by the arm and brought her into the house, where I sat her down. "My name is James Hardy. I'm Alice's father. Tell me exactly what happened. Where's your daughter?"

"Chloe is fine. She came home and told me what happened. They were at the sweet shop on the corner, near our house. It's only a hundred yards away. Chloe goes there all the time on her own. I can see the shop from my house; it's not far. They went together. It was a little treat for them to go and get sweets. Chloe came home alone. She said the policewoman was in uniform and wearing the hat and everything. She showed them her warrant card."

I looked at Monica, who was sitting in an armchair. Faith sat on her lap, staring at Janice and squeezing Monica. Her face was full of fear. Monica looked pale and was trembling.

"I need to speak to your daughter, immediately," I said to Janice. "I need to get a full description of the policewoman, in her own words. I need to know precisely what happened."

I hugged Faith and Monica and told them I'd be back soon. I assured them Alice would be okay and that this was some sort of mix-up. I prayed to God I was right.

I went with Janice to her house and met Chloe. She was the same age as Alice. She was a pretty girl who looked older than her years. She was a little taller than Alice, had dark hair and wore braces on her teeth. Her brown eyes were puffy from crying. Her hands were clenched as she dabbed her nose with a tissue.

Despite how I felt inside, I spoke softly and slowly. "Hello, Chloe. As you know, I'm Alice's dad. I am also a police detective."

Chloe nodded.

I said, "You're not in trouble, let me assure you. Nobody blames you. You did nothing wrong, okay?"

She smiled a little and nodded.

"How about you start at the beginning, Chloe? It would be helpful if you tell me exactly what happened. Tell me in your own words, carefully and slowly."

Chloe explained how they had finished buying their sweets in the little shop. When they came out, a policewoman was waiting for them.

"She seemed to know about Alice. She knew all about you, Monica and Faith as well. She knew about her grandad dying and everything. The policewoman said you were friends. She told Alice things that you had told her. How your house looks, what Alice's bedroom looks like and her toys and favourite colours, things like that, so we believed her."

Chloe started to sob. Between tears, she described the policewoman, then said, "Alice went with her because the policewoman told her it was what you wanted. Alice wanted to call you, but the policewoman insisted there wasn't time. You'd be cross, and she was putting everyone in danger if she didn't get in the police car straight away."

She finished her story and looked at her mother. Janice nodded, and Chloe put out a trembling hand to me. As she opened her fingers, I wanted to fall to my knees. I felt like my body had been cut in two by a terrifying bolt of lightning. I didn't want to believe what I was seeing. *No, not my Alice.*

Chloe's open hand revealed a Scrabble piece. The letter R.

"The policewoman gave me this. She told me that you would know what it meant and that I was to give it to nobody else but you."

I knew what it meant, and I didn't want to believe it. My precious little girl was in the hands of Kelly Lyle.

CHAPTER SIXTY-FIVE

The fake policewoman had brought Alice to a farmhouse, surrounded by fields and opposite a wood, where, she had told her, her dad, Monica and Faith were waiting for her. It was a lie. The woman had tricked her, and now Alice sat at a kitchen table in a cold, smelly and run-down farmhouse.

Alice stared at the woman sitting opposite her.

The woman watched her.

"My name is Alice Hardy, and if you know what's good for you you'll take me home right now."

The woman said nothing. She blinked her eyes and continued watching.

Alice repeated herself with more determination. "My daddy works at New Scotland Yard. Have you heard of the Metropolitan Police in London? He is one of their best detectives. He catches people that nobody else can. He will catch you. But it's not too late for you. Just take me home and we'll forget any of this ever happened, okay? Last chance."

The woman still said nothing. Alice found this frustrating. She didn't let it show.

She tried a different approach. "We used to live in London but recently moved to Dorset. It's really nice now, as I get to see my dad more often. Our house is close to the beach, and we play frisbee and catch with our dog, Sandy. My favourite colour is turquoise. I like watching musicals. I don't like cartoons much, though I do like Disney cartoons. What's your favourite colour?"

Silence.

"My new teacher's nice. Her name is Mrs Beecroft. My new school has its own swimming pool. I like swimming. Do you like swimming?"

Silence.

"My favourite food is spaghetti Bolognese. I don't drink fizzy drinks; only water. What's your favourite food?"

Silence. Then clapping, slow clapping.

"You're a very smart girl, Alice. Very smart. Trying to build rapport with your captor."

"Then why don't you let me go?" suggested Alice.

"You are going to be fine. I know who your daddy is and what he does – I mean, what he did. He retired from the Met, didn't he? You see, he and I are friends. We go way back. You could say we have a special relationship. A bond that ties us."

"Friends don't kidnap one another's children."

"It's complicated, Alice. Like all meaningful relationships. You are a very astute girl. You're too smart for me. I liked the way you tried to build rapport. Did Daddy teach you that? I bet he did. I know all about you, Monica, and your little sister, Faith. I know about your Nana Hardy and your Grandad Hardy. It's a shame about Grandad. I know about your daddy's old detective partner, Rayner. I know about Detective Inspector Cotton – you might have met her. She's eager to prove herself. You see, little Alice, not everyone matters. But it pays to know all you can about those people that do matter. When you understand that, nothing can surprise you. Do you see?"

Alice screwed up her face defiantly. "You think you know it all. My daddy will surprise you. Then you'll spend the rest of your life in prison. Just like all the others who thought they were clever. How does that sound?"

"My name is Kelly Lyle. Have you heard that name before?"

Alice rolled her shoulders. "I've heard Daddy talk about you. You're a bad person. That's all I know."

Lyle pressed the tips of her fingers together and said, "Whether someone is good or bad often depends on your point of view. Never mind all that. We're going to be here together for a little while, and your stay here will be more pleasant if you behave. I know you're a well-mannered young lady, so it shouldn't be difficult for you. I have a couple of rules. I like rules. I bet you do too. The first rule is that you mustn't try to escape. We're a long way from anywhere, so it's pointless and you might get hurt. If you try to escape, I'm going to have to confine you. Do you know what that means?"

Alice shrugged. "Yes."

"It means, Alice, that I'd be forced to do something you won't like. It means I might put you in a box and bury you underground. It means I might put you in a dark, cold, wet cellar full of spiders. It means perhaps chaining you up in a barn full of rats. It means I might hide you somewhere no one would ever find you. Do you get the picture?"

Alice could tell she meant every word. She'd never heard anyone speak with such hostility before. The gravity of her situation suddenly dawned on her. She was alone and vulnerable. Kelly Lyle could do whatever she wanted to her and there was nobody to stop her. She'd overheard her dad say she had killed people. Killed them in horrible ways. Fear welled up inside her, and her shoulders started shaking uncontrollably as she fought to hold back tears. Her bottom lip quivered as she nodded her head. "Yes," she said meekly.

"The second rule is that we treat each other with respect. I'll be honest with you if you will be honest with me. None of this is about you, and I don't need to hurt you. I *will* hurt you, don't get me wrong. But only if I have to. I see no reason we can't be friends. I'd like to get to know you, and I'd like to hear more about your favourite food and your favourite colours and what you enjoy doing. I'd like to hear about your family and the way you live. I'd also like to hear about your mummy who is in heaven. My mummy is in heaven too."

The last part was a lie, but she knew Alice would respond to it. "Let's have a bite to eat, and we can talk some more. And in a little while, we'll phone your daddy. How does that sound?"

Lyle handed Alice a tissue. Alice smiled weakly, nodded and sniffed. "Yes, I'd like to speak to Daddy."

CHAPTER SIXTY-SIX

For a long time, I found it impossible to think. Emma had called me too late. Richter's prediction that Lyle would strike a blow by going after those I loved most had come chillingly true.

It was painful to think of my little Alice crying and calling out for help. She expected me to come to save her, but I didn't know where to start. I was consumed by fear. I was struggling to move beyond the terrifying possibilities of what might come next. I took myself away from everyone around me and retreated to my office. It had never been more critical that my next move be the right one.

I bolted upright as my mobile phone started to ring. "Hello? Alice? Who is this?"

I heard a woman's voice. A woman I knew had to be Kelly Lyle. To my relief, her words confirmed Alice was still alive. "Say hello to Daddy."

Alice sounded scared but strong. "Daddy, where are you? Kelly Lyle took me. I'm sorry; I thought she was a real policewoman."

"Alice, don't be sorry. This isn't your fault. I'm coming to get you, I promise. I promise with all my heart."

Lyle took over the call. "Hello, James. I thought you'd like to speak to your daughter. I think that's very generous of me. She's a spirited young woman, I'll give her that."

"If you harm her, I swear to God I will devote the rest of my life to—"

"She's absolutely fine, James. I haven't laid a finger on her. I have no intention of doing so. Unless it's necessary.

"It's time to up the ante. You and I are heading towards a climax, and so naturally things are intense. Once you see the big picture, you'll thank me. All this time you've done everything except see what's right in front of your eyes. I've left you all the pieces of the puzzle, and now it's time you put those pieces together to reveal what this has all been for. I've given you the name, and now it's time you understand why."

I could hear Alice crying in the background, and it was tearing me apart. "Give me my daughter back, and I'll do whatever you want. Whatever it takes."

"I know. Poetic, isn't it? Intense love and intense hate can be incredible motivators. They cause us to do things we might otherwise avoid.

"I am sorry to hear of your dad's passing. When we are young, a father figure can have a positive or negative influence on our upbringing. But James, right now, mother is key. Mother *is* the key. Do you understand?"

"No more games. Give my daughter back. Harming a child isn't your style. We both know that."

Lyle sighed heavily. "Times change. For now, Alice and I are going to have some fun. We're going to have some girl time. I've always wanted a daughter, so I must cherish these precious moments. You and I will talk again very soon, hopefully face to face. In the meantime, you must go and see Mother."

The call ended, and I found myself standing behind my desk staring at the phone in my hand.

Tormented beyond reason, I roared, grabbed my desk and launched it across the room. It crashed against two filing cabinets. Everything on the desk scattered across the room. I was losing my mind. I sank to my knees and screamed at heaven. I furiously yelled at God and then asked for his help in bringing my baby home safely.

I don't know how long I remained on my knees. My head was spinning, and my heart was pounding. It could have been five minutes; it could have been two hours. I crawled across the floor and picked up a smashed photo frame. I opened the back of the frame and took out the picture of Helena.

I looked at her and said, "Our baby's gone. She's got our baby."

As I talked to Helena about all the mistakes I'd made, Lyle's words forced their way into my head. "Mother is the key."

I kissed the picture of Helena and got to my feet. I unlocked the office door and began running to my car.

With Faith in her arms, Monica came chasing after me. I turned and held them in my arms.

I said, "I know what to do. I'm going to get Alice back, I promise." We held onto each other, and none of us wanted to let go. Finally, I tore myself away. "I had better go," I said, my voice breaking. "When you see me next, it'll be with Alice. You have my word." I kissed them one last time and ran to the car.

As I started the car my phone rang. It was my old Met partner, Inspector Rayner.

"James, I'm sorry. I just heard from DI Cotton. Just tell me what you need me to do."

The sound of his voice and knowing he had my back filled me with confidence. I told him what I had in mind.

"Lyle always chooses her words carefully. When she spoke, she said 'Mother is the key.' I don't think she was talking about my mother; it's more likely she was talking about her own mother. She was trying to tell me something.

"I need you to find out what business interests Kelly Lyle has around Dorset and Hampshire—in fact, anywhere on the south coast. My guess is her mother is close by. I need the address. I need it now. Once you have it, send it to Emma and to me."

"Leave it with me. I'm on it."

"Thanks, buddy. It's bloody good to hear your voice."

"We're going to get Alice back. I'll be in touch as soon as I have something."

I called Emma and gave her the same information. She told me she recalled one of Kelly Lyle's investment companies owned a string of residential care homes that stretched from the south coast to the Midlands.

"That's got to be a good place to start. I'll get the team calling them straight away," she said. "I'll check to see if any of the care homes has a resident under the name of either Lyle or her mother's maiden name, Allerton. We'll start with homes closest to your location and work our way up the country."

Sixty minutes later I was driving up the A31 dual carriageway towards the New Forest at over one hundred miles an hour. Emma had struck gold and found a resident whose surname was Allerton at a care home near there. While she ran a background check and tried to confirm it was Lyle's mother, I decided to take a chance and head towards the home. If it was her, I didn't want to waste a second.

Ignoring the speed limit, I pressed down on the accelerator and leaned heavily on the car's horn to get me through traffic as quickly as possible. I checked my phone repeatedly until Emma's text message arrived with the address. I punched it into the satnav and pressed my foot down harder still on the accelerator.

"I'm coming for you, Alice. I'm coming for you, sweetheart."

CHAPTER SIXTY-SEVEN

Alice felt Lyle's cold hand on her neck. Lyle reached around her with a long, thin key and unlocked the door. She pushed it open to reveal a small bedroom. Alice stepped inside and looked around. The room felt cold and smelled damp.

A large rectangle of chipboard covered the window. The only light came from a small lamp beside the bed. On the floor next to the lamp was a large bottle of water and next to that a bucket.

She turned and looked at Lyle.

"The bucket's in case you need to pee or do a number two. Make yourself comfortable. I'll bring you magazines and some books. And remember, don't do anything stupid. This door will be locked. Knock on it if you need anything. Why don't you try to get some sleep? You must be tired."

"It's cold," said Alice.

Lyle ignored that. "I know you're a clever girl, so I'm going to trust you. If you try to escape or become a nuisance, then I will make things very uncomfortable for you. For your own sake, I'd suggest you settle down, and this will be over soon."

Alice nodded. "Please, just take me home."

Lyle shut the door, and Alice listened as it was locked.

She wiped away her tears and rubbed her runny nose on her sleeve. She lay back on the bed and pulled the blanket over her. Somehow, she managed to sleep.

A noise woke her. At first, she was too scared to move. She heard the noise again. She walked across the room and listened at the door. It was the sound of Lyle talking on the phone. She was laughing and sounded happy.

Alice stepped closer and pressed her ear to the door. The floor creaked. Lyle stopped talking.

She heard Lyle's footsteps approaching the door. She tiptoed back to the bed and pulled the blanket over her head. She closed her eyes and pretended to sleep.

The key clunked and clicked in the lock and the door opened.

Alice held her breath. Lyle's footsteps crossed the room and came close, then stopped by the bed. She kept her eyes tight shut. She could hear Lyle breathing. She felt a finger prodding her. Alice made a small, sleepy sound.

The footsteps crossed the room back to the door. She heard the door clicking as it was locked and Lyle's footsteps moving away.

Alice sat up. For a short time, she heard the mumbled sound of Lyle continuing her conversation. Then there were footsteps outside and the unmistakable sound of a car door opening and gently clunking shut. The car's engine started. She listened to the ground crunching as the vehicle moved. Alice didn't dare make a sound. A pipe rumbled somewhere in the house, then there was quiet. Not a sound. She was alone.

She walked to the door and knocked. She called out and knocked again. She listened. There was nothing but the sound of her uneven breathing.

It took Alice no more than thirty seconds to decide she would escape. It was what her dad would do, and she knew she was brave like him. He'd always said so.

She started checking, doing the obvious things. She tried the door to double-check that it was locked. She kicked and punched it and tugged at the handle. The door wouldn't budge.

She scanned the room for other ways out. She decided the next logical place to test was the window. She ran her fingers along the edge of the board that covered it. Four screws on each side held the board in place. If she could find something to undo the screws, maybe she could get out through the window. She looked about the room for something she could use as a screwdriver. It was useless; the room was empty aside from the bed, lamp, bucket and the water. She swallowed back tears; her dream of a glorious escape and triumphant return home was already over.

She sat on the floor and leaned against the wall with her knees pulled up under her chin. She felt stupid for thinking she could escape. Lyle would have thought of everything, of course. She also had no idea how long Lyle would be gone; it might only be five minutes. That wouldn't be enough time to break out and get across the field to the woods. Even if she did get to the woods, did she really want to be alone in there? What if she got lost or hurt? Would she be any safer out there?

"Don't be negative," Alice told herself firmly. She had to escape, and she had to remain positive. She pulled her feet a little closer. The room was cold. Like the walls and the bedding, her clothes felt damp.

A mouse squeezed under the corner of the door and, staying close to the wall, ran across the room. Reaching the far corner, it stopped and looked at her. Then, with a twitch of its nose, it turned right and continued until it disappeared behind the bed.

Alice wished she were a mouse; then she could squeeze through gaps and disappear down holes. If she were Harry Potter, she could turn herself into a mouse and find a hole to escape through. Alice got onto her stomach and peered under the bed; she was curious to know where the mouse had gone. She took the lamp and shone it under the bed. Where was the mouse?

Alice moved the bed out and could see where the mouse had made a hole in the wall. Crawling closer, she put a finger inside. With her fingernail, she picked at the wall and the floorboard. The floorboard was damp, and splinters of wood came away as she picked at it. She wondered what was under the floor. If she could get the floorboard up, maybe there was a chance to escape. Like the mouse, could she get out?

She pulled the lightweight metal bed frame away from the wall to get a closer look at the floorboards. As she did, one of the bed legs wobbled. The legs were thin metal tubes that slid into holes in the bed frame. Alice pulled the bed's mattress off onto the floor. With a lot of effort, she got the bed frame onto its side and leaned it against a wall away from the mouse hole. She then pulled at the wobbly leg; it wiggled but wouldn't budge. She tried another leg; this one didn't move at all.

She moved to the other end of the bed and tried a third leg. Holding onto the bed frame, she kicked at the leg, causing it to go off at a right angle; she kicked it repeatedly back and forth until eventually the leg came out and slid across the floor.

Grasping her makeshift tool, she began to chip away at the floor and wall. The wall was particularly damp in the corner where the mouse had vanished, and the wood of the floorboard was soft and rotten.

At first, the wood she pounded broke away easily, but it was less rotten in the centre of the floorboard. She worked along the edge, breaking away all she could. It was awkward work, and her hands and fingers soon became sore. After several minutes, unable to chip away at the floorboard any further, she used the bed leg as a lever to prize up the remaining floorboard. As it broke away, she dropped the wood down into the hole.

Alice moved on to the next floorboard. It soon became apparent she wouldn't be able to chip away much of the second floorboard. She would have to lever most of it up. This one was less damp and harder to break up, but the wood was soft around the rusted screws and reluctantly started to move. She put all her strength behind levering it up. She was becoming tired and tearful, and suddenly she fell backwards as the metal bed leg slipped from her hands.

Alice kicked out at it in frustration and then lay back, one arm across her eyes, trying not to cry.

Having taken a few minutes to gather her thoughts, she rolled onto her belly. Sticking her head down through the gap she had made, she looked under the floor.

The gap beneath the floor was big enough for her to crawl around. She pulled the lamp over to get a better look and shone the light around.

Her excitement quickly turned to disappointment; wherever she shone the light, she saw only the stone walls of the building. Exhausted, she got to her feet and walked to the far side of the room. She sat on the mattress and hugged her knees, her head resting on her arms as she looked at all her work. *What a waste of time. Not even Houdini could get out of this place.*

Alice thought of home. She missed Faith. She thought about Faith's birthday party and remembered her own magic trick, the disappearing coin trick. She sat up straight as she recalled how, with magic, it was not always about making the object disappear; rather, the trick was making the audience *believe* the object has disappeared.

She set to work making the hole as big as she could.

CHAPTER SIXTY-EIGHT

Sienna Lasota took back her passport. She watched as Lyle pulled suitcases out of the bedroom and left them at the top of the stairs.

"We're going to need to leave," said Lyle. "It's a little sooner than I'd anticipated, but it's time to move on. If I'm not back by seven a.m., I need you to call a taxi and take your hand luggage. I want you to go ahead, just the way we discussed. I'll join you later. You remember what I told you about these suitcases? We might need to move fast."

"I remember," said Sienna. She tried to recall all Lyle had told her.

"It's not too late to change your mind. If you want to stay here, I understand. It's not too late for you, yet."

"I want to be with you. I'll do it. Whatever you need, I can do."

"Everything is going to be fine. We'll start again like royalty."

Sienna thought about the life she was leaving behind. She thought about her parents and their bickering. She thought about her mum, who had worked at the same job for over thirty years. Her father, who scraped by doing odd jobs, never seeming to get ahead, always getting knocked back whenever he made a bit of progress. An honest, hardworking, decent man with the cards of life stacked against him.

She thought about her career as a high-end property agent. She knew from the way her boss looked at her that she'd only got the job because of how good her arse looked in a tight black skirt. It had had nothing to do with her enthusiasm, qualifications or ambition.

Her parents had been delighted about the job; they'd told her what high hopes they had for her. She had to admit, she'd been happy, too – for a while.

The trouble was, seeing people with so much money could quickly make you feel in want of more. Did she want to spend the next few years showing rich people around luxury homes? Or did she want to be one of those rich people?

Then Kelly Lyle had come along and changed her life. Kelly made her feel desired, alive, excited, important and able to be whatever she wanted to be. There were no limits with Kelly, none, and she liked it. There was no way on earth she was giving that up.

Kelly was complicated; there was a lot Sienna didn't understand about her. It didn't matter. She hoped they'd have years together. Plenty of time to find out all she wanted to know.

For now, she knew all she needed to: Kelly wanted her and nobody else. Kelly's work was important to her, and she was financially successful.

She loved being with Kelly, and Kelly reciprocated that love. She was sensitive, generous, caring and fiercely protective. They were good together.

"Good luck," said Sienna. "Be careful. I love you."

Kelly looked at her oddly and said, "When you have a plan, you don't need luck. Thank you, anyway. Remember everything I told you and we'll both be fine." She kissed Sienna and hugged her and said, "Don't forget. No later than seven a.m. In fact, book a taxi just in case I don't get back in time."

Sienna stood at the front door and watched Kelly drive off into the night.

CHAPTER SIXTY-NINE

Alice lay perfectly still in the darkness. She had to be brave. She'd wriggled as far as she could under the floor. In complete darkness, she held up a couple of large pieces of floorboard in front of her. She prayed it would be enough to stop Lyle seeing her.

The floorboards were a few inches above her head. Her head was bruised and throbbing. She'd hit it twice on the joists as she moved about looking for a way out. Satisfied there was no way she could escape from under the floor, she now lay motionless and waited.

The air was smelly and the ground uncomfortable. Her back was freezing cold on the damp soil beneath her.

In the darkness, her ears found a new acuity, and she felt alert to every sound. Outside, she heard the car return, and her heart immediately began racing. This was it: she must stick to the plan.

Alice studied the sounds. It had become a game, and the prize was to escape. She heard the mechanical clunk of the car locking. The key at the front door, the door opening and closing, a cupboard door slamming, keys dropped on a table, the tap running, footsteps towards her room.

She held her breath. She pictured the long, thin key. *Click-click, click.* The door unlocked. She squeezed her eyes shut and held her breath. Footsteps and movement. She heard Lyle's angry voice. She was moving quickly now. Thuds and banging. Mattress tossed aside. Alice jumped as the bed scraped across the floor to reveal the hole in the floorboards.

She'll find me. She'll hurt me. This plan was stupid.

She didn't dare look. She lay perfectly still, hidden behind pieces of floorboard. She could hear Lyle's heavy breathing. She was close. She was looking under the floor. *It's over*, she thought. *She must see me. She'll realise I'm hiding.* She froze, waiting for Lyle's hand to grab her.

She heard Lyle get to her feet. The sound of fast-moving footsteps as Lyle ran from the room. Hearing her outside the house once more, Alice dared to turn her head.

She didn't see me. It worked.

She moved as quickly as she could. She inched her body through the tight space then rolled onto her back. First putting her arms up through the hole, she pulled herself back into the room. Brushing herself off, she stood and listened.

She walked to the door, which was now open, and looked out. There was no sign of Lyle. She moved quickly and quietly towards the farmhouse's front door. It was within touching distance. She could feel her freedom.

It was night time; her eyes needed to adjust to the darkness. She peered around the doorframe. Now she could see a car. Next to it, looking in all directions, was Kelly Lyle. Alice yanked her head back inside the house and stood still, holding her breath.

She had planned to run towards the woods, which were

straight ahead, then reach the road Lyle had driven along, where someone, she hoped, would help her. But Lyle was blocking her way. She decided instead to go to the side of the farmhouse and move around behind it. Side-stepping carefully out of the front door, she began to inch along the wall, keeping her eyes on Lyle.

Her movement somehow attracted Lyle's attention. Alice froze in horror as Lyle turned and looked directly at her.

"Alice, don't do this. Don't run. I am not going to hurt you," Lyle called to her.

Alice turned on her heels and sprinted towards the back of the building. She knew she would be faster than Lyle. At school, she was always one of the fastest runners.

Knowing Lyle was behind her, following, she decided to circle the building and keep to her original idea of heading into the woods. She could easily outrun a grown-up. She pounded across the hard gravel to reach the grass; she was still wearing her sandals, and they hurt her feet. It didn't matter; she had to keep moving. She had to run as fast as hard as she could. She didn't look back; she focused on the tree line, which she could dimly make out from the light of the moon.

At the edge of the field, she almost ran headlong into a barbed-wire fence she hadn't seen before. It was made up of five single strands of barbed wire between wooden posts several feet apart. *Under, over, or through?* Panting, she quickly assessed the possibilities. Going over was out of the question: too high. The bottom wire was too low; she'd be snagged. Her only choice was to squeeze through. She looked behind her. Lyle was closing in on her fast.

Alice lifted a leg to poke between the barbed wires and immediately drew it back: the wires were too close together. She'd never get through. Her heart began to pound in her chest. She looked left and right along the fence. To her left, two posts along, the space between the bottom wire and the grass widened slightly. The ground had fallen away close to the fence post, leaving a gap she might be able to squeeze through. Beyond the fence, she could see that the ground sloped down towards the wood. Decision made.

She moved quickly to remove her jacket. She rolled it into a ball, got down on the ground and lay flat next to the post. Using her rolled-up jacket to push the wire up, she turned her face to the side and squeezed head first through the gap. She let go of the jacket, wriggled and rolled – and yelped in pain. In her rush to get under the fence, she'd snagged her foot on the barbed wire.

Lyle was only a few metres away now, her face a mask of rage and frustration. Alice got to her knees and tugged frantically at her jacket; she pulled again and heard it tear. Not wanting to lose her advantage, she abandoned the jacket, leapt to her feet and headed down the bank and into the woods. She'd made it.

CHAPTER SEVENTY

Alice wanted to keep moving, but with so little light in the woods, it was almost impossible to see where she was going. The tree canopy blocked most of the available moonlight and the deeper into the wood she got, the less she could see. Soon she wouldn't be able to see her hand in front of her face, and each step had become treacherous. Her foot was throbbing from catching it on the barbed wire, and she realised she was limping. She needed to be careful; a fall or twisted ankle would be bad news. She decided to find somewhere to hide for the night.

For a while she'd heard Lyle calling her, insisting she come back; she was worried for her safety. That had stopped, and she hoped Lyle would give up and leave her alone.

Alice came to a small clearing where a large tree had fallen and the ground was thick with bracken. She waded into the bracken until she felt well hidden. The bracken was tall, some of it taller than her, and as she lay down, it enveloped her. Looking up, she could no longer see the moon or stars, only the tips of the tall plants.

Shivering, she curled up on her side and wrapped her arms around herself. She wished she hadn't left her coat. Feeling miserable, cold and hungry, she tugged at the bracken and tried to cover herself as best she could to keep warm. She winced as she touched the cut on her foot. She could see it had stopped bleeding; that was something, at least.

She thought about home and wished she were in her bed. Too exhausted to cry, she closed her eyes and fell asleep.

When Alice awoke, it was light. It took her a second or two to recall where she was and what was happening. She was icy cold and, at first, found it difficult to move. As quietly as she could, she got to her hands and knees and crawled towards the edge of the thick green bracken.

She smiled; she was pleased with herself. Her dad would be proud. She'd escaped her captor and now just needed to find a way to home or let them know she was safe.

As she emerged from the bracken, she almost bumped into a pony and her foal. The pony's big doe-like eyes looked at her with disinterest, while the foal skip-trotted to the safety of its mother's side.

"Good morning," she said. "Do you know the way out of here?"

Alice noticed the ponies were on a well-worn path, a path probably made by centuries of ponies and cattle moving that way. It made sense to follow the path and hope it came to a road or house, somewhere she could raise the alarm.

After what felt like an hour of walking, she came to a stream. The water looked crystal clear, and she stepped down into it. The cold water on her sore feet felt good. She scooped at the water and drank.

She looked around and wondered which way to go next. The bank on the far side of the stream was muddy, and she could see hoof prints where ponies and cattle had passed that way. She decided that following the ponies had got her this far and it made sense to continue along their path.

As she negotiated the muddy bank, a noise caught her attention. She stopped moving and held her breath. There it was again: the sound of a car. Her heart began to thump with excitement. A car meant people and safety and a way to get home.

Quickening her pace, Alice ran in the direction she'd heard the car. After a few false turns, overgrown paths and dead ends, she reached the road. The sight of it filled her with joy.

She stood on the edge of the tarmac, waiting and listening and looking up and down the road. But after what felt like thirty minutes with no traffic passing, she decided she needed to keep moving. After all, this was a country road and the car she'd heard might be the only car passing this way all day.

It felt natural to go right. Alice stepped out onto the tarmac and began walking. She stepped quickly at first, trying to keep herself warm, then slowed to a comfortable rhythm. After the uneven, muddy paths, the tarmac felt good and solid, and walking was far more comfortable on her scratched and muddy sandalled feet.

After walking what felt like miles, she began to wonder if she should have gone the other way. She'd seen nothing, not even a pony. She stopped at a bridge and stepped down the bank to get some water from the stream. As she got back up on the road, she caught sight of movement far off in the distance at what seemed to be a crossroads. Squinting her eyes, she saw shapes that looked like people.

Yes, they were people: they had bikes. As she stared longer, their shapes fell into place and made sense. They were cyclists, two of them, wearing those brightly coloured, skin-tight clothes that cyclists wear. They were standing with their bikes, leaning against them.

Alice began to run towards them, waving and calling out.

"Hello, help! I need help! Can you hear me? Please help me."

She was too far away. She doubled her pace and waved and called. Her mind was screaming, "Please look up, please look this way. You've got to help me."

As she ran and waved and screamed at the cyclists, a new noise grabbed her attention. She looked over her shoulder. A car was approaching. A terrified murmur escaped her mouth.

Alice began running faster and faster and faster. She knew she had to run like never before. She had to get to the safety of the cyclists and away from the car. And away from Kelly Lyle.

CHAPTER SEVENTY-ONE

Alice could see the cyclists' faces now: a man and a woman who looked about the same age as Nana Hardy. She felt sure they'd have a phone and would let her use it to call Daddy.

Panting, almost sobbing, she looked back and saw that Lyle's car had slowed to a crawl behind her. Lyle was watching her through the windscreen, smiling to herself.

She hoped that if she could get close enough to the friendly cyclists Lyle would leave her alone.

Finally, the cyclists looked up, smiled, and waved back at Alice. Their smiles changed to looks of concern as they realised the young girl running towards them was in distress. They stopped reading their maps and watched her.

The sound of Lyle's car behind her grew louder as it picked up speed.

She was crying now as she ran, tears almost blinding her. Her side was hurting, her cut foot throbbed, her legs ached, but she pushed herself harder, forcing one leg in front of the other. She could hear the car getting closer; it was right behind her. She wasn't going make it; she wouldn't get there in time. The friendly couple were too far away. Alice didn't feel fast anymore. She felt slow, heavy and clumsy. "Please help me," she called. Her voice sounded high and strange in her ears.

Still running flat-out, she looked over her shoulder again. Lyle's car was only inches away from her. Her breath burst from her chest in a guttural sob of anguish and frustration.

Then, to her surprise, the car moved out from behind her and came alongside. Lyle looked at her then looked straight ahead at the friendly couple.

The car began to roar as it accelerated.

Alice watched in horror as it hurtled towards the couple, then suddenly veered off the road and ploughed straight into them.

She was rooted to the spot as she saw the man smashed aside and the woman crushed beneath the wheels of the car. She watched, terrified, as Lyle drove the car back and forth over the helpless couple. Her knees buckled, and she collapsed in shock.

Lyle reversed the car back up the road until it was alongside her. She got out and walked around the car and lifted the sobbing girl like a sack of mail. She carried her to the car, yanked open the rear passenger door and placed her on the back seat.

"They died because of you," said Lyle, leaning over her. "You caused that."

Alice closed her eyes and pictured the bloodied and broken bodies at the side of the road. She began to shake uncontrollably, and her breathing became rapid and out of control. She thought she might be sick.

Lyle stroked Alice's hair and said, "Slow your breathing. You're safe now. I told you you'd be safe with me. I don't know why you ran away. All you've done is waste our time together. You know this means I have to punish you, don't you?"

Alice stared helplessly into space and paid no attention as Lyle popped a tablet in her mouth and asked her to swallow it. She handed Alice a bottle of water.

"Drink this water. The tablet will calm you down. Just relax. You are going to want to get some rest. Why don't you get some sleep?"

Her limbs felt heavy as her body sank into the car seat. She didn't want to give up, but she'd done her best, and it wasn't good enough. What else could she do? Where was Daddy? Why had nobody come to rescue her? Would she ever see Monica or Faith again?

She closed her eyes and heard Lyle put the car into gear once more.

CHAPTER SEVENTY-TWO

The nursing home had once been an inn rumoured to have been frequented by highwayman Dick Turpin in 1736 while he evaded authorities.

Over the years the property had passed through many hands before being converted to a hotel in 1957. More recently, it had been renovated and converted to a premium residential care facility for the elderly. Currently, according to a sign, work was underway to allow an additional twenty-four rooms and a large conservatory. Also, the gardens were being tastefully landscaped, and an outdoor theatre added.

My car slid on the car park gravel as I came to a halt in one of the many parking spaces. I jumped out of the car and ran to reception.

"I'm here to see a resident called Mrs Allerton," I said.

"James Hardy?" replied the duty nurse. "I'm Nurse Holt. I've been expecting you. Follow me."

I followed her along several corridors to the spacious room belonging to Mrs Allerton.

Nurse Holt turned to me and spoke in a low voice.

"I'm not sure how much help she will be. Mrs Allerton has memory difficulties. I did explain this to your colleague on the phone."

I held open the door and said, "Would you mind waiting outside while I speak with Mrs Allerton? A young girl has gone missing, and there is a possibility she can help with the investigation."

"I'll be at my desk behind reception if I can be of any assistance."

I thanked her and closed the door, and Nurse Holt returned to her duties.

Mrs Allerton was seated in one of a pair of armchairs, a blanket over her knees. She watched me with intense curiosity. She pointed a crooked finger at me and said, "They tell everyone I've lost my mind, you know. I might be a little forgetful, I might even repeat myself occasionally, but I haven't lost my marbles. Not completely, as far as I know."

She smiled sweetly and gestured towards a chest of drawers. "I know why you're here, and we'll get to that, but before you sit down, be a dear and open that wash bag. The one on top of the chest of drawers there, next to my books."

I opened the wash bag and showed her a small bottle of brandy. "Is this what you're wanting, Mrs Allerton?"

She grinned and nodded. "Yes, yes. There is a glass and a cup by the sink; you can have the cup. It's been a long time since I've had a drinking partner. And call me Theresa."

I poured us both a stiff shot. Theresa giggled as she took her glass and raised it.

"Good health," she said. "You know, there's a black market in this place for booze. Prohibition always fails."

She sipped the brandy and watched me as I sipped

mine. Patting the seat beside her, she said, "Come and sit here. You look like you have the weight of the world on your shoulders."

I wanted quick answers, and I wasn't feeling patient in the slightest, but I decided the way to get what I needed was to listen to Theresa.

"Kelly was a beautiful baby," she began without prompting. "I couldn't have asked for an easier child. She was never any trouble. All Kelly ever wanted to do was please her father and me. She adored him. She would help him on the farm, and they'd spend hours together.

"Sadly, that all changed when his drinking started. For some reason, it got out of control. He was a good man before that. The drink made him paranoid, depressed and violent. Extremely violent. So much so that I feared for Kelly's safety and my own. I'd been thinking about it a long time, but one night – Kelly must have only been 11 years old at the time – I'd had enough. I waited until he was asleep and I lifted her out of her bed and attempted to leave with her.

"Unfortunately, I woke him when I started the car. He came after me with a shotgun. He fired a warning shot at the car, which caused me to swerve and stall the engine. I got it going again and reversed the car, but by the time I'd straightened up, he was in front of us pointing the shotgun at the windscreen. I can still picture the fury in his eyes. I know he would have killed us both."

Theresa took a long sip of brandy. "He dragged Kelly from the car and pointed the gun at me. He told me to leave and never come back. Leaving Kelly with him is the biggest regret of my life. I can never forgive myself for leaving my little girl with that monster. Kelly is who she is today because of me."

I hesitated before asking, "Do you think she killed her father?"

Theresa took a tissue from her cardigan sleeve and dabbed her nose. "She did what she had to. Don't you see? She was still a child when I abandoned her. I'm to blame for everything that followed, not her. Not my Kelly."

Theresa held out her glass, and I topped it up. I leaned forward and said, "Kelly has my daughter, my little girl. Can you tell me where she is?"

The old lady's eyes brimmed with tears. She reached down beside her chair and pulled out a plain envelope. With a trembling hand, she passed it to me. "Kelly asked me to give you this. She said you'd come."

I took the envelope and feared what I might find inside.

Theresa said, "I am sorry. I hope you find your little girl. I lost my Kelly, the real Kelly, a long, long time ago. I hate the thought of your child being separated from the ones she loves." She took my cup, poured the rest of my brandy into her glass and drank it down.

I got to my feet, put the bottle of brandy back in the wash bag, washed the cup and glass and left Theresa to her thoughts. She didn't look up as I left the room.

Alone in my car, I ripped open the envelope. Inside was the address of Long Meadow Farm. I punched it into the satnav. With my heart pounding in my chest, I prepared myself for getting Alice back and the next stage of Lyle's game.

CHAPTER SEVENTY-THREE

Alice opened her eyes and could see nothing. She was in complete darkness. Her mind was confused. She knew she was no longer in the farmhouse. She could smell the water before she felt it. Terror took over as she tried to understand her surroundings. She tried to scream for help but her tongue felt heavy in her mouth. She splashed awkwardly around and could feel walls all around her, a low ceiling of some sort over her head.

She attempted to move her legs; they felt numb and heavy. Her body felt awkward. She tried to straighten up but couldn't lift herself. After much effort, she shifted herself slightly, which caused her head to slump forward and her face to fall into the water.

Using all her concentration, she managed to lift her face out of the water and tilt her head back. She coughed and spluttered as she gasped for air.

She was scared to move again, but she needed to sit upright. Pushing her feet was useless as she was barely able to feel her legs. Her head began to spin and she felt sick. She was going to vomit.

Alice pressed her hands against the walls. Scratching them with her fingers, she realised they felt like hard plastic. She was in a container, a plastic prison that was filling with water. She tried to stay calm, but she could hear her heart pounding in her ears, almost as if it were outside her body. She took a shaky breath and tried with all her might to stand up, but nothing worked as it should. Her arms and legs felt like rubber. Her head spun queasily and, almost with relief, she shut her eyes.

Alice regained consciousness with her head pressed against the side of the container. For a moment she hoped it had all been a nightmare, that she would open her eyes and find herself back in her room. The smell of plastic and vomit filled her nostrils. *This nightmare is real.*

How long had she been like this? She must get out. Again, she tried to stand. She could move a little more now, but her body was still too heavy.

She tried to scream but once more managed only a faint whisper.

A slow but consistent flow of water was coming from over her head. With a start, she realised it was rising. Frantically, she tried again and again to lift her body higher in the water, aware that if she didn't get out, she would drown and no one would ever know.

After several minutes of unsuccessful effort, she sat still and tilted her chin up to keep her face out of the water.

Outside, she heard a noise. It was definitely a car.

Was it Lyle?

Alice remembered the friendly cyclists and what Lyle had done to them. She realised this watery prison was her punishment for trying to escape.

Swallowing back her tears, she told herself Lyle

wouldn't win. She had to believe it. Alice called out again, and this time her voice was stronger. She yelled over and over until her head began spinning again.

She remembered the tablet Lyle had given her and realised this was why she felt weird. Nodding to herself, she slowed her breathing and focused on getting her emotions under control. Passing out again would be dangerous. If she did, she might drown.

Rain began drumming on the roof of the container. It was loud and getting louder, and she felt the water level creeping up. The storm was bringing more rain into her container.

Staying upright was hard. She tried to lean forward, pulling her feet underneath her, so she was on her knees. If she could do that, she could lift her body higher out of the water. Her arms felt weak, but she managed to grab her left ankle and pull it towards her and then underneath her. She reached out for the other ankle. This leg felt numb, like it didn't belong to her.

She tried to move her right ankle under her, but there wasn't enough room. The sole of her sandal pressed against the side of the container. The more she pulled it, the more her leg became wedged.

Alice tried to lean forward and shift her position, but it was useless. She would have to wait and hope she got rescued or pray that Lyle decided to let her out.

Either way, she realised, all she could do was wait.

CHAPTER SEVENTY-FOUR

Outside, the rain was falling harder and the water around her was rising faster. Alice shifted her shivering body and found that she could move her limbs a little more. She got both feet beneath her and tried to squat. Pressing her hands against the walls on either side, she lifted herself until the back of her head and neck could go no further.

She poked her finger into a hole high up on one side of the container. This was where the cold water had trickled down her back. She ran her fingers up further, along the underside of the lid, and felt several more small holes that were letting in air and rainwater.

Pressing her shoulders against the lid, she placed her hands against the sides for balance and repeatedly pushed. She strained and felt the lid shift slightly. Using her hand as well, she pushed again and felt the lid lift a little more.

She felt sure the lid was thin plastic. She wondered if she could pop it off if she hit it hard enough.

She pushed and pressed and thumped the lid. Her shoulders ached, but she kept going. The lid began to flex on one side. Alice yelled and got angry as she struggled.

She thumped the lid, hitting it with all her strength. *Phwup!* The lid flexed and the seal on one edge released. There was a small gasping sound as fresh air poured in. She breathed deeply. It smelled good and gave her hope.

With renewed energy, she pushed on the lid again, but she couldn't make it budge any more. She slipped her fingers through the gap. Pressing her face to the opening, she breathed deep lungfuls of the fresh, clean air.

She tried to run her fingers under the rim of the lid and release it that way, but the lid got tighter and pinched her fingers the further around she moved them.

She tilted her head and shouted through the gap. "Help! Hello? Can anyone hear me? I'm in here. I need help. Please help me." She yelled and listened and yelled again. Nothing.

She ran her fingers around the edge once more. She guessed the lid was fastened down in some way.

She peered through the gap in the lid for some time. It felt like a little bit of freedom. Occasionally, she called out, but for a long time she simply stared and listened to the noise of the rain as it fell and gathered and trickled.

A noise snapped Alice back into the moment. It sounded like a car door. Had she imagined it? Or was it thunder? She held her breath and listened. The drumming and trickling of the rain were too loud; the sound of the water swishing and splashing, added to the sound of her own heart pounding, made it hard to hear anything.

Whatever it was, she decided she'd imagined it or dreamed it.

A new noise caught her attention. Something was squeaking and rustling. She yanked her fingers in from the edge and sank down in the water.

Rats! Alice recognised the sound. She'd heard it before in the garden of their old London house. The man who had come to poison them told her they were living under the garden shed. She hated rats. They were dirty and creepy. She prayed they wouldn't come down the pipe looking for her. If they did, they'd fall into the water and climb all over her, with their sharp teeth and claws.

Alice took off her sweater and used the sleeve to plug the pipe where the water came out. The hole was probably too small for a rat, but she wasn't taking any chances. She should have thought of that before, she chided herself; it would not only stop the rats but the water too.

The water was up to her neck now, and the rain outside sounded heavier. She decided that was okay, at least for now. If the container filled with water, she could lift the lid and let it flow out; that would stop her drowning.

She wondered what would happen if nobody came for her. If she fell asleep, she would probably drown; she couldn't stay awake forever. She started thinking about all the ways she might die. Would the rats get her? Would she starve to death? Would she freeze to death? She didn't want to die here. Not like this. Daddy would come. He would find her. Yes, he would come. He had to. She hoped he would come soon. The cold was making her feel awfully tired.

Alice began to cry. The tears felt hot on her damp, icy face.

CHAPTER SEVENTY-FIVE

The satnav had got me to the area in which Long Meadow Farm was meant to be situated, but I was now relying on instinct to locate the farmhouse.

The foul weather hampered my progress; the rain and darkness made it difficult to see signs and entrances on the narrow country roads. After a few false turns and a lot of despairing, I saw the sign for Long Meadow Farm. I turned onto a single-track road.

Once I could see the farmhouse, I turned off the headlights and approached slowly. I pulled up at the side of the lane and sat in the car; the only sign of life was a flickering glow from a window. I turned the windscreen wipers back on to get a better view.

For what felt like the thousandth time I looked down at the envelope and card Theresa Allerton had given me. I'd memorised the card, which, beneath the address, read *Come alone, James, or Alice dies. For her sake, the sooner the better.*

I took out my mobile phone and thought about calling Emma. My training told me I should call for backup or at the very least notify Emma of my whereabouts. But Lyle had been one step ahead of me at every turn, and I dared not. I tucked the phone back in my inside pocket.

I turned off the car but left the keys in the ignition. I got out and ran through the mud towards the farmhouse. The front door was slightly open, and as I peered inside I could feel the warmth escaping.

I wiped the rain from my face and gently pushed the door fully open. I took a step inside and looked around. I was in a large kitchen. In the centre was a dining table and chairs, and to my right was an Aga oven. Directly across the room was another door.

I moved quickly and quietly to the second door and listened. I could hear a scraping sound, like something was being moved across the floor.

All I could think about was Alice and getting her away from Lyle. I pushed open the door and stepped inside.

A fire was blazing in a huge stone fireplace. Lyle placed a fire poker back in its stand on the hearth and turned to me. "Come in, James. You got here quickly. And perfect timing – I was just putting another log on the fire." She was dressed from head to toe in black, and on seeing me she spread out her arms to show she was unarmed.

I didn't care one way or another. I ran at her, grabbed her and forced her face down to the floor. I held her down with my knee and lifted her arm high up behind her. Lyle lay still and made no effort to get away. I could hear she was in pain, which gave me a surge of satisfaction. I fastened her hands with plasticuffs.

"Careful, James," she said. "I know you must be cross with me, but don't go hurting me. If you hurt me, I promise you little Alice will suffer."

"Where's Alice?" I screamed at her.

"All in good time. Now, you're hurting me. Let me go. We have a lot to talk about."

"You're not going anywhere, you evil bitch. You're under arrest. And if you don't tell me where Alice is right now" – I pressed my knee down hard on the side her head, pushing her face into the cold stone floor – "I may decide to start breaking every bone in your body."

I moved my knee to allow her to speak.

"That's the spirit – you're going to need that. Alice doesn't have much time; I think you should let me go now. If you hurt me, she will die an agonising death. If you arrest me, she will die. If I sense or see another police officer, she will die. And if you kill me, guess what? Ditto. The only way you're getting Alice back is by letting me go. I intend to walk out of here tonight a free woman. But before any of that, you and I need to talk about the whole point of this little game of mine. You should be excited, James. I am going to reveal why you're really here tonight. Now help me up and untie my hands."

I had all my weight pressing down on Lyle. It took everything I had not to grab her by the hair, repeatedly smash her face into the stone floor and make her tell me where Alice was.

Reluctantly, I got up and lifted Lyle to her feet. I removed the plastic tie around her wrist and watched her brush herself off as she looked me up and down.

"I think you've put on a pound or two. Living the good life by the coast will do that to a person. Don't get me wrong; you're still a hunk, but—"

"Cut your shit. You have my little girl. Where is she?"

"Last time I checked, Alice was fine. Do you really think I would harm your baby? You disappoint me, James. I thought you knew me better than that. Alice is close by; hopefully, you'll get to her in time. We do need to avoid any further delays, as I cannot vouch for her safety indefinitely. Let's take a seat, shall we?"

CHAPTER SEVENTY-SIX

I couldn't believe my ears. From across the table, I stared at Lyle in disbelief. "What are you talking about?"

She didn't take her eyes off me for a second as she enjoyed her moment. She was calm in a way that told me she had been planning her speech for a long time and was in total control of herself and this situation. She spoke soothingly. "It's very straightforward. I want you, James Hardy, retired detective chief inspector, a man who holds himself in such high esteem, to kill someone for me."

I jumped to my feet, and the chair I was sitting on screeched and fell backwards with a disturbing crash.

I shouted across the table at her, "Listen to me. You're playing games with a little girl's life. If you don't tell me where my daughter is right now, I'm going to—"

She remained expressionless. "No, you're not, James. You're not going to lay one more finger on me. If you do, your little Alice dies. Unless I tell you where she is you will never find her. No one will. Alice will die a slow, agonising death. Now sit down and listen to what else I have to say."

I had no choice. I picked up my chair and sat back

down. My mind was racing, trying to think ahead. I needed to find a way to get an advantage or some sort of leverage. I could think of none. There was nothing for me to do but to sit and listen.

"Tick-tock, tick-tock, James. I see your brain trying to find a way out. It's time to accept your predicament and stop wasting precious time that Alice doesn't have."

"Who is this person that you want dead?" The words sounded like a foreign language coming out of my mouth.

Lyle rubbed her hands together excitedly. "Good. Let's get down to business. First, I just want to say, I know you want this person dead. I can deliver the person in question right into your hands. It can be our little secret. I can mentor you. Tell me that wouldn't be exciting."

I felt my face go pale at the word "mentor." Her face broke into a wide smile, and then she changed course. "Did you and dishy Detective Cotton ever figure out the clues I left you? All those who died as part of this game were stepping stones leading to this moment. I want you to take a moment to appreciate the special gift I'm giving you."

My brain was overloaded with worry, and Lyle's words weren't making any sense. "Will you please get to the point."

"Okay. All this time you thought the mother of your children, Helena, was killed by Tony Horn. The truth is he was only the man who stuck the blade into her belly. The little man who had no choice. The man I want you to kill is the man who was really behind your wife's death. The man who gave Horn no choice. Now doesn't that sound like a win-win situation?"

My mind was being pulled in all directions. Was this just another of Lyle's games? Why was she saying these things? What did she have to gain from tormenting me?

"Why do I have to kill him? Why don't I just arrest him and let him face life imprisonment?"

"James, you haven't asked me who it is. You know, don't you? You've always known or at least had your suspicions. You poor man. Carrying that burden. How do you face your children every day while knowing the truth all this time? I want to relieve you of that pain."

I thought about the Scrabble pieces and let my mind put them in order.

R-I-C-H-T-E-R.

I felt my eyes widen.

Lyle was watching my face carefully. "That's it, James. It was Edward Richter who really killed Helena."

A wave of nausea hit me as all the missing pieces from the last few years finally slotted into place. Richter was behind Helena's murder. He was the man who had destroyed my life and the lives of my children, and now Lyle was insisting I kill him to get Alice back.

CHAPTER SEVENTY-SEVEN

Lyle looked at her watch. "I just need a yes from you. More importantly, Alice needs a yes from you. I promise this will be our little secret. You know I always keep my promises. No one will know, ever. You kill him however you want; I don't care how. I know you're a man of your word. Just say yes and you get Alice back, and I'll be on my way.

"A word of warning. If I give you Alice and you fail to kill Richter, I will come after you. First, I'll kill your dog. Then your mother, and then your children, and then I'll make you watch while I kill Monica."

My mind was frantically trying to navigate a way out of this. All I could think of right now was how to get Alice back. I said, "There must be another way?"

"There isn't another way. I give a life; you take a life. It's as simple as that. I'll make it simpler for you. Tell me you want Alice back and let me walk out of here. Say yes, and our deal is done. You'd better hurry."

She had left me no choice. I bowed my head. "Yes, I want Alice back."

Lyle jumped to her feet. "Excellent. I am so excited

about our future together. I'll be in touch with more details very soon. You sit there and don't move. I will step outside and get Alice for you. If you move, you will never see your little girl again."

I pressed my hands flat down on top of the table. I'd done a deal with the devil, and I had to force myself to stay seated as I watched Lyle leave the room.

Everything about this felt wrong, and as I heard Lyle close the front door, I was desperate to go after her. I sat in silence, waiting to hear Alice's voice. My eyes scanned the room, my ears taking in every sound. I prayed Alice was still alive and that Lyle would keep her word. I sat motionless for five minutes, then ten minutes. I looked at my watch; twenty minutes. Doubt crept in. *She's lied to me. Lyle's not coming back. I let her walk out that door. I entrusted Alice's life to a crazy woman. What was I thinking? Lyle was never going to keep to her side of the bargain. What have I done?*

I got to my feet and raced through the farmhouse. I threw open the front door. The rain was lashing down. I stepped outside and looked around frantically. I called Alice's name. I called and called but heard nothing back. I sank to my knees and begged for God's help. I clawed at the muddy soil and cried in despair.

I felt my phone vibrate. It buzzed again. I searched through my pockets and grabbed the phone from my inside pocket. One new message.

The message was from Lyle. I clicked on it and read *Alice is in the water tank xxx.*

I jumped to my feet. Water tank? What water tank?

I looked around in all directions, but it was difficult to see anything in the darkness and with the rain beating down. I switched on my phone's torch to give me some light. Pointing it ahead of me, I ran along the side of the farmhouse until I came to the corner, then sprinted along the rear side until I reached the farthest corner. Nothing. I turned again and again and kept going until I found myself back where I started. No water tank.

I opened my phone and replied to Lyle's message with one word: *WHERE?*

I waited.

No reply.

I ran to my car and found my torch in the glovebox. I turned on the car headlights.

Running back to the farmhouse, I shone the torch around. The beam picked up the shape of the stable block. I ran over and shone the light inside each window. The stables were empty. I ran to the left side and shone the torch around. No water tank. I ran back to the right side of the stable block. I shone the torchlight along the wall and there, halfway along, was a bulky shape. I ran closer and could make out a row of large barrels.

What would I find? Knowing what Lyle was capable of, I feared the worst. My legs felt leaden, as though they were reluctant to move. I had to force myself to get closer.

I called Alice's name as I ran. The barrels, three in total, were raised off the ground on concrete blocks. I climbed up and tried to prise the lid off the first barrel. A metal bar lay across the top. At the end of the bar was a latch keeping the lid down, held in place with a metal pin. I slid out the pin, flipped up the latch and lifted the lid. I shone the torch inside and found nothing but water.

I dropped the lid and moved on to the second barrel, which had the same locking mechanism on its lid. I repeated the process, my hands numb with cold. As I peered into yet another empty barrel, I heard a faint voice calling me.

I looked over at the third barrel. "Alice? Is that you?"

I shone the torch on the third barrel and couldn't

believe my eyes. Little wriggling fingers poked through from under the lid. A weak voice called, "Daddy?" Then stronger and more fearful, "Daddy, I'm here! I'm here! Please, I'm here!"

I wrenched off the lid and took in the heartbreaking sight of my little girl, up to her neck in freezing water. Barely able to form words, I reached over the lip of the barrel towards her. "Come here, sweetheart. You're safe now."

Alice put up her arms and said, "You came. I knew you would. Please hurry. I feel so cold."

CHAPTER SEVENTY-EIGHT

I sat beside Alice while she slept. I held her hand and couldn't take my eyes off her. No child should have had to go through what she'd been through.

Monica, Faith and Mum were on their way. I needed them to see her. I had this inescapable feeling that once they did and our family was back together, this nightmare would be finally over.

Alice's doctor came onto the ward and stood beside me.

I had a million questions but merely asked, "How is she?"

"She's going to be fine. She's a fighter. She has mild hypothermia, which we're treating. And she needs plenty of rest."

I didn't want to ask, but I had to. "You said earlier, doctor, that she is suffering from exhaustion and shock. I sensed something else, something you weren't telling me."

The doctor looked uneasy. "Yes. I didn't want to say anything because we can't be certain. We ran some tests, and it seems your daughter was drugged."

The words hit me like a train. I looked at Alice and back at the doctor and said, "Drugged? With what?"

"The tests were inconclusive, but it's possible she was given something like Valium or Rohypnol. Rohypnol is also known as the date-rape drug…"

"I know," I snapped. "I know what Rohypnol is." I was angry and didn't mean to snap at the doctor.

Neither of us said anything for a moment.

"I'm sorry. Thank you, doctor," I said. "Will there be any side effects?"

"Alice may have limited or no memory of what happened to her. There should be no long-term side effects. My advice is to keep an eye on her, and if you think she's behaving in any way out of the ordinary then speak to your GP. We'll monitor her progress, and when you leave you should schedule a follow-up with her GP."

Voices behind me caught my attention, and I turned to see Mum leading Faith and Monica towards me. "This way. I can see them," said Mum.

Everyone crowded around the bed and looked at Alice. Seeing the shock on their faces brought home to me how frail she looked and how the outcome could have been so tragically different. We all took turns kissing and comforting each other and talking to Alice as she slept.

"She's going to be fine," said Monica. Whether she was talking to us or trying to convince herself, I couldn't tell.

"She is," said Mum. "She's a Hardy. She's as tough as they come. She'll be out playing with her friends again before you know it."

Over Mum's shoulder, outside the ward, I could see Emma hovering. I excused myself and joined her. She looked as tired as I felt. Her usually bright complexion was pale, and she had dark shadows under her eyes. Her clothes looked creased, and I felt sure she hadn't slept for at least forty-eight hours. I wasn't sure how I would ever be able to repay her efforts in getting Alice back safely.

"How is she?"

"She's going to be okay, thanks to you," I said.

"That's wonderful news. Give her my love. It was a team effort. You know how it is," she said modestly.

"What is it?" I asked.

"Hardy, I didn't want to bring this to you now, but I also know you'd want to know."

I could see from her face she had news but was unsure whether to break it to me.

"We know where Lyle's been living," she said. "She's been living right under our noses. I discovered it because the place was purchased by the same business that owns the chain of care homes her mother is in. It's a property on the Sandbanks peninsula. I'm on my way there now to take a look."

"Give me a minute. I'm coming with you. I wouldn't miss this for the world," I said.

As I turned to go inform Monica I was leaving for a while, I thought I caught the slightest glimpse of a smile on Emma's face. She had known I'd want to be there and knew she'd made the right call.

I looked at Emma as we drove at speed across town. We both had a feeling of determination that this was it, that Lyle wouldn't slip through our fingers again.

I couldn't wait to see the surprise on Lyle's arrogant face when I once again had her in cuffs. This time there would be no deal on the table.

CHAPTER SEVENTY-NINE

Emma parked the unmarked Ford Focus across the street. Nodding towards the house, she said, "It's that one. The second floor is pretty much all glass. The back of the property backs out onto the beach. All the properties do on this side of the street."

I reached for the door handle.

Emma said, "Do you want to call for backup?"

I wasn't about to wait. Lyle could be long gone by the time backup arrived.

"I'm going to take a closer look. You're welcome to stay here."

"Not a chance," she said. "You go, we both go. Just hold on one second." She passed me a black leather wallet. I flipped it open to reveal my warrant card. I looked at her and smiled.

"I know the timing isn't great, but welcome to the Dorset Major Crime Investigation Team, MCIT. You'd better carry a badge in case we enter the property."

Holding a warrant card in my hand again felt better

than it ever had, somehow. I tucked it into my jacket. "Thank you, Emma. Come on, let's go get her."

Staying together, we checked the front before continuing around to the back of the property. The ground-floor sliding doors at the back of the house were open. Looking up, I could see the upstairs windows were tilted open. I led the way as we stepped into the house.

Downstairs, the property was open-plan with white leather sofas, a large dining area and a modern-looking kitchen. To our left and right, stainless-steel-and-glass staircases with thick glass steps led to a landing area where I could see two Mulberry suitcases. Silently, I motioned for Emma to take the right staircase while I went left.

We took a closer look at the suitcases as we reached the top. Tags on both bags indicated Lyle intended a trip to Vienna. I couldn't let her leave the country. She had to be stopped.

Working together and watching each other's blind side, Emma and I moved from room to room in silence. Before we entered the last room, I already knew we'd find it empty. Lyle wasn't here. The house was empty, and once again she'd slipped away.

Emma went back downstairs while I read the tags on the suitcases again before checking the upstairs room one more time.

From downstairs, Emma called out, "Hardy, I've got something."

I ran down to where she stood in the kitchen. She handed me two ticket printouts that showed Lyle and another passenger by the name of Sienna Lasota were booked on a flight to Vienna out of Heathrow Airport. "They were among the cookbooks," she said. "There are also other printouts, including pre-booked tickets for the Vienna Opera House next week."

I read the tickets. "We must have disturbed Lyle as she was preparing to leave. Maybe she saw us as we arrived and went out the back way. The suitcases suggest we couldn't have missed her by long."

"We could set up surveillance. There's a chance she'll come back," said Emma.

"It's possible and worth a shot. My guess is Lyle left in a hurry."

"There is a chance we could catch her at the airport. The tickets are printouts. With her passport and another copy of the tickets, she can still get out of the country. I'll get onto the airports; we might still get lucky."

Disappointed, I wandered around the house while Emma made phone calls. I wondered how Lyle was always able to stay one step ahead. It was as though she had telepathic abilities. In reality, I knew her enormous wealth enabled her to buy any information she required. Frustrated, I realised how close we had come to finally catching her.

I thought about the suitcase tags and wondered who her companion was. Sienna Lasota. Did Sienna have any idea who Lyle was? Once Lyle was bored with her, would she be disposed of like so many others had been? Would Sienna become yet another victim I would have on my conscience?

I thought about how Lyle had planned every step of her game. I considered the suitcases, the tickets and the unlocked house.

Emma was about to make another call when I said, "It's all too easy. What do you notice about this scene?"

She looked at me, puzzled. "I'm not sure I follow."

"It's been staged."

"Staged in what way?" She looked at the ticket printouts, which were now on the kitchen worktop.

"We're being spoon-fed what Lyle wants us to believe. The open house, the cases neatly placed at the top of the stairs with tags on. The tickets that were almost hidden. She's not catching a flight to Vienna – I'd bet my life on it."

"Where is she? What do you mean?"

"Lyle knows we'll be monitoring the airports. That's exactly what she wants us to do."

Emma and I started thinking out loud.

"If she's not taking a flight out of Heathrow, do you think she's hoping to disappear within the UK? That's pretty much impossible. In the past, she's always fled the country," said Emma.

I said, "If she is not catching a commercial flight, there are plenty of other ways out of the country by road or by sea or private jet."

Emma added, "She could catch a ferry. The port is no more than fifteen minutes from here. It goes directly to France."

We looked at each other knowingly. That was Lyle's style; she wanted us to waste our time covering airports while she remained right under our noses before slipping away.

Emma said, "I'll find out when the next ferry leaves." While we both ran to the car, she got back on the phone. As I drove, she pointed directions and spoke to security at the ferry terminal.

A minute later she came off the phone and smiled. "We've got time. The next ferry leaves tomorrow morning. We'll work with the port's own security to monitor the ferries. I've also arranged round-the-clock surveillance of Lyle's house in case she comes back. All local and main airports will also be asked to pay special attention and be on the lookout for her."

"Excellent. Let's go and get set up. We can't afford any mistakes."

CHAPTER EIGHTY

The sound of Emma getting back in the car woke me. She placed two cups of tea in the car's cupholders and took the last bite of her bacon sandwich.

"I couldn't wait; I ate mine on the way back to the car. Yours is down there," she said, pointing beside my tea. "I wasn't sure whether you were a red-sauce or a brown-sauce man. I guessed and went brown."

I looked at the sandwich bag resting next to the tea. "Thank you. I might eat it later." I took a sip of tea and looked at my watch. It was 7.46 a.m. The ferry to France would leave in less than forty-five minutes.

We had been watching and waiting all night. If Lyle was leaving the country this way, my hunch was she'd arrive and board at the last minute.

Emma said, "It's getting busy."

"We'd better make a move," I said. "We'll cover more ground if we split up. You know what to do if you spot Lyle?"

"Neither of us should approach her alone." She

switched on her radio. "I'll call you if I see her. And you do the same."

As we approached the terminal building, she said, "I'll check inside in case we missed her going in. You wait out here."

Keeping my distance so as not to be spotted, I checked each car and taxi as it arrived. A concern I had was that Lyle would use a disguise. She was well known for using disguises in the past; we'd have a tough time spotting her if she did the same this time.

A large group of schoolchildren who were late for check-in got off a coach and swarmed past me. At the same time, a taxi pulled up right behind the school coach. I caught sight of a pair of long, slender legs exiting its rear passenger door. As the woman stepped out and straightened up, my eyes moved up her body until they reached her eyes. Eyes I recognised. I stopped dead in my tracks. There, not two hundred yards away, was Kelly Lyle. I looked around for Emma, but she was still inside the building. I tried to reach her on the radio but got nothing but static.

Lyle hadn't seen me. Swinging a small hand-luggage bag onto her shoulder, she turned and paid the taxi driver. She was alone. Without thinking, I stepped off the pavement into the road. A car horn blared, and the driver raised his hands in exasperation. I looked down at the seriously annoyed driver, then back up at Lyle. Our eyes met, and she froze. She looked left and right for an escape.

"Lyle, stop," I shouted. "It's over. Stay right where you are."

Not a chance. Lyle dropped her bag, kicked off her high heels and began to run.

I looked back to see Emma approaching at a run. She was already on her radio to port security requesting backup. She waved at me to go after Lyle. Not that I needed encouragement.

Lyle began running towards the ferry, pushing over anyone in her way. She was fast on her feet, and our paces were evenly matched.

A security guard saw the chase and in a moment of confusion tried to grab hold of me. I sidestepped him, which made me stumble, and shouted back at him that I was the police. I glanced over my shoulder and saw him on his radio.

Lyle had gained some distance. She crossed the car park, and, as she did, a small white delivery van pulled up in front of her. The driver got out, and Lyle jumped in. The driver threw his arms up in despair as he watched his van being driven away. I gained on the van just as Lyle got it moving. Running up alongside it, I began banging on the window and calling for Lyle to stop. She looked at me and smiled. Putting her foot to the floor, she accelerated away.

Another party of schoolchildren streamed off a coach and began crossing the road. Two of the children start playing and chasing one another. One child pushed the other and started running away to avoid being pushed back. Lyle's van swerved violently to avoid them. To everyone's relief, she didn't mow them down.

A mother with two children stopped to attend to one of them. As she knelt in front of the younger child's pushchair, her older child broke free from her hand. She watched in horror as he ran out into the road.

Everything seemed to happen in slow motion, and, like the mother, I could only watch helplessly as the speeding van approached the little boy. His mother screamed and managed only two steps, her arms outstretched, before the van was inches away from the child. At the last second it swerved, missing the boy but causing Lyle to lose control of the van. It heeled over to one side, two of the wheels lifting off the ground.

Dropping back onto all four wheels, the van veered violently from left to right before rounding the side of a red brick office building and disappearing from sight. Dammit, Lyle was getting away again. I took off after the van as fast as I could.

It seemed to take forever to reach the corner of the office building. As I did, I heard an almighty screech and grinding of metal. As I rounded the corner, I saw the van on its roof. Smoke was coming from the engine. It had evidently hit a row of low bollards and tipped over. I had her. Lyle wouldn't be getting away this time.

The smoke was thick and black now. As I took a step to get closer, I felt the hand of a security guard pull me back. "It's going to blow," he said. "I've seen this sort of thing before. There's nothing you can do."

I tried to step away, but he held onto me firmly. And just as well he did.

My body rocked as the van exploded and burst into flames. I didn't know what to do. This wasn't supposed to happen; this wasn't how it was supposed to end. Many people, myself included, needed Lyle to stand trial for her crimes and account for what she'd done.

I tried to get close, but the flames were too fierce and intense. Like everyone else, I could only watch as Lyle perished in the ball of fire.

CHAPTER EIGHTY-ONE

The port was sealed off, and within a couple of hours the whole area had become a media circus. Local and national news teams were vying for snippets of information. The police pursuit and spectacular death of one of Britain's most notorious serial killers was big news. I had seen it all before and wanted no part of it.

I stayed out of the way as fire crews finished dousing the van. It would be a while before Lyle's charred remains could be examined and taken away.

"It's over," said Emma, coming up behind me and passing me a fresh cup of tea. "Between you and me, I hope she died in agony."

I looked at Emma, who continued sipping her tea.

"What will you do now?" she asked. "Will you go back to your writing and lecturing?"

"I'm not sure," I said honestly. "Right now, my family need me. After that, well, I haven't given much thought to what I'll do next." I handed her my warrant card.

"You keep it. It's still okay for a few more months."

· · ·

As Lyle's body was driven away, Emma and I started walking back to the car.

"What about you?" I asked her. "Are you going to be okay?"

"I'll be fine. Once I've had some sleep, a shower and some hot food."

"I know what you mean."

"I'll miss working with a partner. Just as I got used to having a partner around, he rides off into the sunset."

"You make it sound like I'm disappearing forever. We're friends. You helped me get my daughter back. If there's ever anything you need, you only have to ask. I mean that."

She smiled.

"Within reason, of course. I don't want you knocking on my door every other week asking for help on your next big case. I'm retired from all this, remember."

We both laughed, and, tongue in cheek, Emma said, "Oh, yes, I see that. Retired is what I thought as I watched you sprinting across a car park in pursuit of a speeding white van."

"Old habits die hard," I said. "And anyway, where were you? It should have been you chasing that bloody van." I gave her a friendly nudge.

"Me? I was right behind you, ready to take over if you ran out of puff."

"That's enough of your lip. Are you going to take me home or have I got to catch a taxi?"

"Get in. I'll drive you," she said.

"You know you said 'You only have to ask.'" Emma said. "Well, there's an investigation that's been sitting on my desk for a while now and…"

"Nope."

"Just take a look." She was splitting her sides with laughter.

"Nope."

"How about you read a few case files?"

"Nope. Shut up and drive."

CHAPTER EIGHTY-TWO

Emma put the last box in the back of her car and slammed the boot. It didn't amount to much, but it represented the time she and Dave had spent together. She'd kept a couple of photos and the t-shirt she'd liked seeing him in, but everything else she was letting go. The drive to his parents' house she did in silence with just her thoughts for company.

When she reached the house, she switched off the engine and sat deep in thought, staring at the front door. Dave's parents had always been very welcoming to her, and she wondered why she was finding it so hard to see them now. *Of course,* she thought, mentally smacking her forehead. It was because she blamed herself for their son's death.

After a few more deep breaths and heavy sighs, she plucked up the courage to go up the front steps and knock.

Jean opened the door. Emma was shocked at how much older she looked.

"Oh, Emma, it's so good to see you. Come here,

sweetheart." Jean put out her arms and enfolded her in a hug. "How are you coping?"

"I'm okay. How are you and John?"

"You know. Good days and bad days."

"I'm so sorry, Jean."

"I know you are. We all miss him. He had such a big heart. He'll leave a huge hole in all our lives."

"He will," said Emma.

"There's something I need to say, and I don't want you to take it the wrong way."

"Oh?" She took a step back. "What's that?"

"I know you and Dave never actually tied the knot, but I want you to know that for a long time now I've seen you as my daughter-in-law. I don't want that ever to change. I want you to think of yourself as my daughter. Every day, I thank God for you."

Emma tried to smile. How could she ever tell Jean the truth?

"Thank you, Jean. It means a lot."

"Well, come in, come in. John will be delighted to see you."

Emma said, "I have some of Dave's belongings in my car; bits and pieces he'd want you to have."

"That can wait. We're just about to go to Mass. They're going to say a few words. Ask people to pray for him."

"I won't keep you. I can come back another time. I was just going to drop the boxes off. I don't want to impose."

"We can do that later. John will give you a hand after church. He's around here somewhere. Spends most of his time tinkering with his car at the moment. It stops him having to think about it. I suppose that's how men cope."

Emma brushed off her jeans. "I'm not really dressed for church."

"Nonsense. You look lovely. You always do. It would mean a lot to me to have you by my side." Jean put her hand on Emma's arm and rubbed it. "It would really help."

She hadn't been to church since she was a child. Given a choice, she would rather have jumped back in her car and driven as far away from this situation as possible. But right now, she felt an obligation she didn't understand. Jean was a good woman, and she was hurting.

"Let me get my bag."

CHAPTER EIGHTY-THREE

Charles and Patti Gregory were sitting on the terrace of their Spanish villa.

They had risen early and were eating breakfast in the cool of the morning.

Charles turned the page of his British newspaper and scanned the headlines. He lifted his cup of breakfast tea to his lips and sipped it carefully. He placed the cup back down on the saucer and spread out the page he was reading in front of him to get a better look.

"Are you okay, dear?" asked Patti.

He said nothing for a moment as he continued to read. "He's bloody done it."

"Please don't use that language, Charles. Especially at breakfast. You know I don't like it. Who's done what? You're not making any sense." Patti continued to spread marmalade on her English muffin.

"That inspector, Hardy. The one that came here," he said.

"Hardy. What about him?"

"It says here that although the body has yet to be

formally identified, it is believed the prime suspect in a series of murders, Kelly Lyle, died in a vehicle accident while being pursued by retired DCI James Hardy."

Patti felt lightheaded. "I hope she fucking rots in hell."

"Language, Patti," said Charles. "Do we still have his card? I might call him later."

"What good will that do?"

"I don't know. I have an urge to do something. You're probably right. No, damn it; I'm going to write to Hardy and show my gratitude."

Patti no longer felt hungry. She put down her muffin, pushed the plate away and said, "She's dead. That's all that matters. Jacob can finally rest in peace. We all can."

CHAPTER EIGHTY-FOUR

Saying goodbye to Dad was the hardest thing I'd ever done.

After the funeral, Monica and I decided to invite everyone back to the house for the reception. The place was packed with Dad's friends and colleagues as well as our family. Brad, my Royal Marine brother, had been granted leave and was in the front room keeping an eye on Mum and catching up with old acquaintances.

I was taking some time to gather my thoughts and had been joined in my study by Rayner. A knock at the door made us both look up.

Emma put her head around the door.

"DI Cotton," said Rayner, his voice slurred. "Helloo!" He attempted to heave himself out of my old comfy chair to welcome her but gave up.

Seeing three glasses and an almost empty bottle of whisky on my desk, she apologised. "I'm sorry. I didn't mean to intrude. I can speak to you another time." She went to leave but I pointed to a chair.

"Take a seat. Come in. Join us for a drink. I insist. Rayner, get Cotton a glass, would you?"

Emma and Rayner looked at the spare glass of whisky on the desk at the same time. Pointing to it, Rayner said, as though he was letting her in on a secret, "That glass is for Hardy Senior. We're toasting him. Just wait a minute. I'll get you a glass. Just wait. Wait."

She looked at me with an amused smile and we both watched the big man as he concentrated on coordinating his movements.

Rayner twisted his body and leaned back behind his chair and, with a lot of puffing and drunken effort, extracted another glass from the bottom drawer of my filing cabinet. "I know where Jamie-boy keeps his stash. He's a man of habit."

He poured Emma a glass of whisky and handed it to her.

"It was a lovely service," she said, raising her glass respectfully.

"Thank you," I said. "It was great so many people were able to make it. They came from all over."

"The best," said Rayner. The big man drained his glass and poured the last of the bottle into it. I guessed he'd be sleeping in my old comfy chair tonight. "The best service, for the great man."

Emma looked uneasy, so I asked, "What's on your mind?"

She absently stroked her jacket pocket.

Drunk as he was, Rayner didn't miss a thing. He leaned towards her with a broad smile on his face. "Don't ever take up poker. Your body language is an open book."

"I didn't want to bring this up today," she said, "but under the circumstances, I think it's important."

"What circumstances? What are you talking about?" I asked.

She took out a single sheet of paper and handed it to Rayner, who had his hand out and half snatched it from her. He read it, looked at Emma, then at me, and shook his head.

"You've got to be kidding me."

He handed me the paper, which I could already see was part of a post-mortem report.

"Do we know who Samantha Dickson is?" asked Rayner.

"She was reported missing a few days ago. She worked at the nursing home where Lyle's mother is a resident. Lyle must have met her there."

There was a moment of stunned silence before Rayner burst out angrily, "We're all doing the happy dance because we think Lyle roasted until she was good and crispy. Instead, it's some poor kid she abducted."

For a moment I was confused. I'd seen Lyle burn in the van. My mind went back to the chase. I pictured the taxi pulling up directly in front of me. Lyle seeing me before turning and running. The small white van conveniently left with its engine running. The port security guard, holding on to me and slowing me down, giving Lyle the chance to turn the corner and remain out of sight for a few seconds. Enough time for her to jump from the speeding vehicle and disappear. Then, finally, the same port security guard holding me back and preventing me from getting close enough to see inside the van before it burst into flames.

I handed the report back to Emma. "Meanwhile, Lyle slips out of the country while our backs are turned," I said quietly.

"Let's just hope the bitch catches some tropical disease and crawls under a rock to die an agonising death,"

Rayner spat. He reached around to the bottom drawer of the filing cabinet for another bottle of whisky. He twisted the lid off a single malt I'd received for my birthday.

All I could think about was the sick agreement I'd made with Lyle. I thought I'd got away scot-free, but with her on the loose I was still on the hook. If she ever came back, she'd expect me to keep my side of the bargain. If I didn't, she had told me, plain and simple, what the consequences would be.

I looked over at the pictures of the Scrabble pieces that were still pinned to the wall. R-I-C-H-T-E-R. The man Lyle expected me to kill.

I pushed the thought away. I couldn't think about that today. Not today. Today was for remembering Dad.

Rayner topped up our glasses, and we toasted the best father and role model anyone could have.

CHAPTER EIGHTY-FIVE

Monica and I walked hand in hand along the promenade at Flag Head beach. It felt good for us all to finally be out as a family. Alice was recovering nicely, and despite recurrent nightmares she was coping well day-to-day and was happy to be back at school with her friends.

As a family, we had a lot of catching up to do. Each of us was being forced to make significant adjustments to our way of life. But we were a strong family, and I knew we'd get through this together.

Walking and talking, Monica and I watched Alice, Faith and Mum down on the beach collecting shells while Sandy barked and bounced around enthusiastically.

"Penny for your thoughts," said Monica.

"I was just thinking about Dad and how he loved these walks."

"I think he enjoyed collecting the shells as much as the girls do," said Monica. She squeezed my hand.

"You're right. He enjoyed acting like a big kid. I miss him, but I wasn't feeling down about it. I was feeling happy. We have so many great memories."

"That's a lovely way to think about him. He'd want that." She leaned over and kissed my cheek.

"Life is okay right now. Mum is coping. I've got you, and we have our two beautiful little girls. What more could we ask for?"

Monica's face reddened. Her eyes brimmed with tears as she looked at me in a way I hadn't seen before.

I stopped walking and looked at her. I could see something wasn't right. I wasn't sure I wanted to ask, but I had to.

Hesitantly, I said, "Whatever it is, you must tell me. I can take it. I know you're keeping something from me. We agreed we would never keep secrets from one another, and whatever it is, I will deal with it."

"Don't be so dramatic, James. I've been waiting for the right time."

"What is it?"

"I'm pregnant."

"Pardon?"

"You're going to be a dad again. We're going to have a baby."

It took me a moment to register what she was saying. I looked into her big, beautiful, uncertain eyes, and they sent my head and my heart racing.

I felt an intense, joyous energy surge through my body, which culminated in a huge, cheerful roar. I was laughing uncontrollably; I felt giddy. I picked Monica up and kissed her. I put her back down gently and said, "Are you sure? Really? How? When?" I didn't know what to do with myself. I wanted to run and tell Alice, Faith and Mum and at the same time stay and hold this gorgeous woman in front of me.

Monica watched my reaction with delight and amusement. She'd not often seen me acting like a dopey fool. "Yes, I'm sure. We are going to have a baby. I assume you're okay with it? I know we hadn't planned this."

"If you're okay, then I am one thousand percent okay. Let me look at you. You're so beautiful. I love you."

Seeing the commotion and hearing my voice from down on the beach, Alice, Faith, and Mum came running up to us.

"What's going on? You look a bit weird, Dad," said Faith.

"You tell them, Monica," I said.

"No, you tell them. Let's tell them together."

"Tell us what?" demanded a smiling Alice.

Monica and I told them together in a giddy, jumbled way. "You're going to have a baby brother or sister. Monica is pregnant. We're going to have a baby." "You're going to be big sisters, both of you. How does that sound?"

The excitement on the girls' faces told us everything we needed to know.

Mum was smiling and wiping away happy tears. "It's about time we had some good news in this family. And this really is the best news. This is truly wonderful news." She looked up to heaven and blew a kiss to Dad.

"Do you hear that, Dad? You're going to be a grandad again."

INFERNO

A DCI James Hardy Thriller

BOOK 5

CHAPTER 1

Friday, 14 August 2015

Helena Hardy scooped up her handbag and house keys and pressed the phone to her ear with her shoulder as she shut the front door and locked it. She waited for the number she'd called to go to voicemail.

"It's me, again. That crazy-hot woman you share a bed with. This is a reminder, Detective Chief Inspector James Hardy, that it's date night tonight. I haven't booked a table because I know you're busy, so you'll probably be late, and I don't want to sit in a restaurant alone looking embarrassed. That's not a dig about our last date, I promise." Helena chuckled. "Anyway, Alice and Faith will be at your parents' house, and I'll be cooking your favourite. I also have something very special planned for dessert, if you know what I mean. James, I promise – you won't want to miss it." She chuckled again. "Text me, darling, when you get a chance. Let me know you got this message and what time you'll be home. I'll be waiting."

Helena's face was full of smiles as she tucked her phone into her handbag. She thought how funny it would be if James played the voicemail back on loudspeaker in the office. She could imagine him fumbling around, frantically trying to mute it.

Right now, though, Helena needed to get a few ingredients for their romantic meal. It was a short distance to the shops, and for the first time in a couple of days it wasn't raining. She looked at her car and was tempted to drive but decided it would be good to walk, get some exercise. She glanced over the roof of the car and noticed a man across the street. He was wearing a dark-blue or black hoodie and pretending not to watch her. As she watched him, he looked away and started walking. He was talking to himself and scratching his right arm.

Helena watched as the man fleetingly glanced back at her before he picked up his pace. She sighed. It would take longer, but she decided to turn around and walk the other way around the block to the shops. She shouldered her handbag and set off. Before turning the corner at the end of the road she looked back over her shoulder. The man was gone.

She had just rounded the corner when she realised she'd forgotten the list of ingredients for her special meal with James. "You idiot, Helena Hardy," she muttered to herself as she searched pointlessly through her handbag. She could picture exactly where she'd left it – right on the worktop beside her pen. For a moment she considered carrying on without it; she felt sure she could remember most of it. But after running through the list in her mind and knowing she'd come up short, she decided to go back. After all, she was only a few hundred yards from home.

As she approached the house, she unzipped her handbag and reached inside for her house keys. She rooted around for the keys and looked down into the bag. "Gotcha," she murmured. As she looked up, she sensed someone approaching from behind. Out of the corner of her eye she saw a figure moving between the parked cars at the side of the road.

Helena spun around and, in an instant, the man in the hoodie was in front of her. Her hand shot into her handbag for her pepper spray, but she felt the bag being pulled away. She tugged back, then thought better of it.

"Take the bag," said Helena. She shrugged the strap off her shoulder and released the bag from her grip. He snatched it away from her.

"Helena Hardy?" said the man.

"How do you know my name?" Helena edged away, moving carefully along the pavement and closer to the house. He looked in a bad way. Sores on his face and sunken eyes suggested he was on something. She spoke slowly and clearly. "Just take the bag and go. I don't care about the bag. There's money in it. It's yours. Okay?"

The man matched her step for step. "You're the copper's wife, aren't you?"

"Yes. My husband is a policeman. That doesn't matter. There's money in the bag. I'm not worried about the money – take it," repeated Helena. She glanced over her shoulder; she wasn't far from the house. She felt the house keys in her hand. She wanted to run and hoped he'd turn and run in the opposite direction, but, instead, he kept coming.

Helena inched backward, and the man reached into the pocket of his hoodie. Her heart, which was already pounding in her chest, went up a gear as she saw the dull metal blade of a knife appear in his hand. She had to act first. This was no time for self-doubt.

Helena screamed and yelled at the top of her lungs. As the hooded man turned to look around, Helena took two strides forward and hit him in the face with a palm strike, just the way she'd been taught by James and at her self-defence classes. As he staggered back, stunned, she reached in and clawed at his face and eyes before following through with a kick. She'd hoped to hit between his legs, but he blocked her by twisting his body. Even so, his leg buckled and he crumpled to his knees.

Helena took her chance to run. As she ran, she fumbled with the keys, desperately trying to find the one for the front door. Just as she found it, the bunch of keys slipped from her hand and fell to the pavement. She looked over her shoulder and could see that the hooded man was back on his feet and bearing down on her. With a sob of frustration and fear, Helena made a grab for the keys but missed them. Then her hair was yanked up and back, bringing her face to face with him.

Helena gasped as he plunged the knife into her stomach. She stared at him wide-eyed and open-mouthed as he pulled the knife out partway and then plunged it once again deep into her belly. Then he did it again and again and again.

Finally, he pulled out the blade and released his grip on her hair. Her legs buckled, and she collapsed onto the pavement.

He knelt beside her and looked at her. "That's a message for your copper husband, bitch. He needs to back off. Got it? *Back off.*"

He looked up, startled, at the sound of shouts from across the street. He stuffed the knife back in his pocket, leapt to his feet and ran, grabbing Helena's handbag as he went.

A woman appeared beside her, breathless, she crouched down. "Helena, it's me, Karen, from next door. Don't worry, love. An ambulance is on its way. The police too. Don't try to move."

"Call James," said Helena. "Karen, please, call him. You have his number."

Pointing to an elderly male neighbour, Karen said, "Keep talking to her. I'm going to call her husband."

Karen took off her jumper and placed it under Helena's head. "I'll be right back. I promise. You just stay strong. Don't close your eyes. He'll be here before you know it."

"Thank you," said Helena. The elderly man knelt beside her and she closed her eyes. She could picture Karen phoning James's mobile, the call going to voicemail the way it had done for her. She hoped Karen didn't waste time leaving a message but instead dialled the landline number she had for him. *It's my turn to ruin date night,* thought Helena. She lifted a hand from the wound and looked at the blood. *I'm not going to be able to do the school run and nursery run.* Her mind ran through a list of standby mums. Then she remembered that James's mum, Nana Hardy, was picking them up. *That's good. I don't want Alice and little Faith worrying.*

Helena focused on waiting for James, her soulmate, her best friend. She knew he'd come. He'd help her; he'd sort this out.

Over the hum of the gathered crowd, she finally heard James's voice. At first she thought she'd imagined it, then she saw his face. *My handsome husband,* she thought. *James looks scared. Don't worry, my love. It'll all be okay. I just need to close my eyes for a bit. I'm tired. I just need to rest.*

CHAPTER 2

Governor Lloyd Trent stepped into the cell and looked down at the prisoner, who lay on his side clutching his stomach and moaning. Staff had informed him that the bouts of pain had become more frequent, and Trent knew he was duty-bound to ensure the prisoner received proper medical attention. That said, he intended to postpone that decision for as long as he could.

Trent knew all there was to know about the piece of shit in front of him. His name was Edward Fischer, though at the time of his arrest he'd been going by the last name Richter, his mother's maiden name. Seems he thought it had a nice ironic ring to it, what with Richter meaning *judge* in German. His parents were both from Hamburg, Germany, and the family had moved to England when he was four years old; his parents had divorced when he was eight. He had grown up with his mother, Christa, on the poor estates of London. She had never remarried. Died from lung cancer when Edward was nineteen.

The path that had led Fischer to end up residing in Trent's maximum-security prison had started with petty crime at the age of eleven. Over the years, Fischer had moved up the criminal ladder, progressing to high-end burglary in the more affluent areas of London. And when that thrill had become too routine, it appeared he had turned his hand to serial murder.

Prison Officer Terry Farley filled the cell doorway, his eyes moving between Fischer and his boss.

"Give us a minute, will you, Farley," said Governor Trent. It wasn't a question.

Farley hesitated. "Sir? I …"

"I want a moment with the prisoner. Fischer knows better than to do anything stupid. We have an understanding, don't we, Fischer?"

Fischer slowly moved his legs around and sat up with his back against the cell wall. His face contorted with pain, his hands gripping his emaciated stomach. "Yes, sir."

"I'll be right outside, sir," said Farley.

Governor Trent turned to the chair by the desk and sat down opposite Fischer. The usually toned and muscular body of the prisoner had been replaced by a bony figure whose clothes hung off him. Unkempt and unshaven, he looked like he'd aged a good ten years. Trent displayed no concern.

"Why am I here, Fischer?"

Fischer tried to sit up straighter before speaking, the movement causing him to wince with pain. "I'm not right. I've been telling you lot for over a week now. I've got no appetite. When I do manage to eat something, I can't keep it down. And my stomach is getting worse. When I move, it feels like I've swallowed a bag of nails. It's excruciating."

"The doctor says he can't find anything wrong with you."

"I know. But look at me. Does it look like there's nothing wrong?" Fischer held out a skinny, tattooed arm.

Trent sucked his teeth and tilted his head, then leaned forward and spoke in a low, clear voice. "You're in my prison because you're a sick bastard who sliced up young women to the point where they had to be identified through dental records. Forensic evidence put you at the scene with two of the victims, yet you won't give the families of those poor young women the closure they deserve by admitting to the crimes. You still maintain your innocence."

"I *am* innocent. I was framed—"

"Let me finish," growled Trent. "You come into my prison and immediately kill three of my inmates. At great expense and inconvenience, I'm now forced to keep you away from the general population. My point is, if it was up to me, I'd leave you to die a slow, agonising death here in this cell. And while you were writhing around on the floor, I'd invite the families of your victims to come and watch while I piss on you. Do you understand?"

"I need tests. Proper hospital tests."

Trent got to his feet. He lifted his leg and put his foot on the hand Fischer held over his stomach. He pressed down. Fischer gritted his teeth and stifled the cry of pain, not wanting to give Trent the satisfaction.

Officer Farley appeared at the door. "Everything all right, sir?"

Trent removed his foot. His eyes fixed on Fischer, he said, "Yes. Yes. I'm trying to establish the extent of the problem."

Farley watched as Fischer doubled over. "Shall I get the doctor?"

"Yes. Get the doctor. Tell him to increase Fischer's painkillers. If he's no better in a week, I'll review the situation and decide whether he should get an outside evaluation. We're not sending this piece of shit to hospital any sooner than need be. Understood?"

CHAPTER 3

Afternoon walks across clifftops with Sandy – who spends most of her time nose down, tail in the air, searching for rabbits – are one of the great joys of our having moved to the coast. There's far more open space out here than in the city, and the opportunity to go outside and find time to reflect, while surrounded by incredible natural landscapes, is a real incentive to get out and about.

The car park, which was bare chalkstone where the grass had been worn away, was empty except for my car and a sports car, which was parked close to mine. *You've got the whole empty car park and you had to park so close?* I thought.

I opened the back of my car and Sandy knew what was next. She looked around, probably wondering if she could make a break for it. "Come on. Up you jump." She wasn't ready to leave; never is. "Come on, girl." Sandy looked at me then reluctantly did as requested. "Good, girl." I rubbed her over with her towel. She tried to lick my face. "Sorry to break it to you, but you stink. Time for another bath, I think." Sandy put her paw on my arm and tilted her head. "Sorry, no debating it."

As I rounded the car to get to the driver's side, the door of the sports car opened and prevented me opening mine. I stepped back to let the person out. Nobody got out.

I walked up to the open door and peered inside. A young woman in a cashmere sweater and short skirt smiled at me. She pointed a manicured finger towards the cliff edge.

"James!" came a voice ahead of me. "James, darling."

In front of the two cars, beside a fence separating the well-worn grassy path and the cliff edge, stood a woman. Her shoulder-length brown hair blew in the sea breeze. She pulled up the collar of her three-quarter-length camel coat against the chill breeze. She wore black jeans, low heels and sunglasses. She waved, then turned her back on me to look out to sea. I knew immediately who it was. I slammed the young woman's car door closed, almost catching her hand, and yanked open my own car door. I looked around for something I could use as protection. The only thing I could find was a ball-point pen. I tucked it in my pocket, told Sandy to sit tight, shut the door and strode over to the woman on the cliff.

"Kelly Lyle," I said. "Psychopath, sadist, narcissist, millionaire, and deceased."

Lyle chuckled. "You can be so cutting at times, James. You know I prefer to be called a *multi*-millionaire."

"What's to stop me arresting you right here and now, Lyle?"

"If you arrest me, I'll tell the world about our deal. Your glittering career will go up in flames – *poof!*" She made a flicking motion with one hand. "And every investigation you've ever worked on will be brought into question. More importantly, it means we won't be friends anymore, and I've got big things planned for us. It's all very exciting."

"Oh, cut the bullshit," I snapped. "Kelly Lyle, I'm taking you in. I am arresting you on suspicion of murder. You do not have to say anything, but it may harm your defence if you…"

Lyle put out her wrists. I grabbed her right arm and put it up behind her back.

"Do you have cuffs back at your car, James?" she said

coquettishly. "If you're going to put cuffs on me, you kinky boy, we'd better have a safe word." Lyle pretended to think. "What about *Alice*? Yes, Alice is the perfect safe word. Don't you think?"

I stopped. I released her arm.

Lyle lifted her sunglasses and rested them on the top of her head, letting me see her eyes now. She looked at me sympathetically. "Please call me Kelly. A lady doesn't like to be called by her surname; it's unbecoming. I'm not one of your little subordinates back at New Scotland Yard. And anyway, I'd so hoped we could be friends. I've decided we simply got off on the wrong foot, and I'm here to make amends." Lyle pouted. "What's up, James? You look sad. Don't be sad."

Lyle looked me up and down, then stepped close. Her hand hovered close to my cheek, poised to stroke it. I grabbed her wrist and held it.

"Please, don't touch me," I said.

Before I could stop her, Lyle grabbed me and kissed me. She gripped me tightly and pressed herself against me.

I pushed her away. "What the hell are you doing?"

"I've been wanting to know how it felt. You don't disappoint. You're a good kisser, James. A little stiff, maybe, but that's to be expected. Given time, though, I know we'd make incredible lovers. I've given it a lot of thought." Lyle watched my anger rise. "From the very first day we met, in that little cottage, when we sat under the stars together and you held me – do you remember? I've only ever been trying to help you."

"Help me? How have you ever helped me?"

"You really are a tease, James. For a start, without me, you wouldn't know who killed your wife. Please don't tell me you're not immeasurably happier now that you know Richter – or Fischer, to call him by his proper name – is the man behind the murder of your beloved Helena?"

"You nearly killed my daughter. You kidnapped her, drugged her and put her in a water tank, where you left her to die. Is that what you call helping? Christ, why are we even having this conversation? It's insane. You're insane."

"Sticks and stones… You know what your problem is, James? You're so overly dramatic, serious, blinkered, inconsiderate and a little pig-headed. A typical man. You need to lighten up. I was never going to let Alice die. She and I became friends during our time together. She's like the daughter I never had. She's just like you, you know. Strong-willed little thing. A chip off the old block."

"What do you want?"

"Is that our foreplay over already, James? You're going to have to work on that if we're to be lovers."

Lyle put a finger to her face and made out she was thinking. "Tick-tock, tick-tock. What do I want? What do I want?… You know what I want. We made a deal. We've been thrust together, bound by a union of body, mind and spirit. This is the culmination. Can you feel it, James? It's very stimulating. My whole body tingles at the thought of our climax. What a thrill." Lyle tossed her head back and softly moaned. "Oh, James, James." She took my hand and placed it on her chest. "Our connection. We're locked together and it feels so… natural."

I pulled my hand away.

Lyle put on a face of disappointment.

"I'm leaving," I said.

"No, you're not," said Lyle.

"You're not capable of empathy, so all this about helping me is bullshit. You care about no one. You know that. I know that. You have no sense of compassion. So why all the theatrics?"

"I don't know. Fun? Excitement? Exhilaration? Creativity? Challenging myself? Challenging others? Take your pick. But don't be like that – I do care about you. I treasure our relationship. It's special. You're special to me."

"So why threaten me and my family?"

"Leverage. Killing is easy. I want Fischer dead. It's more fun for me these days if I can encourage someone whose moral code prevents them taking such action to do it for me. That someone is you. We're scratching each other's backs, that's all, James. Fischer's an itch. Let's scratch him out together."

"And if I don't follow through, Kelly? What? You'll kill me?"

"You already told me I lack empathy. So yes, reluctantly. I'll kill Alice and little Faith, Monica and unborn baby Hardy, and you. Probably Nana Hardy too. You I'll kill last because you get to watch the others die. Boo-hoo. But a deal is a deal. I gave you back Alice; you get to save your family in exchange for killing the man who sent that nasty little drug addict Tony Horn to murder the mother of your two beautiful daughters. Don't forget – Fischer also killed someone I loved dearly. Two birds, one stone. To me that sounds like the deal of a lifetime. Ta-dah! I give you the opportunity to kill him guilt-free."

"Guilt-free?" I asked.

"It's guilt-free because you have no choice. I'm gifting that to you because we're friends, soon to be lovers. We are friends, aren't we, James?"

"The answer is no. We're not friends, and I'm not killing him. Even if I wanted to kill him, which I don't, he's locked away in a maximum-security prison. Be satisfied with that." I turned and walked away.

Lyle called after me. "Don't worry about little details like prison. I'll make sure he's put in your crosshairs."

I kept walking and didn't look back.

"Bye, James. Nice butt. Love you, James. Don't test me. I will slaughter your family in a blink of an eye. Oh, and my sexy assistant in the car there took photos of our passionate clifftop embrace. I'm sure Monica would love to see how amazing we look together. Don't make me send them. You know how insecure pregnant women can be."

I looked inside the parked car and the young woman held up a camera with a telephoto lens. She was all smiles.

"Kill him, James," Lyle shouted. "Save your family. For both our sakes, I want him dead. You hear me? Dead."

* * *

Inferno, *the fifth book in the series is out now.*
Continue DCI Hardy's journey:
Inferno - Buy on Amazon

ABOUT THE AUTHOR

Born in Dorset, southern England, Jay Gill moved to Buckinghamshire where he worked in the printing industry, primarily producing leaflets and packaging for the pharmaceutical industry. After several years of the London commute, and with his first child about to start school, he realised it was high time for a change and moved back to the south coast of England. This change freed up time for him to write the detective stories he dreamed of one day publishing.

Safe to say, he's caught the writing bug in earnest now. With several Hardy novels under his belt, a growing "family" of characters both good and heinous, and a host of exciting new ideas bouncing around in his head, Jay busily juggles his writing and family life and is hard at work on the next instalment in the DCI James Hardy series of thrillers.

If you've enjoyed this book, please consider spreading the word by leaving a review on Amazon. Reviews help bring the Hardy novels to the attention of other readers.

Many thanks, Jay

If you would like to be kept up to date with new releases from Jay Gill, please complete an email contact form here, or on his Facebook page or website, www.jaygill.net

MORE DCI HARDY

I occasionally send newsletters with updates on new releases, and other bits of news relating to the DCI James Hardy series.

It's easy to join my newsletter mailing list, and when you do, you'll gain access to **free reading**:

1. A profile of James Hardy called 'Who is James Hardy?' *Exclusive to my mailing list: you can't get this anywhere else.*
2. Bonus scenes from *all* my James Hardy novels: For example, you'll find out what happens to Melvin Barclay, a particularly nasty piece of work featured in *Hard Truth*, when Kelly Lyle catches up with him again. (Hint: Brace yourself. *It isn't pretty!*). There is also a scene from my latest book INFERNO which has been described as taut and nerve-shredding. *(Again, it's exclusive to my mailing list, you can't get it anywhere else.)*

Visit my website at www.jaygill.net

Made in the USA
Middletown, DE
06 October 2022

12161682R00213